IN MY SISTER'S HOUSE

Praise for **The Bachelorette Party**

"Don Welch must have really studied 'sistahs.' I mean, how else could he be so on target when it comes to how we interact? He put his foot in this one . . . or at least in somebody's high heel!"
—*Vanessa Bell Calloway, actress*

"You will laugh, cry, and celebrate while connecting with this story of irreplaceable friendships, personal transformation, and the flip side of love. An enlightening and very enjoyable read."
—*Hill Harper, actor and author of* Letters to a Young Brother

"This story really grabs you and never lets go until the very last line. Readers will get so involved that they will do everything but get up and testify: 'OH YES!' " —*Loretta Devine, actress*

"The writing is SUPERB! . . . The biggest laugh and cry I have had in a long time." —*Freda Payne, singer*

"Don's writing brings to life the diversity of women's issues with honesty and emotion." —*Kenny Lattimore, singer*

"*The Bachelorette Party* convinced me that Don Welch bugged the ladies' room and has been listening to all our dirt for years."
—*Anna Maria Horsford, actress*

"*The Bachelorette Party* is a wild ride on the secret side of what we ladies laugh about, cry about, try to hide from our friends . . . and even at times ourselves! The stage play is a must see. . . . this book, a must read!" —*Dawnn Lewis, actress, singer, composer, producer*

"Don's writing is that of a fly on the wall in a group therapy session hearing firsthand details with nothing left out."
—*Fred Thomas, Jr., director, filmmaker*

ALSO BY DONALD WELCH

The Bachelorette Party

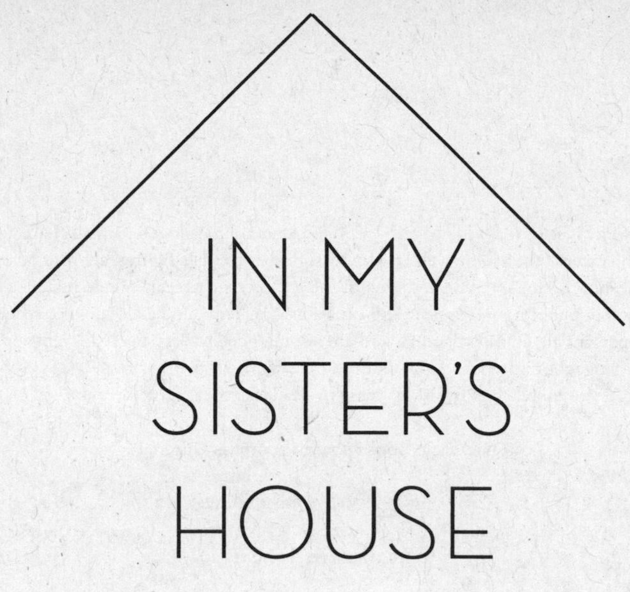

IN MY SISTER'S HOUSE

A NOVEL

DONALD WELCH

ONE WORLD
BALLANTINE BOOKS • NEW YORK

In My Sister's House is a work of fiction. All incidents and dialogue, and all characters with the exception of some well-known historical and public figures, are products of the author's imagination and are not to be construed as real. Where real-life historical or public figures appear, the situations, incidents, and dialogues concerning those persons are entirely fictional and are not intended to depict actual events or to change the entirely fictional nature of the work. In all other respects, any resemblance to persons living or dead is entirely coincidental.

A One World Books Trade Paperback Original

Published in the United States by One World Books, an imprint of The Random House Publishing Group, a division of Random House, Inc., New York.

ONE WORLD is a registered trademark and the One World colophon is a trademark of Random House, Inc.

Library of Congress Cataloging-in-Publication Data

Welch, Donald.
In my sister's house: a novel / Donald Welch.
p. cm.
ISBN 978-0-345-50162-2
eBook ISBN 978-0-345-51970-2
1. Twins—Fiction. 2. Sisters—Fiction. 3. Women ex-convicts—Fiction. 4. Co-heirs—Fiction. 5. Nightclubs—Fiction. 6. African American business enterprises—Fiction. 7. Family-owned business enterprises—Fiction. 8. Philadelphia (Pa.)—Fiction. I. Title.
PS3623.E4623I52 2010
813'.6—dc22 2009044065

Printed in the United States of America

www.oneworldbooks.net

2 4 6 8 9 7 5 3 1

Text design by Diane Hobbing

To my mother, Gloria Welch Pollitt,
who continues to stand strong and
steadfast with her love and support
of all that I do

Dear Readers,

Boy, how time flies. Seems like it was just yesterday that I sat down and began writing my first novel, *The Bachelorette Party*. I was excited, nervous, scared, and happy all at once. But I got through it with the support and love of so many of you, and God's ever-present grace. As a write this, I am listening to the great Aretha soar through the gospel hymn "God Will Take Care of You," from her landmark *Amazing Grace* album, reminding me that Aretha possesses possibly one of the greatest voices ever given to a woman, and that God truly does take care of all of us.

A lot has happened since *The Bachelorette Party* was published. Not only has my faith been strengthened immensely, but America elected its first African American president. As pleased as I am personally that this has come to pass, I could not be more elated that it happened in my mother's lifetime. She migrated to Philadelphia from the South many years ago, and lived through Jim Crow. On the night of the presidential election she called me as they announced that Obama was the winner. My mother said she had gotten out of bed and was running around in circles in her bedroom, wildly clapping and flapping her arms in joyous glee that "the Lord had moved." (Christians will know what I mean by that [smile].) There was nothing better than sharing that precious moment in American history with my mom.

And that sense of family and love brings me to *In My Sister's House*. In this novel, I wanted to show the importance of family, friends, and lovers and their impact on our lives. Even though life has many trials, tribulations, and ups and downs, at the end of the day, what really matters is love and support. Isn't that what we all want? I am ecstatic with how this story turned out. The characters are as real as the day is long. Some are outlandish and unforgettable, others, colorful and unpredictable. But I hope you find them all familiar nonetheless.

I also have great news to share. I am still in love! Yes, I wake up each day in love with my life, my career, the people close to me, and God. Now if I could only find someone to share it all with (smile). But the future remains bright: I have a slew of new projects on the table—stage plays, TV and film projects—and I know there are more novels in me. So you'll soon hear more great news and receive blessings from Don B. Welch.

To the countless fans—old and new—book clubs, friends, and family around the country, thank you so much for traveling on this journey with me. I don't take any of you for granted.

Now sit back and relax with your favorite snack while you laugh, cry, and hopefully are entertained by *In My Sister's House.*

With all that life brings us, "be not dismayed, God will take care of you."

Donald

< PROLOGUE >

Time in a Bottle

Philadelphia County Jail for Women

An agitated Storm paced the floor of the visiting area at the Philadelphia County Jail for Women. Her red eyes were puffy and swollen from crying and lack of sleep, and her one-piece orange uniform hung loosely on her small frame. Her unflattering white slip-on sneakers were too big for her, and she had to make a conscious effort to keep them on because the powers that be didn't allow shoestrings in case an inmate tried to hang herself or strangle someone else. Her attorney was late and Storm was pissed! Her hair was pulled back into one single braid held together by a dirty rubber band. She undid it and smoothed her hair back neatly. Her long hair was her pride and joy. And it was all hers.

Wasn't nothing fake about Storm Morrison. She never understood how women could get cheap weaves. She believed you should either wear your own hair, no matter how short it was, or get a good weave. And if you can go to the corner store and buy a Pepsi and a bag of hair, then you aren't getting a good weave. That shit was crazy to her: A headful of hair from some bitch in Indonesia on a bitch's head from the hood.

She looked down at her hands. The clear pink shade of polish she had favored since her college days had either faded or been eaten away by her nervous energy. A manicure was definitely in order.

Catching her reflection in the Plexiglas window that separated inmates from freedom, Storm knew her appearance was not on point. She was a far cry from the chick once heralded as Philly's "baddest-dressing bitch in stilettos."

Although too short to runway model, print work was readily available to her. Talent scouts from *KING* magazine and *SMOOTH* begged her for photo spreads. Her knockout body boasted two perfectly shaped breasts, a set of legs to die for, and an ass known to make a man's eyes water when she passed him on the street. She turned all the magazines down, saying, "When you niggas pay what the white people pay for *Playboy* and *Hustler,* maybe. Until then, fuck no!"

But not today. Today she wouldn't even be considered for a *JET* centerfold. But all that would change. *As soon as I get the fuck out of here.*

Once her attorney, Clara Bow, was seated and picked up the phone receiver, Storm lashed into her. "My preliminary hearing was supposed to be weeks ago. What the hell is going on?"

"I asked for more time to build your case. It didn't happen overnight, Storm."

"I don't give a fuck, MISS CLARA BOW! I've called your office time after time and you have not returned my calls. And who names their kid a stupid-ass name like Clara Bow anyway?" Storm's eyes bulged larger, and her nostrils flared to resemble the tip of a loaded .45 ready to go off any second.

"I was named after my mother's favorite actress." Attempting to calm Storm down, Bow explained, "I have not ignored your calls. If I remember correctly, you told me not to bother you with particulars, that you would rather know for sure what our plan of defense would be. I had to wait for the formal charges from the DA." She gave Storm a moment and then continued. "But I do have some good news. After weighing all the evidence, or lack thereof, the DA was sympathetic to your case and has agreed to reduce the charge to involuntary manslaughter. I think—"

"What does that mean?" Storm cut in.

"If you plead 'No Contest,' he'll ask the judge to reduce the charge to involuntary manslaughter. There isn't sufficient evidence to support intent on either one of the charges. With an involuntary charge, you'll get no more than three years, which you will start serving immediately. Stay out of trouble, you'll do half. Hell, Storm, you already have sixty days served. You'll be out in less than eighteen months."

"Bitch, are you crazy?! I couldn't do that! Do you have any idea what kind of hell I've been through in this pig hole? Huh?" Storm shouted loudly enough to prompt the female guard on watch to step forward and tell her to lower her voice or her visit would be cut short, attorney privilege or no attorney privilege.

Looking over her shoulder Storm rolled her eyes and continued talking to Clara. But before she got a word out, Clara reprimanded her. "We're going to stop the name-calling. I have never allowed a client to call me out of my name in the seventeen years I have been practicing law and I refuse to start today. Now I know you're upset, but I am doing the best that I can, as quickly and as effectively as I can. If the day arises that you feel that I'm not, then perhaps we need to have a discussion on my resigning as your attorney. Am I clear?" Clara glared.

Storm paused. "I'm sorry. I didn't mean that. I'm just frustrated at this whole thing. What other options do I have?"

"We go to a jury trial, which could take up to a year. And they could try you for second-degree murder, which carries a mandatory fifteen to life. As I told you before, Pennsylvania is a no-bail state for murder charges. Look, take the deal, Storm. We won't do any better."

As tears welled up in her eyes, Storm pleaded, "But I'm innocent and you know it!"

"Yes, I do. But my job was to have everyone else believe it, too, and I couldn't do that with the material I have."

Two days later, Storm found herself dressed in a two-piece burgundy suit, a lilac blouse, and conservative pumps, with just a hint of makeup, looking older than her twenty-six years. It was not her choice of suit, not at all her style, but when her attorney suggested that Storm needed to come to her arraignment with a subdued appearance, she knew that there was nothing in her closet at home quite appropriate for the occasion. Storm caught a glimpse of herself in a mirror as she was being led into court by two burly female guards, and was reminded of the scene from the movie *Monster* in which Aileen Wournos, a prostitute–serial killer, is led into court for her sentencing. *Difference is I'm no prostitute, and I damn sure ain't nobody's killer,* Storm thought to herself.

As she approached the table where her lawyer stood, Storm noticed that her family was there. Her father, Dutch, looked at her with weary, sleepless eyes, seeming as if he had aged overnight. Feeling responsible, Storm glanced at him and gave him a slight smile before dropping her eyes in shame. Nettie, a family friend who worked at the restaurant, waved at her. Standing at the very end of the row with a solemn expression on her face was Skylar, Storm's twin sister.

"Your Honor, the defendant is willing to plead guilty to an amended count of involuntary manslaughter," Clara Bow said. "We've agreed to a three-year sentence in state prison. The sixty days she has served in county would be credited to the overall sentence." After the lawyer spoke, Dutch's shoulders slumped and his legs looked like they'd give out on him any second.

Looking through a pair of half-rim glasses barely clinging to the bridge of his nose, Judge Randell Reinhart shuffled through the paperwork at his bench. "Miss Morrison, do you understand that this conviction could be used against you in any future violation or convictions, resulting in additional time attached to your sentence?"

"Yes, Your Honor."

"Upon completion of your sentence, you will be on a five-year probation, and during that time, you will not be able to vote in any election or leave the country without authorization. Do you understand these terms?"

Vote!? Who the hell cares about voting? Obama is already in office. What really pissed Storm off was that she wouldn't be able to go to her favorite vacation spot in the Cayman Islands for five years after getting out of this joint. "Yes, Your Honor," Storm answered.

"Therefore, Miss Morrison, for your conviction in count one, the court sentences you to three years in Muncy State Prison for Women, with a credit of sixty days already served. Good luck to you, young lady. And may I say that I hope this unfortunate event has turned your life around." The judge banged his gavel so hard that his glasses fell off completely.

IN MY SISTER'S HOUSE

< ONE >

When I Think of Home, I Think of a Place

Storm had long ago decided not to call anyone to come pick her up on the day she was released. No, she needed to make this journey back into society the same way she left it three years ago, by herself! Besides, the one thing she didn't want or need was pity from anyone, especially Skylar.

The smell on the prison bus was a familiar one. Although it had been three years since she was last on one, it was just as she remembered: funky and stale with a mixture of recognizable scents, like cheap perfume, cigarettes, body funk—life and death. But all that didn't matter now. She was on her way out of this cage.

There were only ten people on the bus including her, but Storm chose a seat in the back by herself. She didn't know any of the other girls getting released anyway. None of them were from her cellblock. Besides she needed this time to think about all she had to do when she got home. *Home. Do I even have a home anymore?*

Storm had plans and they were already in motion. First, she needed to find a job. Sidney, Skylar's man, had assured her there would be a job at the club for her if she wanted to work there. She had never met Sidney, but felt she knew a little about him. He was usually the one who accepted her collect calls from the prison. Over the years, they had had lengthy conversations. Skylar was usually too busy, or not there when the calls came through, and when the two sisters did manage to speak on the phone, they seemed like strangers. Storm heard that Skylar had turned Morrison's, the family restaurant, into some type of nightclub. *Things are going to be* real *different back home.*

< TWO >

Get Here if You Can

"So, do yourself a favor and stop by Legends for an unforgettable evening of sheer entertainment, dancing, and the finest in Southern cuisine." A tear formed in Skylar's eyes as she read aloud the ending of the review that *Philadelphia* magazine had given her very popular nightspot. She had worked her ass off this past year trying to make Legends the number one spot for entertainment in the Philadelphia club scene. The two-storey burgundy- and amber-colored brick building almost appeared out of place, nestled among a string of neatly adjoined row homes and positioned proudly on a corner in the working-class community. The fact that *Philadelphia* magazine had done a feature story and review on an African American business was a rare accomplishment—and rarer still, it was a *positive* review. But there it was, in black-and-white—a glowing review and profile ranking Legends number one.

Although Legends catered to an affluent, sophisticated crowd, its atmosphere was elegant, not bourgeois. Everyone felt at home here. Exquisite artwork by such noted artists as Jacob Lawrence, Romare Bearden, and Annie Lee adorned the walls. There was also a special rich royal blue tribute wall where eight-by-ten black-and-white portraits of legendary black entertainers of yesteryear, like Lena Horne, Ella Fitzgerald, Johnny Mathis, Sidney Poitier, and Dorothy Dandridge, hung in gold-colored picture frames. It was a conversation piece among the guests dining and dancing the night away. So much so, Skylar was planning to add to it and highlight legendary artists of today, like Whitney Houston, Beyoncé, Usher, Mary J. Blige, and Sade.

Looking at all she had accomplished, her mind went back to when she was a child. Dutch had been head chef at Morrison's, and people came from far and wide to savor his food. As it became more successful, everyone encouraged him to expand. But he always politely declined, convinced that the restaurant would lose the down-home family feel that he and Lady had dreamed of and created, even if it meant that periodically there were lines of people outside waiting for seats. After a difficult pregnancy, Lady lost her life during childbirth, and Dutch doted on his two baby girls from the start—they were the only family he had left aside from his regular customers—showering Skylar and Storm with more love and attention than any father could ever give his daughters. And now he was gone.

Roebuck Cicero Morrison, a retired navy man, worked as a short-order cook during his time in the service. He opened Morrison's Family Restaurant back in 1979 after marrying his longtime high school sweetheart, Barbara Evans. From the moment they laid eyes on each other in Spanish class at Ben Franklin High in Philly, there was no doubt they would be together forever. When Dutch enlisted in the Navy, Barbara enrolled at Cheyney University and promised to wait for him. Dutch called Barbara the love of his life and she reciprocated the feelings. Because they were complete opposites, no one really expected their romance to last, and some even passed it off as puppy love. He was laid-back, quiet, and gentle. She was eccentric, controlling, and what some deemed "a little off." But none of this bothered Dutch, not even Barbara's decision to change their names—especially his, because she couldn't for the life of her understand why someone would name their child Roebuck. She became Lady and he became Dutch. Together they purchased the building at 1625 South Street during a period of aggressive gentrification in South Philly.

Skylar's tears of joy over the review now turned into tears of sadness for her father. How she wished he had lived long enough to see her follow in his footsteps and become so successful in this business. When he decided to retire, his goal was to sell the place, but when she approached him with the idea of keeping it in the family by allowing her to open up a nightclub, he didn't hesitate to say anything but "Yes!" Hence, Legends was born. Thank God for Sidney, her fiancé and best friend. She couldn't imagine the past few years without him. And yet she still felt lonely at times. Not because Storm had been incarcerated for the past three years—they were never close anyway.

But so much for loneliness, for now Skylar had a business to run. She had not become so successful sitting on her butt. So she gathered herself together and prepared for the night's opening. Glancing at her watch she wondered where Nettie was. Nettie was never late.

Nettie was Legends' main bartender. But she was much more than that to Skylar. Day-to-day operations would not move as smoothly without the no-nonsense, outspoken, take-no-shit Nettie Flowers. Standing a little under five foot two and weighing about one hundred and five pounds, she was curvy, youthful, and sexy. One wouldn't have guessed that Nettie was in her late forties. Nettie looked good. A night never went by when some unsuspecting fool who came into the club didn't try and holla at her. Stopping them dead in their tracks, she never had a problem letting them know her weakness was young Puerto Rican women. Especially ones who dressed like stone-cold dudes and walked like they were carrying ten-inch dicks. The thought of it made Skylar chuckle to herself.

"Hey, baby, I'm sorry I'm late," Nettie said, rushing past Skylar directly to the bar to make sure it was set up right for the evening.

"Hi, Nettie," said Skylar, who sensed that she was upset. "What's the matter?"

"Nothing!" Nettie snapped.

"Is it June?" Skylar asked. June was Nettie's partner of two years.

Slamming down the wet cloth that she used to wipe the bar down with, she looked at Skylar and rolled her eyes. "What else could it be?" Nettie hissed. "I swear I'ma leave her ass in a minute. She got on my one good last nerve today."

"What happened this time, Nettie? Come on over. Let's sit down and talk about it." Skylar moved over one seat at the table, making room for Nettie next to her.

"Girl, I ain't got no time for that. I'm late as it is. We open in less than an hour and you know my station is always set up by now!"

"It's okay, Nettie. Take a few minutes. Here, come over and sit down."

Checking her watch first, Nettie sat down next to Skylar.

"We've been having a problem in the apartment with the cable. So for the last few days the cable company had been sending this guy over to try and figure out what it was. Well, today he finally realized that the root of the problem was the wiring in our bedroom. So we were in the room and because it was the same brotha had been dispatched for the last three days, well, we started conversing. Just talking shit, you know, like, 'Where you from? How long you been living in Philly?' A real nice, respectable brotha. And he had just finished telling me this joke when June came home from lunch. She walked in and heard all this laughter in our bedroom and started trippin'. Asking what was so funny and why was he in the bedroom and shit like that."

Skylar started to laugh.

"The shit ain't funny, Skylar!" Nettie glared at her.

"I'm sorry, Nettie," Skylar apologized. "But you two go at it all the time! Why was she so jealous?"

"I don't know!" Nettie shouted. "If I even look at a dude, the bitch's eyes cross! I'm like, 'Baby, if I wanted a man, I'd be with a man. I'm gay. I like women—but right now, you acting like a little girl!' I told her, 'If you're so damn insecure about a dick, then why don't you get your ass a penile implant?' "

"No you didn't, Nettie." Skylar couldn't contain her laughter.

"I sure did! I'm tired of this shit. I'm forty-seven years old and I'm taking this kind of shit from some twenty-five-year-old. Fuck that.

So she started packing up some of her shit and told me she was going out. Like that shit was gonna faze me. I was like 'Okay, well you just leave my keys on the kitchen table.' " Nettie crossed her arms and leaned back in the chair.

"Nettie, tell me you didn't say that." Skylar probed for more.

"You want me to lie to you? I said it and I meant it. She then got smart and said the reason I wanted her to leave the keys was because I wanted to give them to my 'cable man.' "

"You two ought to stop."

"So you know I had to fan the fires, girl." Nettie started to laugh. "I was like, 'Naw, he already got a set. I'll just put yours aside for the mailman.' " Nettie and Skylar laughed hysterically.

"Well, where did she go?" Skylar asked.

"The hell if I know! And do I look like I care? She'll bring her fat ass back home crying like a little bitch in a day or so." Nettie rolled her eyes and continued her rant. "These young bulls are something. They want to be the man so much. Talking 'bout how they can put a bitch's back out during sex, that it's so good. But when things don't go their way, they start whimpering like some spoiled pampered child! That's what I get for dealing with somebody that damn young. The next one I mess with is going to be old, settled, and on SSI."

Skylar and Nettie shouted their laughter together, nearly doubled over in stitches.

"It seems like yesterday when June and her brother came in here for lunch. I remembered thinking, What a cute teddy bear of a guy, with the prettiest smile," Skylar said. "It took me a while to notice that he was a she."

"Aw hell, girl, I clocked that shit when she walked in here." Nettie said matter-of-factly.

"Really? How?" Skylar quizzed.

"Gaydar, girl!" Nettie said. They laughed so much that Nettie almost completely forgot the mood she was in when she came into the club, that is, until her phone started to ring—with an Alicia Keys ringtone. June. Nettie frowned.

"See, there she goes now! Blowing up my damn phone." Nettie rolled her eyes and dismissed the call with a wave of her hand. "Let her ass sit over there and look at her ugly-ass momma!"

"Nettie!"

"What?" Nettie shouted. "Makes me sick! I'm too old for this shit, Skylar. Besides, I'm at work. I need to get ready for work." The phone continued to ring and Nettie continued to ignore it.

"Answer the phone, Nettie. The girl probably wants to apologize," Skylar pleaded through a series of chuckles and snickers.

Her plea fell on deaf ears as Nettie started to get up and go toward the bar. "Well, that's what voice mail is for!" Nettie sneered. After the ringing stopped, Nettie changed the subject. "Hey, did you see the article in *Philadelphia* magazine?" she beamed.

"Yes I did, girl! And tomorrow they're running a piece on the Channel 3 midday news, right?"

"Yup!"

Skylar smiled.

"Well you deserve all the success you get, baby. You've worked very hard to make this place what it is. Your daddy would've been so proud. I know I am." Nettie gave her a motherly embrace.

The mention of Dutch brought tears to Skylar's eyes. "You think so, Nettie?" Nettie assured her that not only would Dutch be proud, but that she felt his spirit around all the time, so she knew that he was looking after her. "No disrespect, Skylar, but your father was a 'one-of-a-kind nigga.' Let me just say that!"

Normally Skylar would have barked at anyone referencing her father as a nigger, but she knew that this was just the way Nettie talked.

"He supported me when I was at my lowest. Broke as a three-legged table." Nettie let out a hearty laugh, prompting Skylar to do the same. "Seems like yesterday that I came into Morrison's and asked your daddy for a hot meal." Just the thought of that dark time in her life made Nettie shake her head in disbelief. Skylar, careful not to interrupt, took Nettie's hands in hers. "I was practically on the streets. Correction—I was on the street. I knew I had no business coming into an establishment like Morrison's. Let's just say my reputation preceded itself. Nobody wanted to be bothered with me around here. Girl, I was like *The Scarlet Letter.*"

Ever since she was a child, Skylar had heard rumors about Nettie. But it never bothered her if they were true or not because, as far as she was concerned, Nettie was as near to any mother she had ever known. And she always felt a loving closeness to her.

"None of what was said about me bothered your daddy," Nettie said. "Even if most of the shit niggas was saying about me was true anyway. After he helped me get back on my feet, I asked him why he did it. And he looked at me and said, 'Nettie, every one of God's children deserves a second chance. And no matter what you may feel, you *are* one of God's children.' " Tearing up, Nettie used one of the table napkins to wipe her eyes. "I don't know where it came from, but somehow deep inside I believed him. Your daddy helped me and didn't expect nothing from me for it either. And I wasn't used to shit like that. Niggas been wanting shit from me since I was a child. Dutch was just a giving spirit." Nettie smiled and turned to Skylar. "And you're the same way, Skylar. You always helping people. Shit, you helped me, too."

"What you talking about, Nettie? All that you do around here for us? Please!"

"But I wouldn't have had that chance if you didn't keep me on when you opened Legends. When Dutch announced his retirement and said he was looking for a buyer for this building, my heart sank. I had no idea what I was going to do. Girl, where was my ass going? No formal education, and the only full-time job I had ever held was on my back! Going back to that shit was not even an option. And not because I was older or washed up, 'cause we all know I still look fabulous. Sshhiitt . . ." They both laughed. "I'm not ashamed of my past, because that's exactly what it is, my past. Besides, your pops made me so hopeful about my future. Dutch was the only man I ever trusted."

"Dutch loved you, too, Nettie. You've been family as long as I can remember," Skylar said, missing her father more than ever. "I've always appreciated the love you showered on me and Storm."

Saying her twin's name abruptly changed Skylar's mood. Nettie sensed this and and asked, "You thinking about Storm aren't you?"

"Huh? Yeah, I guess. Don't get me wrong. I'm happy she is getting released. I really am." Trying to sound convincing, Skylar continued, "I just don't know what to expect. Has she changed? Has she gotten herself together?"

"I'm sure she has changed some, Sky. Let's hope it's for the better. Being confined can make a believer out of even a housefly. Put one a 'em in a jar with a lid, and punch a hole in the top for a little air to get in. No matter how much he buzzes around, once he realizes he can't go anywhere, he'll settle down. Storm had three years to think about her life. And settle down. By the way, have you spoken to her lately?"

Skylar bowed her head. "The last time she called, Sidney answered. That's when she told him about her release date. I think it's any day now. She'll call for one of us to pick her up, I'm sure," Skylar said. "I just pray she has a new outlook on life, and won't fall into old habits."

"Storm is a sweet girl, Sky. She just ended up on the wrong side of the street a few times too many, that's all." Nettie gave her a comforting smile. "Everything will be fine, baby, you'll see."

"Thanks, Nettie, I don't know what I'd do if you weren't around."

"You'd keep on living! That's what you'd do," Nettie declared. And with that Skylar smiled, and wondered if this was what it felt like when a daughter had one of those intimate moments with her mother. She wished that she could have known her own mom. But she thanked God for Nettie.

Nettie's cellphone started singing Alicia Keys again and jolted the both of them out of their melancholy states. After glancing quickly at the display panel, Nettie snatched up her phone and turned on the Mute button. Skylar just shook her head and smiled. "You two."

< THREE >

Heartbreak Hotel

Exhausted from the prison bus ride, Storm checked into the Libby, a cheap hotel on Arch Street in downtown Philly, as soon as she was dropped off. Not exactly the Ritz-Carlton or Four Seasons that she was used to, but this would have to do . . . for now. Besides, she had had only $249 on the books at Muncy and that's exactly what they gave her when she was released. She could not believe that this fleabag of a joint was $99 a night. Sure, she thought of calling Sidney or Nettie to come pick her up, but she decided against it, opting to spend her first night home alone. She had spent the last three years locked up in a place where she had no privacy at all. Bitches even watched you when you peed. No, she needed at least twenty-four hours to regroup and plan her next move.

There were a few scores she had to settle. Besides, she didn't feel like having to answer anyone's questions about what things were like while she was locked down. Fuck, aside from Nettie, they hadn't cared enough to come visit her ass much when she was in there. Especially Skylar. Storm wasn't surprised, but she really didn't want Skylar's condescending ass coming up to the prison on family day anyway, sitting across from her with a frown on her face. Storm knew the only reason she came up to see her was because she drove

Dutch. But now he was gone. Storm could never forgive herself for being incarcerated during the final weeks of her father's life. Dutch had been the best father any child could have.

She wondered how he did it all—being a single parent raising two baby girls, running the family business and dealing with his ongoing health problems. But Dutch did it and never complained one time—at least not within earshot of his girls. Despite the differences between the twins, Dutch gave them the same amount of love and attention. Skylar was the more serious and focused one. She knew early on what she wanted out of life and her career. She was a planner, a list maker. On the other hand, Storm drifted through life with as much ease as she was afforded. She graduated from college with a degree in fashion design. But as of yet she hadn't done much with it. In fact, short of picking out the designer threads she once wore, she hadn't done anything with that degree.

Storm never considered herself a "problem child." She just had a mind of her own and did what she wanted to do. And Dutch encouraged this in both his girls. "Be the captain of your own ship," Dutch would say. "Be a leader, not a follower." He felt most parents of twins made the mistake of forgetting that they were two individuals, not one. Dressing them alike, involving them in the same activities, and acting as if they were one was never cute to him. Sure, twins were similar and shared a lot of the same interests, but they were still separate people with their own goals, aspirations, likes, and dislikes.

The only thing that bothered Dutch was that his girls were never close with each other. It was almost like they were born into the world as total strangers. No matter how much he taught love, togetherness, and sisterhood, the two girls seemed to have a vast amount of disdain for each other. Once they became adults, the only time they even pretended to like each other was when the three spent a holiday together, like Thanksgiving, Christmas, or his birthday. Other than that, they had little to do with each other.

God only knows what it will be like once we see each other again.

That she even had to ask Skylar for a little job to get back on her feet made Storm nauseous. But a bitch had to do what a bitch had to do. And besides, it was only temporary.

Glancing down at her watch, Storm decided to venture out for a bite to eat. She hadn't eaten anything since her last breakfast at Muncy that morning. If you want to call plastic-tasting powdered eggs and two overcooked scrawny pieces of sausage that resembled hard Chihuahua turds breakfast, well, then she had had breakfast.

Pulling her cap down low on her head and donning a pair of cheap sunglasses, she took the elevator down from the fourth floor to the small, smelly lobby. After being confined to a twelve-by-nine cell for three years, she felt uncomfortable in small, cramped places. Cursing herself for not taking the stairs as she had upon her arrival, she prayed she could get off soon. The elevator came to an abrupt stop at the lobby, and when the door opened, Storm headed straight to the front desk. An overweight light-skinned girl with a headful of cheap braids sat behind the desk talking on her cellphone. Nearby was a half-eaten bag of pork rinds and a can of Pepsi. *Typical!*

"Excuse me," Storm said. The girl never looked up. *Is this bitch ignoring me, or didn't she hear me?* Noticing the name "Pumpkin" on her nametag, Storm decided to give it another try, this time addressing her by name and a tad louder. Pumpkin stopped her conversation and glared at Storm.

"Hold on, Boo." Pumpkin put down the phone and looked up at Storm. Storm immediately caught the attitude Pumpkin was giving her. *Now this bitch does not know me, because I will snatch her fat yella ass from behind that desk and beat her like she stole God's supper.* Returning the stare, Storm decided to calm herself down and appease this ho, and tell her what was wrong.

"Yes, I just wanted to let someone know that there may be something wrong with the elevator—it took forever to get down to the lobby, and it actually got stuck midway between the second and the first floor," Storm offered.

"Okay, *and?*" Pumpkin shook her head like a fat bobblehead doll.

"*And*—I thought you might want to let the maintenance person know or whoever is in charge." Storm forced herself to smile.

"Aight, thanks. I'll leave a note, 'cause don't nobody get in till in the morning," Pumpkin said. "That's why when I went to the vending machine, I took the stairs down there, 'cause that thing gets stuck all the time." With that she resumed her conversation.

Storm disgustedly stared at her for a moment longer. Realizing that Storm was still there, Pumpkin rolled her eyes and again asked her person to hold.

"Anything else?" she asked Storm.

"No, it's fine. I won't be in this hellhole another night anyway. Like I said, I just thought you might want to know." With that, something caught Storm's eye. A roach had crawled into Pumpkin's Pepsi without her noticing it. Storm decided to fuck with her.

"Girl, it sure is hot down here in this lobby. That Pepsi looks so good and cold. I think I'll get me one." She chuckled.

"Yup." And with that Pumpkin lifted the can to her mouth and took a swig. Delighted at what she just witnessed, Storm started on her way out the door. She reasoned that the two belonged together: a fat, nasty, yella rat, and a germ-carrying roach. She let out a hearty laugh and stepped into the night air.

< FOUR >

This Joint Was Jumping

As the pulsating beat of the new Chris Brown joint filled up the club, the dance floor got crowded quickly. Judging by how fast everyone took to the floor, it was definitely a crowd favorite. His fans weren't just teenage girls. Often compared to Usher and Michael Jackson because of his vocal style and dance moves, this twenty-year-old also had some cougars wet-dreaming about him, wishing for the opportunity to break him in. Posing bare-chested on an *Ebony* magazine cover hadn't hurt, either. Suddenly, mature women who once spoke of him like a sweet doting son for their daughters wanted to bed him. All of this was before the whole Chris Brown–Rihanna episode that had had Hollywood tabloids selling out quicker than the Saturday morning hot cakes special at Denny's. Certainly not one to condone his actions, Skylar had even forbidden Brown's music to be played at Legends. But Quince, the club's DJ, convinced her that she had to separate the artist from the man. Hadn't she been guilty of still listening to R. Kelly? And *his* alleged despicable act was beyond forgiveness. She had innocently seen the video, sent to her in an email. She'd had no idea what it was until she opened it. And unless he, too, had a twin, there was no denying that it was him.

A stylish Skylar entered the packed club amid a flood of hellos, stares, whispers, and well-deserved compliments. As Tupac's classic said, "All Eyez on Me." She smiled. Along with all of the usual Friday night regulars there was a flurry of new faces—obviously, the magazine article and newscast profiles had worked.

Attempting to make her way to the bar, Skylar glanced briefly at herself in one of the wall mirrors and liked what she saw. Dressed in a tasteful black Dolce & Gabbana catsuit that complimented every curve of her body, with a multicolored scarf tied symmetrically around her waist and a pair of three-and-a-half-inch Jimmy Choo pumps, she was a striking presence. Her honey-brown hair was pulled back into a long, loose ponytail. Because of her flawless bronze skin, she needed little makeup.

Moving across the floor, she couldn't help but sway to the music. But not too much. She was the owner and always had to set an example. Bumping and grinding and sweating like Whitney Houston on a dance floor was not professional. Among the bodies swaying back and forth, she noticed her man standing at the bar talking to Nettie. It was as if he knew someone was watching, because with a slight tilt of his head, he noticed her looking at him. His face lit up once he saw that it was her. Sidney Francis, a strikingly handsome six-foot-four chestnut-brown brotha with a killer smile, beamed at her. *Boy, have I hit the jackpot with this one.*

Usually a fine brotha like this had some shit going on with him. Like he knew he was fine so he walked and talked like you must *also* know it. Or they would look like Flava Flav and Jimmy JJ Walker combined, but be gentle, kind, and loving. Rarely did a sista come across a single, straight, educated, and spiritually connected brotha who gave you body and face and was available. But there he was. Skylar smiled. And to think, this fairy-tale romance almost hadn't happened.

At thirty-one years of age, Sidney Francis knew he had found his African princess as soon as he spotted her at a small business seminar in Cherry Hill, New Jersey, back in 2005. After being with the Jackson-Wilder accounting firm in Philly for the last five years, he was ready to open his own business. Although he doubted there was anything new that he could learn from this seminar, he had decided to sign up and attend anyway to obtain useful contacts. The all-day lecture was to begin at 9 a.m. and go to 5 p.m. Because Sidney arrived at 8:45 a.m., there was limited seating available. In fact, there only seemed to be two seats still left. One was in back of a twenty-five-ish girl who was reminiscent of Amy Winehouse, complete with a ridiculous beehive-type sixties hairdo, tattoos, and gothic makeup. Sidney couldn't tell if she planned on opening a salon or a tattoo parlor. The other seat was next to an older, heavyset white gentleman who had an oxygen tank beside his desk and breathed like he was in a porno. *Amy Winehouse, here I come, baby.*

Nestling back in his seat next to the faux British pop / rock singer, he took a quick scan of the room. *What the hell am I doing here?* Then he saw her. Right then and there he knew the real reason he had paid $349 for a seminar he didn't need. His wife-to-be was seated directly across from him. It was as if God himself planted her there for him. Not wanting to seem rude, he tried in vain to catch her eye without being obvious. He would smile at her. *Yeah, that always seems to do it. Momma always said I had the prettiest smile this side of Philadelphia. Never mind the fact that Momma hardly ever left the state of Pennsylvania.*

Just thinking about that, and her, made him chuckle. This caused "Amy" to turn around and stare like he had disturbed her or something. "Sorry," he said. Not missing a beat, she turned back toward the speaker at the podium. He felt that he should do the same. Periodically, he'd attempt to steal a glance at the beautiful sista, who reminded him of a better-looking Gabrielle Union, which was hard to imagine, because Gabrielle was his ideal woman. He remembered seeing her in Tyler Perry's film *Daddy's Little Girls* and leaning over to his sister, Dawn, in the theater, saying, "Now that's wifey material right there!"

Two hours and forty-five minutes into the seminar, the moderator stopped for lunch. Everyone headed to an area set up like a cafeteria. Sidney would work his magic on "Gabrielle" during lunch. Hell, by the end of the seminar, they would be planning their engagement.

"Excuse me, was this seat taken?" Sidney asked. Without even looking up, Skylar replied that it was not. Sitting down, he noticed that she was engrossed in a book.

"What's that you're reading?" he asked. This time, looking up, Skylar felt like time was standing still. She was literally speechless. She swore to herself that she had never seen a man so handsome in her life. "Oh, it's just a novel my book club is reading," she said, not taking her eyes off him. "*The Bachelorette Party.*"

"Oh, I see. Were 'we' thinking of having one of those soon?" He lifted one eyebrow curiously.

"No, not me, I am happily single," she lied. "It's the book club selection we decided on. Our group meets tomorrow, and I have a few pages to finish up. It's pretty good."

"Who's the writer?"

"Donald Welch. He's actually from Philly. It's his first novel, and it's making quite a buzz. Will Smith has even optioned the film rights," she proudly stated, as if she knew the writer and the megastar.

"Will Smith, wow, that's impressive. Well it must be pretty good. Sorry, I haven't heard of the brotha Don, but that's not saying much. If it isn't a book on business or stocks and bonds, I'm afraid I have no idea what's out there," he said. "I didn't mean to disturb you. I'll let you get back to your reading." And with that, Sidney turned on his BlackBerry and retrieved some emails. Skylar smiled and returned to her reading.

Why didn't he say something else to me? Skylar thought to herself, stealing a glance at him while he appeared to be texting someone, scanning as much of him as she could see, as quickly as she could see it. She didn't want him to think she was interested or anything, although she clearly was. After all, she had not been able to concentrate on anything she was reading since she first laid eyes on this heavenly creature. She noticed he wasn't wearing a ring—that was a good sign right there. Or was it? Playas often didn't wear their wedding bands when away from their wives so they could appear single. But there was no tan line either, so it seemed safe. She liked his nice, strong-looking hands, clean nails, smooth, even skin, close, fresh haircut. Even through his suit jacket it was obvious that he worked out—his chest was *on point*. The scent of his cologne was ambrosia. She needed to see his shoes. Dutch said you could always tell a successful man by what was on his feet. Moving her chair back, she pretended to drop something and looked under the table. He was wearing a pair of stylish, expensive soft black leather loafers. Smiling to herself, she returned to her upright position at the table, wanting to ask about the cologne, which by now had inebriated her senses, but deciding against it because of her womanly pride.

Say something, dammit! she screamed to him in her head. *I know you're interested.* She could tell by the way he had approached her. Looking around she could see that there were plenty of seats available, even a few vacant tables, however, he had chosen to invade her space. She laughed to herself and wondered, *Why must we all play these childish games?* Okay, fine, she'd break the silence.

"Excuse me, what's that cologne you're wearing?"

"Oh, it's Unforgivable by P. Diddy. Not sure if I like it or not, but my sister got it for me. Do you like it?" His broad smile made Skylar blush like a teenage schoolgirl.

"Why, yes, I do." Looking up at him with doe-like eyes, she returned his smile, hoping this would reopen the door for a more in-depth conversation. But he only thanked her and resumed fidgeting with his BlackBerry.

Oh no, he doesn't! an annoyed Skylar thought to herself. She wouldn't say another word to this pompous jerk. The next few moments seemed like hours going by, and nothing else was uttered between the two. Skylar couldn't keep her mind focused on the book. She could have sworn she had read the last paragraph three times. Checking her watch, she noticed that the lunch break would be over soon and was determined she'd leave "Mr. Right" wishing he had said more to her. Thoughts of Dutch came into her mind. He used to tell her not to jump to conclusions. "Things aren't always what they appear," he'd say.

Stealing another glance at him, she reasoned that perhaps he was just trying to be respectable and not too forward. She despised pushy men, anyway. But somehow she knew he wasn't that way. No, this was a decent man. One she hoped to know better.

"Gosh, it looks as though it's time to go back inside," Skylar offered.

Still not looking away from his BlackBerry, Sidney told her he thought he was done for today, especially after receiving an email that needed his immediate attention.

"Oh, I'm sorry to hear that. I hope it isn't bad news," she said.

"No, nothing like that, but I probably need to take care of it sooner than later." He started to gather his briefcase, turned off his phone, and excused himself. And with that, "Mr. Perfect," "The One," was gone, probably for good.

Watching him walk away, it suddenly occurred to Skylar that she didn't even know his name. "How rude!" she said loud enough just for her own ears. For a second she even thought about calling out something—anything—to him. But what? Inquire about his cologne again? Tell him that she wanted to get it for Dutch? Yeah, that's it. . . . No. She nixed that idea with a chuckle because she knew very well that Dutch only wore Old Spice, a scent he'd enjoyed as long as she could remember. Too late now anyway, her Prince Charming was disappearing among the bevy of pedestrians going in all directions.

Returning to the seminar, she mechanically sat through the last half, oblivious to anything that was going on or being said. Embarrassed, she quietly cursed herself for being so smitten with the handsome stranger.

Later that evening, while readying herself for bed, Skylar heard her cellphone ring. Trying to identify the source of the John Legend ringtone, her attention made its way over to her handbag. Rummaging through it, she grabbed the phone and noticed the word "Private" on the keypad. Frowning, she immediately shut it off and put it on the coffee table. She had a practice of not answering private or unavailable calls. Standing up, she noticed a tan-colored business card had fallen on the floor. The name Sidney Francis, CPA, was inscribed in gold lettering on the front. It didn't ring a bell so she started to discard it, but after flipping it over she noticed some unfamiliar handwriting. "Was great meeting you at the seminar. Would love to take you to lunch sometime. Please call! — Sidney 1–267–555–0234." Covering her mouth with her hand in disbelief, Skylar couldn't contain herself and fell back onto her bed, letting out the loudest scream she'd ever made. Knowing she was in the apartment alone, she jumped up and started running around in blissful glee.

"Oh, my God, what in the world will I wear?" she thought. Rummaging through her closet, tossing designer dresses and blouses haphazardly about, she suddenly realized how silly this was. Plopping down amid the designer wreckage, Skylar shook her head in innocent embarrassment. They didn't even have an actual date scheduled yet. Throughout the entire ordeal, she did not let go of his business card. She stared and stared at it, knowing she would indeed call him. Speaking out loud, "Yes, Mr. Sidney Francis, I will have lunch with you. Perhaps I'll call you in a day or two, but not today." She didn't want to seem too anxious. Ecstatic, Skylar got up, decided on a lingering hour-long soak with lavender and vanilla bath crystals. As her body descended into the toasty calm waters, she dreamt of the man with the beautiful smile.

A romance had blossomed almost instantaneously after their first lunch date. A lot had happened in those two years. Dutch's death and Storm's incarceration had certainly taken their toll on Skylar. But meeting and falling in love with Sidney was definitely a highlight. His hypnotic, insatiable smile mesmerized her, and the love he showered her with brought her welcoming comfort daily, even at the times he annoyed her—like when he left the cap off the toothpaste after every use no matter how many times she reminded him, or when he left their computer signed on and retired to their bedroom. These were small nuisances compared to what she got in return.

As Skylar fell in love with his smile all over again, looking at him through her impressively crowded club, she reassured herself, *Yes, yes, I can live with this.* Yes! Today was a good day to be Skylar Morrison.

Just before reaching Sidney at the bar, Skylar saw Flynn, the house comic, waving her down. "Hey, Sky, hot night, huh?" With his jovial, easygoing style and winning personality infused with impeccable comedic timing, Flynn had been with Skylar since she opened Legends.

"Hey, Flynn. Yes, I'm very happy about that. I'm sure you are, too." She smiled.

Flynn loved performing in front of crowds. The bigger the better. It wasn't that he was that funny. Some of his jokes fell flat. But it was just Flynn. He'd tell a joke, and even if no one else thought it was funny, his infectious laugh bellowed through the club, prompting everyone else to follow suit. Sometimes his joy spilled onto the streets of South Philly, and eager patrons lined up awaiting entrance would start laughing, just knowing that Flynn was onstage doing his routine. He never made it to the big time—his only claim to fame had been a lone appearance on HBO's popular *Def Jam Comedy Show* in the early '90s. Unlike Bernie Mac, D. L. Hughley, Martin Lawrence, and Chris Tucker, Flynn Wilson didn't see the offers come in. He did manage to go on the small club circuit a few times as the opening act for B- and C-listers like Chris Spencer and Ralph Harris. Even they worked more than he did. After a while those jobs had dried up, too, and he came to work for Skylar at Legends. It wasn't the Comedy Store in L.A. or a showroom in Atlantic City or Vegas, but it was better than nothing. Still he had dreams of making the big time. He would just have to keep working at it. Will Smith, Patti Labelle, Bill Cosby, or some other famous Philadelphian would surely come through one night and hook him up.

The one time Will Smith had been in the house, Flynn was home with the flu. When he found out that Will had been in the audience, he got sicker. Will had a reputation for helping so many people, especially those from Philly, and Flynn remained hopeful. Skylar had promised as long as she had Legends, Flynn would have a job.

Knowing he would never have a chance with a girl like Skylar didn't stop him from thinking of her as much as he did. Not the same way he did in the beginning, though. No, Skylar was more like his little sis. This was why he gave so much attitude to Sidney once he saw that Skylar was smitten with him.

"I don't know about yo pretty boy, Skylar," Flynn said one night before they opened.

"What do you mean, Flynn? Sidney is really a nice man," she assured him.

"Yeah, well he better know I'm watching his ass, and if he slips up one time on some stupid shit, I'ma be right here to take care of his ass!"

Smiling and shaking her head at Flynn, Skylar gave him a hug and a light peck on the cheek. "That's very sweet of you, big brother, but I don't think you'll have to worry about that. But I know you got my back."

It wasn't long after that Sidney had won over Flynn, too. Once Flynn found out that Sidney was a Phillies fan, he was all right with him. If he couldn't have Skylar for himself, well, then, he was cool with Sidney becoming the lucky man. In the end, Sidney asked Flynn to be one of his groomsmen at their wedding, which was taking place next year. Of course, Flynn said yes, but jokingly said it might be a double wedding because he had planned on finding him his "special girl" by then, too.

"Yo, Sky, any special announcements you need me to make tonight?" Flynn asked.

"No, I don't think so." Suddenly remembering something, she stopped him before he reached the stage area. "Flynn!" she shouted. "Can you remind everyone that we are holding auditions in the morning for two new dancers? Here at the club at 10 a.m. sharp—and emphasize 10 a.m. *sharp,* would you please?" She folded her arms across her chest.

"Aw, girl, if I do that, well, you gonna be here by yo'self. You know black folks don't know nothing 'bout being on time," Flynn joked.

"And as long as we play into that stereotypical excuse, they *will* be late! So let's stop that right now!" she laughed. Flynn went up on-stage just as Mariah Carey's voice trailed off at the end of a song. Signaling to Quince to end the music, he grabbed the mike and started his routine.

"Yo-yo-yo, welcome! Welcome! Is everyone having a good time?" Although the deafening screams were proof that everyone was, Flynn insisted on asking again, "I said, is everybody having a good time?" Again, screams were heard throughout the well-dressed crowd of people aged twenty-five and over. "That's more like it." His face lit up. "As you all know, I am Flynn Wilson, comic extraordinaire here at the number one nightspot in Philly, Legends!" The crowd roared louder than the cheering section at a Sixers' game. "LEGENDS, LEGENDS, LEGENDS!" they all chanted in unison. Flynn told a few mediocre jokes that went over well, despite not being funny. The crowd still responded favorably, more to Flynn's rambunctious laugh than to his punch lines. Flynn moved into his favorite segment of his act: targeting members of the audience and making them the butt of his jokes. Standing off by the bar, a relaxed Skylar and Sidney watched in anticipation of what Flynn had cooked up.

Skylar knew that the audience did not always take kindly to Flynn's antics—like the time he decided to tease what appeared to be a very pregnant woman sitting at one of the front tables. He did an almost five-minute-long act on this woman, who looked like she was in her final trimester, even going into the audience and insisting the woman stand up while he told a joke about how her man could still have a little fun in the bedroom with her, despite her intrusive girth, without it harming the baby. The club roared in laughter. Even Skylar marveled that Flynn had hit a home run with this one.

But the woman wasn't pregnant, not pregnant at all. She had just gained some unflattering weight, mostly in her midsection. When she started crying, at first Flynn thought it was one of those times when a joke had been so funny that even the person on the receiving end couldn't resist the flow of tears. Not that he knew what that was like, because it had never happened during any of his routines, but hey, a first time for everything, right? He poured it on thicker, telling the woman how now her stomach matched her ass. "Baby got back *and* front," he shouted, as he twirled her around for the whole room to get a look.

At this point, her boyfriend had heard enough; he stood up and punched Flynn in the mouth and then proceeded to jump him. As pandemonium struck the crowd, Head, the buff six-foot-five 330-pound security guy, scurried across the floor and pulled the guy off Flynn. Skylar remembered how Head had effortlessly used one hand on the dude and his other hand on Flynn. She and Nettie immediately went to the crying woman and led her back to the office to calm her down, while Sidney maintained order in the crowd. The look of surprise on Flynn's face revealed that he had no idea what had just happened.

Fortunately, the police did not have to be summoned. The couple left quietly after several apologies, including one from a bleeding and swollen-faced Flynn. Needless to say, after that night, Skylar forbade Flynn from picking on any audience member at all. He would have to come up with a new routine. Though discouraged by Skylar's choice—and being physically beaten; his nose never did return to its original shape, even after the rhinoplasty that the club paid for—Flynn would find another way to keep this part of his act, a way in which he wouldn't have to worry about any repercussions from his boss or an angry boyfriend or husband. He wasn't looking for any more trouble or alterations to his face. He decided to play the dozens.

"Everybody knows that I have a habit of picking on peeps in the audience," Flynn said as he surveyed the packed house, looking for his first victim. "So if you can't take the heat, bounce now, 'cause it's about to be on and poppin' in here!" An excited but nervous audience cheered loudly. Just as Flynn was about to go on, a heavyset woman wearing rhinestone sunglasses and a skintight fuchsia spandex dress stood up. She appeared to be gathering her things to leave. Flynn noticed her immediately and flashed a sly smile toward the audience, letting them know he'd just found his first victim. The crowd started to egg him on.

"Aw, damn!" a hysterical Flynn zeroed in on her. "Now what the hell do we have here? You know you are wrong!" By this time, no one could contain themselves in anticipation of what was about to come. The woman had a nervous look on her face and started toward the exit.

"Oh, shit, I see I may have stepped on someone's toes!" Flynn teased. "Hey, baby, you ain't got to go. I'll be good to you." Again Flynn threw a sinister smile to the audience, indicating that he was ready to let loose. But the woman had no intention of leaving yet. She had something else on her mind, like confronting Flynn. Carrying her purse, a drink, and a large envelope, she approached the stage.

"Oh, you gonna be real good, Flynn Wilson," the angry woman snapped. Handing the envelope to him, she said, "Here, take this!" A confused and somewhat worried Flynn reached for the package and asked what it was.

"Papers from my attorney. I'm pregnant and you's the daddy, nucka!" With that she snatched off her glasses and stared him down with her hands on her hips. A stunned and shocked audience reacted to this revelation with gasps, laughter, and outbursts of "OH, SHIT!" and "NO SHE DIDN'T!"

A speechless Flynn stuttered and stumbled over his words, trying to find the right thing to say. Skylar, with her hand over her mouth, pulled Sidney close to her side and gave him a look like, "What the hell?" Sidney shrugged his shoulders and turned his attention back to the stage, where all the action was taking place. Nettie stopped serving drinks and wondered what could possibly happen next.

"Peaches?" Flynn managed to spit out the name with caution.

"Naw, nigga, its Beatrice. Peaches was my sister. She's knocked up, too!" Standing toe-to-toe with him, she waited for a reaction from a panic-stricken Flynn.

"There must be some mistake. I never slept with you!" A nervous, pop-eyed Flynn scanned the room only to immediately focus on

Beatrice. A brazen Beatrice snatched the microphone from him and bellowed, "Who said we went to sleep?" And with that the laughter reached fever pitch. The crowd couldn't tell if this was all a part of Flynn's routine or if it was real. Even Skylar didn't know and she always knew when Flynn was pulling a prank. She was hoping to lock eyes with him long enough for him to give her an indication that everything was cool. But he didn't. Flynn was a nervous wreck. He continued one-on-one with Beatrice.

"I-I-I must have been drunk," he stuttered. "I-I don't understand. This is all too crazy!"

"Are you calling me a liar?" Not waiting for him to respond, she continued. Tossing her head back, with weaved hair going everywhere and both hands on her hips she screamed, "Well, I never!"

With that, Flynn offered that this was his sentiment exactly. "Well, *I* never!" The audience burst into laughter, appreciating the irony. They were enjoying this comedic interchange.

Beatrice, clearly upset by what was taking place, informed Flynn that she would meet him on *The Maury Povich Show* for a DNA test. With that she started toward the door, the back of her dress rising higher and higher. As she walked, she threw one more dagger at Flynn. "You will *never* taste the fruit of my womanhood again!" She then waved her pinky finger at him, visible for all to see. "See you on the set of the show little man." Then Beatrice swung back the door of the club and left.

A rush of hot air blew through the room. No one could tell if it was the hot air of the summer night or the heat from Beatrice's ample body as she whizzed by. An apologetic Flynn attempted to quiet down the audience.

"Okay, okay, enough of that. Now, everyone makes mistakes, right? I mean it was only one night. She looked better under the club lights, and under the influence of that fifth of Hennessy!" He laughed. "Brothas, you know what I mean, right?"

The men in the club all started shouting "Hell, no!" and "Were you crazy, man?"

Realizing that he was alone on this one, Flynn decided to chastise the entire audience. "Now wait a minute here. Y'all didn't say nothing when Janet Jackson hooked up with Jermaine Dupri. And he look like Webster with glasses." Only a few found this one funny, so Flynn continued. "Nor did y'all make any noise when Beyoncé got with Joe Camel—I mean Jay Z." This time a few more started to laugh, but no cigar. Flynn proceeded. "*And,*" he raised his voice, "nobody said shit when you found out that Condi Rice likes 'Bush.' " He sheepishly smirked and waited for his joke to sink in. However, he got more playful boos than laughs.

Someone shouted from the audience, "BRING BACK BEATRICE!" As laughter erupted, some of the audience started to chant, "BEATRICE, BEATRICE, BEATRICE . . ."

Flynn pretended that he was pissed. But this scene couldn't have pleased him more. Unbeknownst to the crowd, or Skylar, Sidney, or Nettie, "Beatrice" was part of his new act, and the entire routine was a setup. The crowd had been punked. "Oh, so you want that ol' battleaxe Beatrice, huh?" he playfully joked. "Yeah!!!" someone shouted, and with that Flynn introduced his new comedy partner, Beatrice Boston. A much different Beatrice reemerged into the club: This time, she was stylishly dressed in a Baby Phat silver-and-gold jumpsuit that flattered her buxom and curvaceous body. A pair of Manolo Blahnik pumps fit snugly on her petite feet, and what everyone had thought was a weave had actually been a wig. It too had been discarded and she was sporting a stylish pixie haircut, reminiscent of the actress Melinda Williams of *Soul Food* fame. Beatrice was rather attractive and received several catcalls from the male audience. One full-figured sista in the audience shouted, "BIG GIRLS RULE!" and started to pump her fists in the air like she was at a rap concert. When the cheers simmered down, Flynn turned the microphone over to Beatrice, who proceeded to do a fifteen-minute routine that kept most of the crowd in stitches.

Once Beatrice finished, Flynn brought up Skylar who tearfully thanked the crowd for all of the support given to Legends and said how proud she knew Dutch must be. "I don't take my success for granted, I want you to know. I am fully aware that in our present economy, businesses of all sorts are folding. But your loyalty, and the fact that we abide by the unspoken, yet universal rule that 'the customer is always right,' is our key to success. I also have a 'bomb' staff, wouldn't you say?" Waving her hand toward them she thanked all of them, especially Nettie and Head. Turning her attention to her "rock," she asked Sidney to join her onstage. Everyone could see these two were in love. No matter how much they attempted to remain professional while standing before the crowd, they couldn't keep their hands and eyes off each other. Before leaving the stage, Skylar reminded everyone about the new dancer auditions. That drew some catcalls from the male clientele, but not as many as when she sprung a surprise: As part of Legends' upcoming anniversary celebrations, the club would host the official V.I.P. afterparty for an upcoming Flo Rida concert at the Kimmel Center. One overzealous fan, known as Miss Shoes because of her unique selection of stylish footwear, shot directly up from her seat, with screams of delight, and snapped her fingers in a Z formation, as she strutted across the floor in a pair of lavender Prada ankle boots. On her way back to her seat, she slapped five with several other women, who were all excited about the sexy new bad boy of hip-hop. With that Skylar and Sidney instructed everyone to continue enjoying the rest of the evening. As they left the stage a light jazz tune filtered from the speakers overhead.

< FIVE >

Help Me Make It Through the Night

Trying to nestle into the uncomfortable single bed, Storm drifted in and out of a restless slumber. After lying on a cheap bed pad on a metal frame for three years, she thought at least she'd be able to get a little rest in the quiet of her hotel room—especially after not getting more than three or four hours' sleep on any given night in Muncy. Inmates learned early on in the joint that you never slept too soundly. You never knew when some crazy or jealous bitch would decide to shank you for no apparent reason. Or ransack your personal belongings in an effort to steal cigarettes or a snack. She remembered one incident in particular when the nagging urge to pee awakened her late one night and she found one of her cellies, Rosa, bent over with her stank ass in the air, going through her trunk. Not caring whether she woke up Carrie Ann or Deshanna, their other two cellmates, or not, Storm sat up on her bunk and screamed at Rosa. "Bitch, what are you doing?" Normally, one would think that if they got caught red-handed doing something like that, they'd react like a deer caught in headlights and make up some kind of lie. Not these brazen hos. "I'm looking for a clean sponge," Rosa whispered in an annoyed tone. Sponge was a term women used in the slammer to describe tampons.

"Well, did it occur to you to ask my ass for one?" Storm hissed.

"I didn't want to wake anybody up. Sorry—damn! Now you got one or not, Mommie?" Rosa said in her thick Spanglish.

The only reason Storm decided to oblige this bitch and not make her butt bleed to death was that she didn't want to smell Rosa's contaminated ass till morning. "Look in the second drawer and get one!" she snapped. "And tomorrow you take your Puerto Rican ass to the commissary and get you a box!" With that Storm laid back down, still facing in Rosa's direction, however. She had to make sure the tampon was the only thing that Rosa's sticky fingers picked up.

"Ain't nobody got 'paper' on they books like you do, Ma!" Rosa chuckled in a hushed tone as she scurried back across the room to the bottom bunk.

"Well, that's yo broke-ass problem!" Storm spit out. "Now that's the last one I'm giving you, so either you get your own or start using your bedsheet to stop up that big-ass hole!"

Deshanna, who obviously was also awake in the next cell, started laughing. "Damn, Storm, you a cold-ass trick, you know that?"

Rosa didn't like being the butt of jokes and vowed to herself that she'd pay back Storm for what she'd said.

The memory of Deshanna's laughter filled Storm's head as she tossed and turned on the uncomfortable bed in her Libby hotel room. *Wait, were those footsteps?* Hearing a noise in the hall outside her room, Storm perked up and she strained to hear where they would stop. Had she locked her door? Not remembering, Storm got up and quietly tiptoed toward the door. Once she saw that the door was secured, she pressed her eye to the peephole, wondering if she'd see anything. A very intoxicated woman was standing in front of the room across the hall, unsuccessfully trying to find the keyhole with her key. Her cheap, foul-smelling perfume seeped through Storm's door, almost blinding her. Deeming the woman harmless enough,

Storm retreated to her bed more wide-awake than before. Who could sleep anyway? Lying there in the complete quiet of the night, she tried to enjoy the solitude, because come sunrise, some *shit* was about to jump off that would surely be legendary. Burying her face in the pillow, she smiled to herself.

< SIX >

Brand-new Day

During the day, with all the lights off, the sound system silenced, and its tables bare of fancy and festive coverings, Legends didn't quite look like the luxurious five-star showroom it was. Less than twelve hours ago, a crowd of two hundred–plus had enjoyed themselves way into the night. Now even the ornate crystal chandelier seemed out of place as it hung in solitude over the limited dining area. Two of the club's regular dancers, Princess and Lovely, stretched and warmed up on the dance floor. Princess, the smaller of the two, was a little shorter than five feet, with a compact dancer's build. She sat in a lotus position, with her eyes closed and back arched. Her honey-brown, somewhat curly mane stood at attention all over her head like a light and airy wheat field. Even untamed, it complemented her small oval face and features. Normally, Skylar would not have considered hiring someone so young looking. Princess was twenty-six but looked all of sixteen, and every so often a first-time patron would come into the club, see Princess onstage dancing, and assume that Legends was hiring underage dancers. But her talent was undeniable. There wasn't any style of dance that Princess couldn't master. For the last two years, during the fall pilot season, Princess would leave Legends and Philadelphia and trek off to Hollywood, where she choreographed hopeful dancers on the popular Fox show *So You Think You Can Dance*. She got the job after appearing on the show herself as a competitor the first season, and although she didn't win, she impressed the producers so much with her grace, style, and beauty that she was asked to come on board as one of the choreographers. The show paid her quite handsomely, so she really didn't need to return to Philly and her job at Legends, but she did.

Legends and the city of Philly had that kind of effect on you. If you were born and raised in Philadelphia, no matter where you went in the world or what career path you chose, Philly was always home—although in the past few years Philadelphia had not been depicted in the press as the city of brotherly love and sisterly affection, with its almost daily murders. Nonetheless, Philadelphians loved their town, its famous cheese steaks, soft pretzels, and rich American history—there was the Liberty Bell, the Betsy Ross house, the Constitution. So Princess maintained residences on both coasts. The only problem Skylar ever had with Princess was her attitude. Since her instant fame in LaLa land, there were times when she could be unbearable to be around. Nettie would say to Skylar, "Princess believes her own press releases." But as far as Skylar was concerned, as long as Princess performed well at the club, there was no problem.

Lovely was christened with her name by an ex-boyfriend and was physically the complete opposite of Princess. Standing around five-feet-eight, buxom and proportionately thick, the rich chocolate beauty had a body much like Serena Williams's. Her athletic build belied a softness and very ladylike presence, and her shoulder-length, bone-straight, toasty-tan-colored hair lightly touched her perfectly round shoulders. Her body stopped dudes right in their tracks whenever she'd walk by. But it was her full, red, juicy lips, like Chaka Khan's, that drew the most attention. Whether she was talking to you or her mouth was closed, her lips always looked ready to kiss you.

By day, Lovely was a nurse at Thomas Jefferson Hospital in downtown Philadelphia. Her nurse's salary provided her with more than enough to live comfortably. Dancing was just something she had always enjoyed. To her it was a way not only to relieve the day-to-day stress of being an active nurse, but also to help her deal with the unexpected death of her college sweetheart, Anthony Davis. Although somewhat secretive about her life, she had shared a little about Anthony's death with Skylar. He had collapsed while playing an outdoor basketball game with a few of his buddies one very hot Saturday afternoon. Lovely and their two-year-old son, Tony Jr., witnessed the entire event.

Because Tony was a known prankster, no one rushed to his aid while he lay motionless on the ground. His buddies thought he was merely being dramatic after missing a shot that had cost his team the game. However, even from the stands, Lovely knew something was wrong. Taking Tony Jr. by the hand, she made her way down to the court. By the time she reached him, other teammates and a few people from the sidelines were crowded all around him. Handing their son to a friend of Tony's, she knelt down over him and began talking to him in a frantic tone. "Baby, wake up! Tony, Tony!" she cried. Lightly slapping his face in an effort to revive him, she continued talking to him. "Baby, it's Lovely and Junior. Hold on, baby!" Tears formed in her eyes—she felt helpless. She remembered hearing a siren in the distance, and the baby crying nonstop, but not hearing anyone shouting to call 911. Just before the paramedics reached Tony, he half-opened his eyes enough to see Lovely peering down at him, her salty tears falling directly onto his face. "I'm sorry, baby," he said softly and slipped away. Her deafening screams matched their baby's, as friends pulled her away so that the paramedics could prep him for departure.

Anthony "Tony" Davis had died of a heart attack. It was discovered that the physically fit, strong, gym-conscious twenty-seven-year-old had had an undetected heart problem, and obviously the rigorous ball game in the hundred-degree Philadelphia heat triggered a fatal reaction.

It was now three years after that dreadful life-changing day, and Tony Jr, the spitting image of his father, was a daily reminder of her lost love. In fact, looking at their son at age five, Lovely's family often joked with her that she'd had nothing to do with his birth but to push him out, because the boy not only bore a direct likeness to his father but inherited almost every one of his traits. Not one week would go by that the handsome little boy did not point up to the eight-by-ten portrait of the three of them taken shortly before his father's death, and declare, "That's my daddy."

At times, out of nowhere he'd ask his mom, "Where is Daddy at?" Lovely's unchanging response—that Daddy was in heaven—only satisfied him for a moment. Other times he would ask her, "How come we can't go see him?" or "Could we visit him in heaven?" The exchange was so painful some days that Lovely had considered taking Tony Sr.'s picture down and putting it away. Of course she always decided against this, deeming it selfish. She never wanted to erase memories of the man who loved her and his son more than life itself.

Lovely and Tony Sr. were not legally married, though toward the end of his life she had finally decided to agree to the idea; after all, he'd been asking her about it almost from the very beginning of their relationship. She never really knew why she hadn't said yes sooner. She planned to. It was inevitable that the two of them would spend the rest of their lives together, but Lovely just didn't feel like they needed a piece of paper from City Hall saying they had a commitment. Many a night she beat herself up for not doing it sooner. Tony had always been supportive of anything she wanted to do in her life. If going through the formality of obtaining a license and making things legal meant so much to him, why did she have to be so selfish and deny him that?

Some of her girls thought she was crazy. "Girl, you're gonna lose that man, keep it up," they warned. "Tony is gonna leave you one day." Tossing back her head in laughter and with a wave of her hand, she dismissed their innocent warnings as girlfriend gossip with no merit.

"Tony ain't going nowhere, chile! He loves me too much." If she'd only known that these words would come back to haunt her.

Anthony Davis was a rare man. Most brothas had to be coaxed into matrimony. She remembered telling him that her secret passion was to become a dancer. He never laughed or thought she was crazy. He would simply say, "Well, baby, do it if it's what you want. Take classes on your evening off. Me and the little man can hold down the fort until you come home." Holding her close to him one evening while lying in their bed, watching the burning flames of the fireplace, he said, "You know, babe, you don't want to wake up one day and feel sorry for not going after something you want. So I say, go for it!" And with that he pulled her to his chest tighter, gently rubbing her arm up and down, as she inhaled the sensual blend of amber and tropical fruits in his cologne, before melting in heavenly bliss.

Some nights after putting little Tony to bed, she would spray one or two spritzes of that scent on her pillow and lie awake in their bed quietly crying herself to sleep. Longing for the closeness of his body and his comforting touch, she'd often prop two or three pillows directly behind her like security barriers and lean back against them, pretending that he was still there holding onto her, protecting her, loving her. Dreaming of yesterday lost.

Not long after his passing, Lovely vowed that she would never put off anything that she wanted to do or say ever again. She decided that she would dance. But where? How? When? It was while she was out on a rare evening after work that she decided to join a few of the nurses for happy hour at Legends. Although she had only been there twice, both times with Anthony, she remembered it being a very nice spot. Her sister agreed to watch Lil Tony and told her to go and have a good time. She read a flyer that was placed on each table announcing upcoming auditions for dancers. Examining it more closely, she thought, *Why not?*

Assuming the girls coming through would most likely all be professional, Lovely shrugged her shoulders and dared herself to do it. Imagine her surprise when she got a call from Nettie, informing her that Skylar would like to see her again. She couldn't believe it. She imagined Tony smiling down on her and saying, "Do your thing, baby!" That was a year ago. Lovely was now one of the top dancers at Legends. And she loved it!

Unlike a few of the other girls, she didn't complain about the salary. Each dancer received two hundred a night, for no more than two hours each night. And tips weren't allowed. Little did anyone know, but Lovely would have done it for free. Once she took to the stage and heard the music, she'd let her body's inner rhythms take over.

Legends dancers were no strippers or go-go dancers. There weren't any lewd or overtly suggestive dance moves either. These ladies were more like Vegas showgirls. Theme nights would find them bejeweled in extravagant costume jewelry, with boas and feathers, moving to the sounds of salsa, reggae, hip-hop, and Broadway tunes. This eclectic mix, coupled with the large percentage of female clientele, dashed the illusions of any man expecting Legends to be a gentlemen's club. Such notions dissolved almost as soon as they walked in the club. In fact, Skylar had mentioned on more than one occasion to Sidney and Nettie that maybe they should hire a couple of male dancers as eye candy for the women—a suggestion that brought frowns to both of their faces, for almost the same reason. Neither Sidney nor Nettie looked forward to seeing men dance at the club. After a little coaxing, Skylar got them to at least agree to the possibility, and today she hoped that a few brothas might respond to their open call.

Princess and Lovely were overseeing the audition process today. Skylar had a hair appointment at Zenora's salon at eleven that morning and probably would not be back in time to see all of the would-be dancers that were coming through. But she trusted these two would make the right choices. Rainey and Vanessa, the other two dancers, were not required to be in attendance until their regular shift this evening. Nettie assured Skylar that she would also come in a little earlier to make sure things were cool. This made Skylar laugh because she knew the real reason—Nettie would never pass up a chance to see beautiful girls dance.

Auditions went rather smoothly most of the morning; a few potentials came with impressive routines, but no one bowled Princess and Lovely over. Either girls came in off the street doing the nastiest, most sexually charged moves—what they *thought* Legends was looking for—or they came in full starlet gear, looking for an opportunity to be spotted by some local Philly rapper or national hip-hop star scouting for video hos. Young, old, fat, skinny, Asian, Black, Hispanic, and white: They'd filed in one by one. Handing over their song of choice to Quince, they launched into a two-minute routine.

But then came Treasure, a six-foot-two, pencil-thin pre-op transsexual, demanding an opportunity to audition. Princess started to say no, but when Lovely noticed that Head, the club bouncer, was not in the room, she nudged Princess and whispered under her breath, "Let him / her audition."

With that, Treasure broke out into some wild 1990s voguing moves, complete with flat-on-her-back twists and turns. It took all of Princess's might not to laugh, and Nettie—from her seat behind the bar—had stopped trying to hide her amusement. Princess thanked Treasure for coming, "But I'm sorry to say you're not the type of dancer we're looking for." This did not go over too well with Treasure, who lashed out at both girls.

"You dirty bitches don't know real talent when you see it. I've been dancing for fifteen years and am recognized as one of *the* best in Atlantic City. You bitches come by Studio's, where I work, and see some girls that will put *all* you tricks to shame," she hissed. As her rant got louder and louder, Princess gave Nettie the eye that she might need her to call the police. Knowing that girls handle rejection differently, Princess and Lovely at first thought the best way to handle this situation was to not say anything in reply at all. Nettie felt quite differently however, and when Treasure breezed by her, she leaned in.

"Baby, let me give you some womanly advice. The next time you answer an open call for *dancers,* make sure, if you want to be believable as a female, that you don't wear Spandex," she whispered.

"Why?" Treasure sarcastically asked.

"Because it looked like you got a lopsided sack of nickels in your private area. It's a dead giveaway, baby!" Nettie remarked. "But even that isn't why they won't hire you," she went on. "Bitch, you couldn't dance!" Everyone howled at this, and Treasure was clearly embarrassed.

These were fighting words for Treasure, who swiftly pulled a straight razor from her bra, just as Nettie pulled one from her wig. Holding it in a striking motion, she peered up at Treasure and said, "What's up?" A surprised Treasure backed down and warned Nettie that she better not ever see her on the streets of A.C.

"I'll be there next Tuesday night as a matter of fact, at Bally's doing a little gambling. So you bring your man ass to the nonsmoking section and you'll see me on the blackjack table. We can settle this shit right then and there out on the boardwalk!" Nettie bellowed. "I don't fight on my job. But I'll beat yo ass till times gets better on the street. Now git out of here."

With one last glaring look, Treasure pointed her finger at Nettie, turned, and assured her that they would meet again. At least four more girls were waiting to be seen, so, burying her razor securely back in her wig like a bird's egg in a nest, Nettie turned to Princess and Lovely and instructed them to proceed with the auditions. Without saying a word, they motioned for the next girl to come in while Nettie wiped down her bar, calm as ever.

"That could have been so much worse. Where was Head?" a nervous Princess whispered. Looking over at Nettie, Lovely remarked, "Who needs Head? Next!"

A few more girls came through and they still had not found what they were looking for. A stunning white five-foot-seven brunette with what appeared to be fake boobs, and sporting an ass like a sista, marched in, extended her hand, and in a Southern twang declared, "Hi, I'm Gidget! Is this where the auditions are poppin' off?" Princess tried not to laugh, but Lovely didn't seem to care and let out a howl. "Yes, Gidget—is that what you call yourself? This is indeed the right place, and we're ready to see your routine if you are." Princess figured that this would most likely be a quick audition, assuming that the cheerleader wannabe would probably be more suited for an Eagles tryout.

As Gidget handed her CD over to Quince, Princess leaned into

Lovely, saying, "Okay, bets on she'll do some Hannah Montana number."

Staring Gidget down, Lovely disagreed. "Naw, I'm thinking Hilary Duff or a Spice Girl routine." They both laughed. But the joke appeared to be on them. Girlfriend took center stage against the beats of a Mary J. Blige jam and rocked one of the hypist solo routines either of them had ever seen. Smiles left their faces and looks of disbelief took over. Princess and Lovely tilted their heads at an angle as if they were watching dance magic happen before their very eyes. Even Quince was shaken. "Oh, *shit!*" he shouted as he covered his mouth with a closed fist. He spun around sharply in a quick circle before returning his fixated stare to Gidget. Nettie looked up and mouthed "Work, bitch!" just loud enough for her own ears. After about a minute and a half, Princess gestured with her hand in a horizontal motion under her throat for Quince to cut the music. Cheers and exuberant clapping erupted in the room. Even Lovely stood up to give the white girl props. "Girl, that was off the chain! Where the hell you from? And why ain't you already dancing?"

"Why, thanks, I appreciate that. I'm from Pennsauken, New Jersey, by way of Nashville, Tennessee." Gidget displayed a wide toothy grin like she was doing a Colgate commercial. All that was missing was the tube of paste, a camera, and someone shouting "Action!" Princess acted less enthused than she was, calmly telling Gidget they would like to see her at callbacks on Monday. She also told her it might be a good idea for her to come by the club that night to see the type of show they put on.

"I can assure you I'll be there," Gidget said, and thanked them both again for the opportunity.

After Gidget disappeared into the outside world, Lovely turned to Princess. "Can you believe that shit?"

"Believe what?" Princess said.

"C'mon, Princess, you got to give it to her. That girl was bad!" an excited Lovely stated.

"She did all right. But let's see how she handles our routines. What she did in here was a routine she's probably been doing for years and had a whole lot of time to rehearse before coming. She'll be expected to do much more here and learn it in a shorter time. I'll just wait a while before I get too excited over *Miss Girl from Pennsauken*!" And with that, Princess gathered up her things, told Lovely she'd see her later, and thanked Quince and Nettie for their assistance. Not uttering anything else she exited the club, leaving behind a quiet atmosphere. Her behavior didn't affect Lovely or anyone else; they were well aware of how Darlene Withers, aka Princess, could be sometimes.

Shaking her head, Lovely went over to Nettie, who witnessed the whole exchange. "Dag, I don't know why she acts that way. She knew that girl came in here and rocked it!" Lovely said to Nettie. "I mean, I have to admit that I am shocked, too, but it is what it is. You take can't that away from her."

"Chile, that's just the way that girl is. People act like that when they don't like themselves," Nettie offered. "All that beauty, talent, youth don't mean shit, if you can't wake up in the morning, look at yourself in the mirror, and *like* what you see. And I'm talking from experience." With no intention of elaborating, Nettie quickly changed the subject. "Look, baby, I got to finish up here and prepare for tonight. You go on home for a few hours, because before you know it, you'll need to be right back here reporting for work. And bring my little man by to see Auntie Nettie sometime. It's been way too long."

"I will, Nettie, I will. He always asks about you. Especially when he gets mad at me after I've scolded him for something. He'll warn me he is going to tell Auntie Nettie on me," Lovely laughed.

"That's right. He knows his auntie will take care of everything. You better leave my baby alone," Nettie playfully said.

"You ever think about having any children, Nettie? The way you love kids, I know you'd make a great mom," Lovely said.

"Girl, I'm forty-seven years old! My day care center has been closed for many years," Nettie laughed as she pointed to her private area. "Naw, baby, mother *loves* kids, as long as they are not hers," she added.

"What about June? Has she ever talked about it with you?"

"Yeah, she did, and I talked her ass right out of it, too!" Nettie barked. "We already fight every other day over some type of shit. Imagine if there was a child involved. Hell, at times I feel like I already got a child—her!" Nettie said sarcastically.

"I don't know, Nettie, a lot of same-sex couples are having children and raising them in a family environment. Statistics show they're usually well adjusted."

"Yeah, yeah, I know all about that," Nettie said, waving her hand to dismiss the idea. "But that will never happen over here, baby. For one, I'm too old to get up on anybody's table and start pushing. Second, June is too butch and thinks she is too much of a man to allow her body to carry a baby. That would make her have to deal with the reality that although she's a lesbian, biologically she is still a woman. Chile, that would just put her under!" Nettie laughed. "Naw, we got some friends who have gone that route and they seem real happy about it. So I say hooray for them. But like I said, it ain't happening over here. And I thought I told you to get outta here anyway! How did we get to jaw jerking 'bout me, huh?"

With that they bid each other good-bye. Nettie stayed behind tending to what she needed to as Lovely stepped out into the bright sunny morning.

< SEVEN >

Afternoon Delight

Philly is known for experiencing some brutal days in the summer, but not today. Today couldn't be more perfect. The humidity was surprisingly low for the month of July, and by one in the afternoon, the temperature was a comfortable eighty-four degrees. After checking out of her hotel, Storm stepped out into the sunlight. Immediately a city cab approached her and asked if she needed a ride. At first she said yes, but then changed her mind, opting to walk the twelve blocks to South Street. The cabbie frowned, rolled the window back up, and sped off, but not before spitting the word "Cunt!" out of his mouth. Normally this would have pissed off Storm; she thought that was the lowest name to call a woman. Even she refrained from using that word and she held a dictionary of cuss words in her head. She would have screamed obscenities right back at him, but she let it roll off her back. A foul-mouthed disgruntled cab driver was not going to spoil her mood. Not today.

Today she was *free* and the taste, smell, sights, and sounds of freedom wrapped around her like a comforting soft sweater as she turned off Chestnut Street onto Walnut. She couldn't believe all of the trendy new shops and restaurants that had opened since she went away. She barely recognized anything. Where was the Philly she used to know? She had known all the businesses on Walnut when she was on the street. Everything had changed. A twinge of sadness crept over her as she tried to remember which store used to be where, what restaurant had closed and what new one replaced it.

Storm was headed for her old apartment building, walking up to the corner of Eighteenth and Walnut, where The Rittenhouse Claridge stood. Not ready to be recognized by any of her old neighbors or Ernie, the doorman, Storm walked on the opposite side of the street until she was directly across from the eighteen-story place she had called home before Muncy. Watching the comings and goings of all the people brought back memories of Storm's society days. Days when she'd step out of The Claridge in a Donna Karan mini jersey print dress, with a Dior handbag, Prada boots, a Movado watch, and Fendi earrings. And that was just for a Saturday afternoon brunch with friends. How she longed for the return of those days.

Deciding on a park bench across from her old residence, she sat down and took in all the scenery. As long as she had lived on Rittenhouse Square, she never fully realized how beautiful and scenic it was. A stone's throw from the South Philly neighborhood in which she grew up, Rittenhouse Square sat in the center of the downtown area, surrounded by numerous high-rise office buildings, shops, and condominiums. The square was adorned by ten-foot trees, some with white and pink blossoms, and manicured patches of rich green grass, and in its center sat an ornate Roman-style fountain. During the summer, birds and squirrels would perch themselves on the edge of the fountain or dip their faces in the water, oblivious to the assortment of urban professionals, businessmen, moms with strollers, and folks sitting around having lunch or chatting endlessly on cellphones all around them. Storm was enjoying all of this for the first time. *This must be what they call taking time to smell the roses.*

Before prison, her life was so full that sitting down in a park watching other people wasn't even a consideration. If anything, they would be watching her. There was another reason Storm chose to sit idly in the park, taking a moment or two to get herself together. She was preparing to see her sister, Skylar.

< EIGHT >

Sunrise, Sunset

Nettie entered the club, stylishly dressed in a pair of hip-hugging black slacks, red three-inch pumps, and a solid red silk tank top. She carried several bags in her hand and was in mid conversation on her cellphone. Her mood was jovial. It was obvious that she and June had patched things up because they were flirting the night away.

"Okay, so you gonna make me tell Skylar that I have an emergency back at home, yeah, that my *space heater* has overheated and I may have to go home a little early to have it taken care of." Putting the bags down on the table, she let out a hearty laugh. "Oh, really, you're going to do all that, huh? I see. Well, I tell you what, you just make sure you're awake when I get there and you can show me how badly you've missed me, okay?" Nettie said while clicking on the lights and heading over to the bar.

"I love you, too, baby." She softened her tone, "And I'm sorry, too. It was both of our faults, baby. I'm not the innocent one here," she cooed. "Okay, well, let me go. You know we are going to have another packed house tonight. I can already see the flashing light on the phone. We've got reservations up the ying yang! Okay, sweetie, see ya later. Bye-bye."

Even with all the fussing and fighting they went through, Nettie had always known that June loved her. Even with all the jealous behavior and insecurities, there was no mistaking that June Alvarado adored her some Nettie Flowers. The thought of this brought a smile and chuckle to Nettie's lips.

Although Nettie had known for years that she was attracted to women, June was normally not her type. For one, June was overweight and short. Second, she was entirely too young for Nettie. But June pursued her and wouldn't take no for nothing in the world. In short, she wore Nettie down until she gave in. And Nettie had to admit: She was glad she did. Nettie knew she could be a handful in relationships. Her abrasive, controlling, foul-mouthed ways would normally send women screaming for the exit. She certainly wouldn't tolerate the mess she dished out to June if the tables were turned. Thinking about this brought a touch of guilt, and Nettie mumbled to herself, "I promise . . . I'll try to be better from now on." She would try to not fly off the handle as quickly as she usually did and understand that there was a generational gap. Perhaps she would be more patient with June when she went on her jealous binges—and she had to admit that it was a bit flattering.

Putting her cellphone away in her oversize purse, she noticed a small gift-wrapped box with a card attached. She assumed that it was something from June. *What has this girl gotten me now?* The card read, "Nettie, I know that sometimes we argue and get mad at each other, but I just want you to know that I love you more than you'll ever know. This is a little something for you. I hope you enjoy it. I had no idea who these women were or ever heard of their music except for the lead singer, and you play a lot of their old-school tunes in the house. But I know what they mean to you. Enjoy, June."

Ripping the paper off the small package in anticipation, Nettie opened the box to find that it was indeed what she was hoping for. The rock and soul group Labelle's reunion DVD. She had gotten the CD in 2008 when it was released, but was waiting for the tour DVD. Patti Labelle, Nettie's favorite singer, had reunited with group members Nona Hendryx and Sarah Dash after thirty years for not only a CD but a series of concerts, and this was the DVD of the group's one-night-only appearance at The Apollo Theater in New York.

"Yes!" an ecstatic, hand-clapping Nettie shouted, and she got lost for a moment, reading the text on the back of the case. She thought of calling June right back and telling her thank you and how much she appreciated the gift, but more important, her. But she decided against it after looking at her watch and remembering that there was no such thing as a quick call with June. She would thank her later, when she got home. In more ways than one.

Approaching the bar, Nettie noticed that someone had bumped the picture of Dutch that hung directly on the wall above the bar. The lopsided frame seemed to be hanging on by a thread; it looked as if a mere touch would send it crashing to the floor.

"I wish people would leave my shit alone!" Nettie said, annoyed. "This is my area. I don't bother nobody's shit, so they shouldn't bother mine!" Straightening the photo, she continued fussing out loud even after the picture was returned to its rightful position. "Whoever it was, they better hope that I don't catch 'em over here! Make me sick." She bent down behind the bar to retrieve a few unopened bottles of Ciroc vodka, and did not notice that someone had quietly entered the club.

"Excuse me," the stranger said.

Without standing up or missing a beat, Nettie matter-of-factly stated, "Sorry, baby, we ain't open yet. Come back around eight o'clock, okay?"

It was Storm. She decided to tease Nettie by disguising her voice. "But I just want a beer or something," she growled in a low voice, trying not to laugh.

"Well, get you some water!" Nettie snapped. "The fountain's out in the front lobby. Now I don't want to sound rude, but we're not open now, shit!"

"I heard this was a classy, sophisticated joint and that the staff was *professional.*" Storm dragged out the word for dramatic effect. "That must have been before they hired you!"

Nettie, now really annoyed, stopped what she was doing and prepared to confront the stranger. She was in too good a mood for a verbal battle but *someone* needed to be put in their place.

"I know one thing, before I turn around you better haul ass . . ." Before she could finish she turned and saw that it was Storm. Tears quickly formed in her eyes as she lit up with joy. "Over here and give me a hug!" They both screamed in delight and rushed toward each other, arms spread wide open for an embrace.

"Hey, Nettie, gotcha!" Storm said gleefully as she hugged her old friend.

"Girl, you damn sure did." Without letting her go she continued, "How did you get here? Did Skylar pick you up?"

Relaxing in the embrace but still holding on to Nettie's hands, Storm told her how she'd wanted to surprise everyone.

"Girl, now you know I would have come and got you. What the hell's wrong with you?" She playfully hit Storm on the shoulder.

"I know, I know. It's okay. I'm here now aren't I?" An excited Storm smiled and thought about how much she had missed Nettie.

"Lawd have mercy, look at you. You look good, Baby Girl." Nettie's eyes gave Storm a motherly once-over.

"I'm okay, Nettie, I'm okay," Storm replied. There was a quiet moment between the two of them as Storm glanced around the place.

"Well, it sure is good having you back. Did you get all my cards and letters I sent? 'Cause if I remember correctly, I think I maybe got like, what, two or three from you the whole time you was down," Nettie said as she stepped back with both hands on her hips, waiting for an answer or an excuse.

"I'm sorry, Nettie. You know I was never much of a writer. But I did send you a card for your fiftieth birthday. Did you receive it?"

"*Bitch,* I know you crazy. You know damn well I ain't fifty," Nettie said, rolling her eyes. "I turned forty-seven and yes I did get that *one* ol' cheap card!"

"I'm just playing, Nettie, you know that!" Storm said as she demanded another hug from Nettie. Nettie steered her over to one of the tables and they sat down and played catch-up.

"Nettie, I'm just so glad to be out of that place and I never plan on going back."

"I know, chile." Nettie shook her head. "Prison ain't no joke. You know I've been down that road. Shit, there was a time I was locked up more times than a bank vault." They both let out a hearty laugh. "Shit, I don't know where I'd be if yo daddy didn't accept me off the street."

Storm's expression became solemn and her gaze drifted to the framed portrait of Dutch on the wall.

"Well, that stuff is all behind you now, Baby Girl." Nettie tenderly rubbed Storm's hand. Baby Girl was what Nettie always called Storm. Hearing that name again soothed and comforted Storm instantly. "You're gonna work here, ain't you?" Nettie asked.

"For a while, I suppose. I spoke to Sidney and he said there would be something available," Storm added.

"Oh, that's right. Well, let me run upstairs and get the new menus your sister had printed up." Nettie stood, gave Storm a hug, and started to leave.

"Menus? Y'all selling food, too?" Storm asked as she scanned the club.

"Yeah, girl, just some little hors d'oeuvres and appetizers—shit like that. Your sister hasn't decided on a full menu yet."

"Sky's doing it like Dutch, huh? Serving food like we used to when it was Morrison's?" Storm managed a nervous smile.

"A little bit." Nettie winked. "I need to run in the back and get a few more supplies, Storm. I'll be right back. Settle yourself in. Your sister should be here soon."

"Okay. Cool."

Reaching the door that led to the second floor, Nettie suddenly stopped and turned toward Storm. "So glad to have you home, baby. You know, you and your sister are like family to me," she said tenderly as tears formed in her eyes.

"I know, Nettie. I know," Storm said and smiled at Nettie.

Storm decided to take a tour of the club. Checking out the decor and layout of the main room, she made her way over to the Legends wall with its photos and paintings of musicians and artists and actors. As her eyes scanned the wall, she zeroed in on another black-and-white photo. It was a picture of two little girls, holding hands and smiling broadly at the camera—her and Skylar at age five. Dutch had taken the girls to Hershey Park, the amusement park outside Philadelphia, the summer they finished kindergarten. In one hand each girl was holding a few miniature Hershey's candy bars; with the other hand they were holding on to each other.

No mistaking that these girls were twins. Although dressed differently, they had the same excited expressions on their faces. Even the way they were pointing their left feet and leaning back was identical. Storm remembered Skylar telling her that when taking a photo, you must stand like Janet Jackson. Janet was the only common interest the girls shared. They were both huge fans, especially after Janet released *Control* in 1986. *That's how I remember* you *that day, Sky. Controlling.*

Storm touched the photo gently and laughed at the memory. At this moment, the door swung open and Skylar entered. She was on her cellphone and unaware that Storm was there. Although Storm didn't turn around, the sound of her sister's voice paralyzed her for a moment.

"Okay, so you're saying we should expect the delivery of the tablecloths *and* the matching chair covers by tomorrow morning? Okay, thanks, bye." Skylar hung up her cell, relieved that at least one headache had been cured. She was startled by the silhouette of the woman whose back was to her, facing the Legends wall.

"Hello, may I help you?" She couldn't make out who the woman was because the limited lighting threw a shadowy edge over everything, but there was something eerily familiar about her posture. At that moment, Storm slowly turned around and stepped out of the shadows.

"*Storm?*" Skylar's eyes widened in surprise as she whispered her sister's name.

"Hey, girl," Storm answered. Neither one of them made a move or gesture toward the other. Their eyes locked and they both stood still for a few more moments. Skylar nervously broke the silence.

"When did you . . . ? How did you get here? Why didn't you call me?"

"Slow down, girl. Which of these questions am I supposed to answer first?" Storm managed an innocent smirk.

"You look good, girl. You look good." Skylar smiled.

"I'm doing okay. Thanks," Storm said.

"Where are all your things?" Skylar looked around Storm.

"Right over there." Storm pointed to the table where she'd sat with Nettie earlier.

"Oh." Skylar saw the lone tan duffle bag on the floor by the table and wished she had not asked. Skylar stepped a little closer toward Storm, but not too close. Just close enough for her to get a good visual of her sister.

Prison life had not been that kind to her. There was a hardness in her face and a sadness in her eyes that Skylar had never seen before. After a few more moments, Skylar informed her, "We have the guest room ready for you, and you're welcome to use my car, you know, to help you get settled in and all."

"Thanks, Sky, but I'm fine. I already have a hookup for a spot to stay."

"Oh, okay, fine then." Skylar wondered who the hookup was, but dared not ask. She really didn't care.

Storm could tell that Skylar was happy. That she was in a good place in her life. Success, a good man—everything appeared *perfect* in Skylar Morrison's life, which was in direct contrast to what Storm's own life was like, to what it had been like for the last three years.

"Look like you've stayed in the gym, missy." Storm gave her a once-over and smiled.

"What?" Skylar said coyly. She knew damn well she looked good. She didn't need Storm's validation. Working out and eating right had been a longtime practice of hers.

"Yeah, but it gets harder and harder to maintain, the older I get," Skylar offered.

"Don't I know it. I mean, we are the same age, right?" Storm laughed, and the statement drew surprising laughter from Skylar as well. Changing the subject, Storm brought up the job situation.

"Listen, I was wondering if you could spot me for a while. You know, like a little job around here until I get back on my feet? The last time I spoke to Sidney, he said that he was sure that something could be found to do around here. Did he speak to you about it?"

"Yes, yes he did, and sure. Let me think on it. We can always use a little help around this place. Let me talk to Nettie. She's more involved with the day-to-day operations around here," Skylar said. "Have you seen her yet? I thought she was already here . . ."

"She is, I saw her. When I came in she was over at the bar area fussing about something." They both laughed.

"Well, as you can see, much hasn't changed. She's still Nettie," Skylar declared.

"But that's what we've always loved about her, right?" Storm's voice lowered.

"Yeah, you're right about that," Skylar agreed. "So what are your long-term plans?" Skylar asked, folding her arms across her chest while giving her the eye. Immediately recognizing the familiar condescending manner with which Skylar approached a question confirmed for Storm that she was right: Nothing much had changed.

"Actually I've been thinking about taking a few culinary classes. You know, maybe becoming a chef." Without thinking, Storm mirrored her sister, folding her arms across her chest and smiling at Skylar.

"Culinary school! Storm, you know you can't cook!" Relaxing her stance, Skylar laughed.

"Don't laugh, I can burn, girl!" Storm offered.

"Yeah, burn shit up!" Skylar added, still laughing.

"Naw, seriously, they have all these different kind of courses and trades in the pen. I assume they call themselves rehabilitating a sista!" she laughed. "But it was cool."

Shaking her head in an approving manner, Skylar said, "That sounds good. Maybe you can even whip up one of your specialties around there. But you have to test it first before I'll allow my customers to eat it."

"Wow, it's like that, huh?" Storm laughed.

"I'm just kidding. Seriously, I think that sounds great, and I am glad you found something constructive to occupy your mind in there." Skylar threw this out while walking across the room. Seeing a stack of mail on the table, she started sifting through it. Storm knew all too well that she was being dismissed. She thought of giving her sister a piece of her mind but decided against it . . . for now. There would be plenty of time for her to let Skylar know how she really felt.

"By the way, if last night was any indication of what tonight will be, we are expecting a huge crowd, so I need to get a few things together. Make yourself at home. Go in the kitchen, grab a bite to eat or do your culinary thing or whatever. It's cool. I'll be back in a few hours, introduce you to the staff, and we'll move on from there." Skylar said all of this without ever looking Storm's way. One envelope seemed to catch her eye and she retrieved a letter opener from behind the bar.

"Okay, you need any help with anything?" Storm started moving toward her, but stopped short.

"We're good. Thanks. Tonight, you just chill, sit back, and check out the show. I'll have Nettie talk over a position with you tomorrow." Then Skylar pushed the door leading into the kitchen, but not before Storm stopped her.

"Fine. Oh, by the way . . . Sky," Storm called out to her.

"Yeah?" With her hand still on the door, Skylar still didn't turn around.

"Thanks," Storm said.

"For what?" Skylar slowly turned around and faced Storm.

"Hooking me up," Storm said as she waited for a reaction.

"Sure thing." And with that she nervously disappeared into the kitchen. All that was heard for a few seconds was the flapping sound of the door going in and out. Storm patiently waited for it to stop. She found herself alone. Just like she had been for the last three years. Without uttering a word, she smiled with the same devilish smirk she displayed to the hotel desk clerk upon seeing that roach go in her soda can. *You know what you have to do.*

On the other side of the door, Skylar leaned against the wall and tried to catch her breath. She wasn't sure if she was having a panic attack or a heart attack. Whatever it was, she was afraid. Where was Nettie? Sidney? Flynn? She was alone. "Think happy thoughts, girl, calm yourself down," she managed to whisper. In a matter of seconds, she calmed down, but still felt hot. Unfastening the top button of her blouse, she fanned herself, trying to cool off as the sweat that had collected on her forehead in tiny beads evaporated and disappeared. Something she wished she could do.

< NINE >

Night Shift

The club was packed with an audience roaring in laughter as Flynn and Beatrice went through their routine. This wasn't the usual response to his material, and Flynn was beginning to wonder if he'd made a mistake in bringing on Beatrice. Granted it had been fun playing off another comedian, especially a female, because the material and subject matter were endless. But he'd be damned if he was going to lose any of his shine to some unknown comic that *he* discovered at an open mike competition—one *he* had judged down at Larry's Laugh House on Germantown Avenue. Yes, *he* would be cutting down *her* material and less time would be granted for *her* to do *her* thing. He wasn't trying to be a hater or anything. He knew she was funny, funny as hell. But Legends was *his* club. He was the main comic and no matter how funny another one may be, they have to know right from jump that they're only making *guest appearances*. Too many hard-knock years had passed, and Flynn Wilson was not playing second fiddle to anyone at Legends.

After winding down his twenty-minute act with Beatrice, Flynn introduced Princess, who danced one of the hottest salsa numbers anyone had ever seen. As the music pulsated to a Caribbean beat and lights flashed in step with the rhythm, Princess strutted, kicked, twisted, and gyrated her body with uncontrollable speed. She was lost in the music. Princess ran and jumped, thrashing her body about like she was possessed by some unruly spirit. Locking eyes with as many people in the audience as possible, she cast a spell. The audience hooted and hollered their approval. From the third row, the ever-present Miss Shoes showed her delight by taking off one of her purple Ralph Lauren pumps and hauling it at her, barely missing Princess, who was in mid-flight. Miss Shoes screamed, "Work, bitch!"

Lovely and the other dancers watched in awe as Princess built up to a climactic ending, sliding across the floor and finishing with her head buried in the crease of her arm. As she lay stretched out on the floor, both legs straight out—*bang!*—the music concluded. A puff of smoke filled up the stage area and the lights went black, leaving the crowd in complete darkness. Their thunderous applause picked up where the music dramatically left off, completing Princess's routine.

Watching from the sidelines, Gidget stood with her mouth open wide in shock as a tear rolled down her cheek. She wondered if anyone else could hear the sound of her heart beating over all of the hoopla taking place. Quince brought the lights back up. Princess had disappeared and all that remained were traces of smoke in the air and a few beads from her costume that lay solemnly on the dance floor. Everyone was drained! A disoriented Miss Shoes hobbled up to the front of the stage to retrieve her pump. Waving her hand high in the air and shaking her head like she was at a church revival, she weaved in and out between tables looking for where it had landed.

Grabbing the mike to address the crowd, Flynn spotted the shoe and handed it over to her. Miss Shoes couldn't even say thank you—she was still speechless, as everyone else seemed to be. If any one of the other dancers ever doubted before tonight why Princess held the position she did at the club, they got their answer with that performance.

"Okay, okay, settle down. Settle down." Flynn motioned to the crowd using both arms to demonstrate. He continued: "I don't know about y'all but I ain't never seen any dancing like that. What about you?" he shouted. The crowd erupted once more with deafening sounds of approval. Looking toward the dressing room door Flynn shook his head and shouted, "Give it up one more time for Princess! That girl was finer than the horsehair on that woman's weave!" He pointed to a random woman in the audience to more laughter. *This is more like it,* he thought.

Once everyone settled down, Flynn introduced a new addition to the Legend family, a new waitress, Alexia Adams. A slim, attractive, tan-colored sista with platinum blond hair, thirty-ish and about five feet eight, stepped from behind the bar, waved, and nodded to the audience. Flynn eyed her seductively. "Lord, have mercy. You are hotter than fish grease off a food truck in Harlem! You single, girl?"

Alexia just smiled and bashfully turned away.

"Don't nobody want you, Flake! I mean Flynn!" an obviously intoxicated Beatrice shouted out from a back table.

Everyone laughed. The look on Flynn's face showed his disapproval at Beatrice heckling him while he was onstage. He cut his eyes at her—if looks could kill, those daggers would have slayed her. He would definitely deal with her later. Beatrice, unaware she had done anything wrong, lifted her glass high as if offering a toast, nodded her head at him, and them downed her drink in one gulp.

The lights dimmed, and the cool jazz sounds of Cassandra Wilson filled the air as more patrons filed in. Waitresses descended upon tables almost in unison with pads in hand, taking food and drink orders from waiting and willing customers. Horace "Torch" Wells, a small-time thug, and Cleet James, his show monkey–acting flunky, entered the club. Not waiting to be seated by Ruta Lee, the house manager, they strolled over to a table directly in front of a dancer's podium, where an attractive, well-dressed middle-aged couple were already planted securely in their seats, enjoying drinks and each other. As Torch stood erect to the side of the table surveying the crowd, Cleet leaned in and whispered something to the man at the table. The man's lighthearted and upbeat expression quickly faded and was replaced by fear. Glancing over at Torch, he suddenly nudged his wife, indicating that they should probably move to another table. Torch and Cleet took their newly hijacked seats, and

Cleet tried to get the attention of a waitress while Torch made a call on his BlackBerry. A nervous Alexia approached Nettie, who was busy behind the bar.

"I hope I do everything right," she said to Nettie.

"Girl, you're dong fine. What are you talking about?" Nettie said. "I see how you've been handling folks. You know what you're doing. Listen, you got the looks and attitude. Just don't let any of these jokers walk all over you, because they will try to," Nettie said and winked at her.

"Don't get it twisted. I might be nervous as a hooker in church, but only because it's my first night. It's been a minute since I've done this type of job but I am far from being a pushover," a confident Alexia stated. "I keep to myself, do my job, and then take my ass home!" she said as she thought about what brought her to Legends.

Alexia Adams had only been in the city of Philadelphia for about two weeks and was stressed about finding a job. She was staying temporarily with her cousin NeNe in a one-bedroom apartment in the working-class neighborhood of West Oak Lane. Not that she didn't appreciate NeNe's hospitality, because she did, but NeNe didn't keep a very tidy home. In fact, she was downright nasty and trifling. The bathroom was always dirty, and no matter how many times a day Alexia washed the dishes, there were always more.

"Girl, I was going to get that," NeNe would say whenever she heard Alexia running water in the sink.

"It's okay, I don't mind," Alexia lied.

NeNe didn't work, either. She was on *relief.* For the life of her, Alexia could not understand why this thirty-three-year-old grown-ass woman was getting welfare and food stamps. NeNe spent most of her days on a prepaid cellphone watching the array of courtroom and talk shows on television. From *Judge Judy* to *Judge Mathis,* she watched them like she was studying law. But her favorite was Maury Povich. She didn't miss Maury. "Girl, I don't know what I'm going to do," she said one day.

"About what?" Alexia asked.

"Chile, these crazy-ass TV people done put Maury on the same time as *The Young and the Restless,"* she sniped. That shit makes me mad 'cause now I gotta decide which one I'm gonna watch and which one to drop. Damn!"

"Maybe you could tape one and watch the other," Alexia offered. "I see you have a VCR over there."

"That shit don't work!" she said, rolling her eyes at it.

Alexia thought, *Well, you don't either so you couldn't be but so mad.* Alexia laughed to herself.

"Matter of fact, I'm thinking about writing a letter to the network about that shit 'cause it ain't right," NeNe said defiantly. "Girl, you gonna have to show me how to use your computer." She eyed Alexia's laptop over on the kitchen table. Alexia told her, sure she could use it but she needed to sign off first because she had spent most of the morning like she did every morning, searching online for a job.

"Let me know if you see something for me on there, too" an unenthusiastic NeNe stated.

"Sure," Alexia said as she rinsed off the last glass and put it on the dish rack. Wiping down the counter with some bleach, she saw a roach bravely crawling right out of the cloth she was using. Slamming the cloth down hard she instantly killed it. The sudden loud sound didn't raise a look from NeNe, who was biting her nails awaiting the DNA results on the latest Maury couple's paternity test.

"Was that another one?" she asked.

"Yeah," Alexia said disgustedly.

"I sprayed yesterday," NeNe proudly stated. "I believe it's that nasty bitch Monica next door bringing all dem roaches over here. I ain't never had *one* till she moved in. I'ma tell Gracie she gon' have to do something about that."

Gracie worked in the rental office downstairs but never seemed to be on call. If you wanted to know where Gracie was during the day you just knocked on 102 and she'd come to the door—with an attitude, like you were bothering her or something.

Yes, Alexia had to get out of here as soon as possible.

"Aw, *hell naw!* This bitch done had dude number nine up on here, saying he's the father, and the shit done come back that he ain't!" NeNe shouted as Maury read the results.

"Look at this bitch running off the stage and falling on the fucking floor like she ain't got no damn sense." NeNe was getting a kick out of this. "Come here, Alexia, and look at this bitch. She don't know what to say now. Looking all stupid up in here. That's what you get, ho!" she screamed at the girl.

Alexia appeased her by looking over at the TV where a sobbing young girl about twenty years old was laid out on the floor while Maury was consoling her. In the background a jubilant black dude was doing the Crip walk and flashing a gold-toothed mouth in front of the audience. Alexia thought of what her granny would say—"he's just a sugar-coated coon"—but NeNe felt differently.

"And he cute, too!" she declared. Alexia shook her head in disbelief. Her cousin was a lost cause. "But she did take me in," Alexia thought out loud. NeNe had her back no matter what anybody said. She could not forget that.

Alexia had a few extra dollars with her when she came to Philly. She wasn't broke entirely, but her savings would not last forever. Still, she treated herself a couple of times by going downtown and enjoying a nice meal at Ruth's Chris Steak House or Miss Tootsie's Soul Food Café. She had even taken NeNe to Ruth's Chris one time. However, when NeNe saw the bill for her ribeye steak, baked potato, and salad she was pissed. Never mind that Alexia was the one paying.

"Oh, no, I would never had paid this kind of money for that little bit of food they gave us," she said, loud enough for the couple sitting in a nearby booth to overhear. "Chile, they got over on us," she declared. "Shucks, we coulda went to the Chinese restaurant up on Germantown and Wayne and got some fried wings, shrimp fried rice, egg rolls, and a can of soda. You woulda had money left over for, like, three more days. But I appreciate it though," she said, licking her fingers.

Alexia decided today that she'd swing by Delilah's restaurant to look for a job as a hostess, but only after getting her hair done. She'd recently seen an ad in the *Philadelphia* magazine she'd picked up for Zenora's, a hair salon where you could get the full treatment—hair, manicure, pedicure, and a facial. It looked like a classy joint so she made an appointment. While waiting her turn a very attractive sista walked in. Alexia could tell by the way she dressed that this sista had a little *bank*. It seemed that all of the stylists in the shop knew her, too. Parking herself down next to Alexia, Skylar smiled.

"Were you waiting for Zenora?" Skylar asked.

"No, I believe they gave me Rocky," Alexia said.

"Oh, well, Rocky's good. You'll be very happy with him." She smiled again and picked up an *Essence* magazine with Jada Pinkett-Smith on the cover. Flipping through, she asked Alexia if this was this her first time at Zenora's.

"Yes, it is. I saw an ad and I'm looking for a shop since I just moved here, so this looked like a pretty cool place to try," Alexia replied, smiling.

"You've come to the right place. Zenora's is the hottest salon, and sista, girl over there"—she pointed to an attractive full-figured light brown stylist—"owns four of them. But this is the only one that she actually works in. She's so successful that she could stop if she wanted to, but she just loves doing hair." Skylar marveled at Zenora. "I'm sorry, where are my manners? I'm Skylar Morrison." She offered to shake Alexia's delicate hand.

"Nice to meet you, I'm Alexia Adams."

"So you're new in the area?" Skylar asked.

"Yes, I am. I haven't been here that long," Alexia said, wishing that Skylar would stop with the personal questions already.

She didn't. "Oh? Where are you from?"

"Not too far from Philly," Alexia said, planning on ending it right there.

The two conversed for the next thirty minutes or so and discovered much more about each other. Alexia found out that, like Zenora, Skylar was a successful businesswoman, who owned and operated a nightclub. Alexia confided that she was looking for employment and having the toughest time securing any kind of job. In fact, she told Skylar, she'd be willing to do almost anything at this time because her funds were low.

The two hit it off quite well. In fact, they finished their appointments around the same time and Skylar insisted that Alexia join her for lunch. They grabbed a quick bite at Reading Terminal Market, and Skylar asked if Alexia had ever worked in a club before. There was a waitress position open and if she wanted to give it a try, Skylar would be willing to help her out. Stunned by the offer, Alexia happily accepted. "I used to waitress, but that was a long time ago," she said.

"Fine, then you'll start tonight, deal?" Skylar once again extended her hand to Alexia.

"Sure thing! Wow, thanks, Skylar," an ecstatic Alexia responded. Before excusing herself from the table, Skylar gave her the club's address and told her to come by around six that evening and ask for Nettie. With that, they bid each other good-bye, and a few hours later, here she was, loving the atmosphere despite her nerves, and taking a moment to give thanks to the Almighty. She knew if this job worked out it would only be a matter of time before she said good-bye to cousin NeNe and the roaches. *Yes, maybe the move to Philly wasn't a bad idea after all.* She could start all over again. She would do things differently this time for sure.

Cleet began hitting his spoon against his drinking glass loud enough to get the attention of both Alexia and Nettie, who were standing at the bar.

"You know what? Let me handle this one. He can be a little trouble. I'd hate for you to get Cleet James on your first night. Watch the bar for me?" Nettie said to Alexia.

"No, no, Nettie. He's at my station. I'll handle it. He most likely craves attention," she laughed. "Besides, if he's a regular then I better get used to him, don't you think?"

"Okay, but if he gives you any problem, call me or signal Head and the problem will be handled," Nettie warned. On her way over to Cleet's table, Flynn stepped into Alexia's path. Alexia did not notice him until they collided.

"Oh, excuse me. I'm sorry," Alexia said.

"Not a problem. So, how's your first night?" he asked, smiling.

"It's cool. I'm getting the hang of it," she said, returning the smile.

"Let me say that we love nothing more than having another beautiful lady in our establishment or on staff." Flynn was flirting. "Your man is a lucky dude."

"Why thank you . . . and just so you know, I don't have a man."

This revelation couldn't have sat better with Flynn, who continued with the small talk. Alexia didn't want to be rude, but she needed to go, especially after peering over Flynn's shoulder and seeing Cleet squirming in his seat looking for another waitress. She was flattered by the attention Flynn was giving her but she couldn't let anything jeopardize her job.

"I bet you flirt with every girl who comes in here," Alexia said.

"Hmmm. Yeah, I do." Flynn laughed. "But I only ask the *ladies* out for a date."

"You're smooth. I got to give it to you, my brotha. You don't waste any time." Alexia giggled.

"You have a pretty smile," Flynn said. "If it's not too forward, would you like to go on a date sometime?"

Alexia was surprised by the invitation, but let Flynn down easy. "It's nice of you to ask, but after my last situation I've decided to do the single thing." Seeing the look of disappointment on Flynn's face, she added, "Please don't take it personally. Now, I've got to go help a customer."

Flynn didn't seem to be fazed at all by this. Watching her walk away he could sense that there was something special about Alexia and he aimed to find out what it was.

"She'll come around," he said in a low tone. "Especially when she sees how debonair and charming I can be." Besides, she'd get to know that Flynn Wilson was a warrior. He didn't give up a fight easily.

Quince put on a Flo Rida jam and several patrons headed for the dance floor. As Alexia maneuvered through the crowd, a lanky guy with pronounced freckles and an old-school Afro, dressed in a pair of charcoal-gray slacks and a white button-down shirt, grabbed her by the hand, coaxing her to dance with him. He actually managed to twirl her around at least once before she freed herself. Laughing, she reached the table where Torch and Cleet were seated. Retrieving pad and pen from the pocket of her slacks, she took their order, but not before apologizing.

"Good evening, gentlemen. I'm Alexia, I'll be your waitress this evening. Sorry for the delay. May I take your order?"

Cleet glared at her. "Not a great way to start your first night on the job, now, is it? We've been waiting for service for some time now."

"Again, I'm sorry. Your order, sir?" Alexia forced a smile.

"Yeah, well, recognize! Now git me a Hennessy and Coke!" He got louder with each word. "And some of dem coconut shrimp and jerk wings."

Alexia restrained herself from telling this joker off. Maybe she *should* have let Nettie or one of the other girls handle this table.

"And you, sir? What will you be having?" she said turning her attention to Torch.

"I'll take a little . . . Cutty on ice." Getting his first look at Alexia, he stared at her for a moment. "Do I know you from somewhere? You look awfully familiar. You have any family around here? Brothers, Sisters?" He couldn't take his eyes off her.

"No," Alexia said. "In fact, I just moved to Philly."

"I don't usually forget a pretty face." He smiled at her. "It'll come to me." Alexia shrugged her shoulders and began to leave when he stopped her again.

"By the way, have you seen DuBoy and Storm?" he asked.

"Who?" Alexia seemed puzzled.

"Storm. She's the owner's sister? DuBoy is her ol' man." He threw a sly smile to Cleet.

"Oh, sorry, we haven't met yet. But I'll let Nettie know to send them right over to your table when they arrive." And with that, Alexia left to place the order.

Torch never took his eyes off her, while Cleet seemed to be spellbound by the dance moves of Lovely, who had taken the podium, moving her curvaceous body to the beat of the music.

"I know that bitch from somewhere, Cleet," Torch said. "Damn, this shit is gonna bother me all night." He watched Alexia at the bar conversing with Nettie.

"Forget that bitch, Torch, man. What we gon' do 'bout Legends? Yo, you sure DuBoy is down, man?" Cleet grabbed a handful of peanuts and gulped them down all at once.

"Nigga, you let me handle DuBoy. That nigga is down. Everything is gonna be fine. You can believe that shit!" Torch raised his voice to emphasize his point.

"Yo, I hope so, man. I'm ready to make this *paper,* baby!" Rubbing both of his hands together, six-foot-three Cleet reared back in his seat, grinning broadly, displaying one of the most beautiful sets of pearly white teeth ever seen. His smooth, midnight skin glistened in the club like the coat of an African panther. A pronounced jawline and almond-shaped eyes made it easy for him to be mistaken for a model. "Your problem is gonna be Skylar," he added.

"Listen, the bottom line is, Storm owns half of this bitch. All DuBoy gotta do is convince her of what is rightfully hers and we good to go, nigga!" He reached over and pounded Cleet on the back.

"Look, I'ma hit the stall, make a few calls, and I'll be right back." Torch stood up, maneuvering his large frame through the crowd with ease. His tailor-made Sean John cranberry single-breasted suit fit loosely against his six-foot, two-hundred-and-twenty-five-pound frame. The reflection of the disco ball overhead bounced off his clean-shaven head as several dancing couples made way for him to pass like a parting sea. He didn't have to ask anyone to move, they just did. Torch got his name because as a child he was known for setting fires in the neighborhood. As a matter of fact, he'd burned down a corner store at the age of six by lighting a newspaper with a match and putting it in the mail slot on the front door. When the fire trucks arrived, they found Torch sitting across the street on a neighbor's steps with his head in his hands, watching the comings and goings like he was looking at *Sesame Street*. Still holding the box of matches, he didn't deny starting the fire. When asked why he did it, Torch said, "Ain't nothing like a good fire." He ended up doing five years in juvie.

Glancing over his shoulder, Cleet noticed Head standing against the wall, arms folded, overseeing all the activity in the club. Cleet decided to amuse himself by taunting him. "Punk, is that all you do? Standing up there like you the damn Rock or Hulk Hogan or some shit?" He started to laugh. "Ain't nobody scared of you, man. What you make, like ten or twelve bucks an hour?" With that he took a twenty-dollar bill out of his wallet and tossed it at Head's feet. Head neither reacted nor seemed the least bit bothered by Cleet's antics. "Nigga, git a real job. You oughta come work for me and Torch. Hell, it don't matter, we gonna own this dump in a minute anyway. Then I'ma be your boss. You big-head muthafucka!" He howled at his own joke.

At that moment, Lovely completed her dance and stepped down off the podium. As she passed, Cleet said, "Damn, baby, yo ass move like a stripper's bowels, slow and steady."

Lovely ignored him and continued toward the dressing area. He followed her every move, transfixed by her ass until Alexia interrupted with his drink.

"Here you are. Will this be a running tab or would you like to pay now?" she asked. This seemed to infuriate Cleet.

"Running tab? Shit, it should be on the house, much as we spend in this muthafucka!" Taking out his wallet again, he handed her a fifty-dollar bill. "That's cool though, here you go. But in a minute, all this up in here is going to be free for me—including you—know that shit!" he warned her. Alexia told him that she had no idea what he was talking about but that the bill was twenty-two dollars. Her dissing him only got him more angry.

"You know, you got a smart-ass mouth on you. A nigga just trying to conversate with you and you got yo ass all up on yo back!"

"Now see, that's your first mistake," Alexia spat at him. "I don't deal with niggas. You see, a *real man* knows how to get the attention of a sista without disrespecting her or hog-calling her out her name!" She placed the drinks on the table, but something told her this was not over yet. She mentally prepared for whatever was about to go down.

"Who you think you talking to?" he screamed. "Bitch, I'll slap the taste outta yo mouth!" At this moment, Cleet jumped up to confront Alexia, who swiftly pulled a compact switchblade out of nowhere. The sight stopped Cleet. Laughing, he told her, "A bitch with balls, that makes my dick hard. Ho, where you from?" he asked, sitting back down. "Torch swears he know you."

Leaning in close to him, Alexia offered him some advice. "Listen, don't fuck with me. Because as bad as I need this job, I'll fuck you up. Now you play that shit with those tricks you meet on the *stroll,* not your girl," she pointed to herself. "So let me try this again. Can I get you *anything* else before I go?"

"I'm cool. I'll holla if I need you." Cleet sneered.

Alexia leaned in even closer to him, offering one more piece of advice. "Oh, and another thing," she whispered. "You can tell Suge Knight—he don't know me from nowhere, you feel me? My advice to both of ya'll is to go play in somebody else's playground." Looking around, making sure no one heard her, she continued. " 'Cause, see, in my playground, niggas get cut up from the knees up!"

From across the room, Skylar noticed some activity at Cleet's table that might need attention. She started to signal Head to go over but after seeing Alexia walk away with a smile, she dismissed it, though she knew she needed to have a word with Cleet. She passed Alexia on her way and asked if everything was okay. Alexia assured her that things were fine, that she was just getting to know the regulars, that's all.

"Okay, well, you're doing a fine job. We're glad you're with us."

Alexia smiled and thanked Skylar again for the job opportunity. She excused herself after seeing another customer attempting to get her attention. Something made Skylar feel that the interchange between Alexia and Cleet had not been as smooth as she was letting on. Reaching his table she didn't waste words.

"I don't want any trouble in here, Cleet," she warned. "I run a top-notch spot and I aim to keep it that way. Now, you and Torch are welcome here as long as this is understood."

"We cool, baby. Everything is everything, girl, you know that," he teased as his eyes zeroed in on her cleavage. "Yo, by the way, where is your sister? DuBoy said she was out." He looked around attempting to spot Storm.

The mention of DuBoy's name sent chills up Skylar's spine. She had never cared for the no-good two-bit hustler that had Storm sprung before she went in the pen. "DuBoy?! What makes you think he knows anything about Storm's comings and goings?" Not waiting for an answer, she walked away. She hoped that Storm had not contacted DuBoy to rekindle their sick and twisted relationship.

She passed by Torch, who was returning from the restroom. He acknowledged her with a nod of the head. She ignored him and walked toward Sidney, who was calling her over to one of the side tables. He was sitting with a well-dressed Asian couple who she assumed were husband and wife.

"Hey, baby, come over for a minute. I want you to meet someone." Sidney motioned for her to join them. Approaching the table, Skylar smiled. Sidney introduced her to Mike and Sara Chin. The young twentysomething couple seemed excited and eager to meet Skylar. Sara vigorously shook her hand and said, "Sidney's told us so much about you. Your club is amazing! And congratulations on your engagement—Sidney is a very lucky man."

Mike said, "We're big fans of this guy," pointing at Sidney, "and there are so few successful minority-owned accounting firms in this town. Sidney Francis is actually shaking up a few of the high-powered white firms, too, aren't you?" He playfully ribbed Sidney and went on. "I'm just another Chinese Philly boy, a few years out of U. Penn, but I love what Sidney's doing. I really admire him."

"And I, you," Sidney countered. "Mike and I, we hit it off immediately, and I think your smarts and perspective are just what we need at The Francis Group. It would be an honor if you agreed to come on board as our newest junior analyst."

Mike graciously accepted, and he and his wife looked excited. Holding onto Sidney's hand, Skylar was so proud of her man and happy for Mike and Sara Chin. For a moment she had forgotten all about what Cleet said to her about DuBoy, until she looked up and saw Storm entering the club with none other than Joshua Tillman, aka DuBoy, at her side. She tightened her grip on Sidney, who, after looking at her, knew something was wrong.

Sensing that Skylar knew that she had come in, Storm looked through the crowded room until their eyes meet. Sidney wouldn't let go of Skylar's hand and decided that they should all have a toast there at the table to celebrate Mike's good news. Skylar calmed down long enough to relax her hand and joined in on the toast.

Storm's entrance caused a stir. Not because she was known, but because she was stunning! Wearing a simple black Nicole Miller minidress and a pair of Antonia Melani high-heeled sandals, and carrying a black beaded Louis Vuitton purse, Storm looked as if she had stepped right off the pages of *Vanity Fair.* DuBoy's thuggish b-boy appearance seemed almost acceptable to the crowd witnessing this unexpected entrance. He was in a pair of loose-fitting Sean John jeans, a clinging black wife beater, and a pair of black Tims. A black leather belt with an oversized gold and silver belt buckle, a skull with tiny sparkling gems entrenched in each eye socket, gave the illusion of expensive jewels.

Nettie noticed Storm and immediately went over to her with her arms outstretched. She greeted her warmly and gave DuBoy a quick disapproving nod. He returned the sentiment. When Storm took off her sunglasses to give Nettie a peck on the cheek, it caused several customers to do a double take. Some were speechless at the resemblance to Skylar. Some had heard that Skylar had a sister; certainly most of the employees knew of a sibling; but no one outside of Nettie and Sidney knew that she was a twin.

"Excuse me," Skylar said to the Chins and Sidney as she stood up.

"Baby, be calm, okay?" Sidney whispered to her.

"I'm fine, Sid. Everything is fine," she assured him. With that she headed over to the table where Storm and DuBoy were sitting down. Ruta Lee told them a waitress would be right over to take their order. Skylar signalled to Quince to lower the music. As she approached the stage, Flynn handed her the microphone.

"Ladies and gentlemen, please join me in welcoming home my sister, Storm Morrison." At that moment a light shined on a surprised Storm, who managed a nervous smile. "You'll be seeing quite a lot of her, because as of next week, she will be our new assistant house manager. Our regular colleague, the wonderful Ruta Lee, will be traveling back West for a while on some family business."

Skylar continued. "I can assure everyone that Ruta Lee *will* be back and that this is only temporary. But I can also promise you that Storm will be just as great in the position. We're all lucky to have her here."

Nettie couldn't hide the gleeful look on her face upon hearing this news. Skylar caught Sidney's eye and his trademark smile indicated his approval. He was proud of his woman for this gesture.

As the cheers and congratulations simmered down, Skylar motioned for Quince to start up the music. "Okay everyone, enjoy the rest of the evening." With this she started to leave the stage, when Storm stopped her.

"Skylar, I . . . I don't know what to say. I mean, I really appreciate this to the highest." Storm was shocked. "I wasn't expecting—" Not allowing her to finish, Skylar assured her that she could handle it. That they would spend the next few days having Ruta train her and show her the ropes.

"Wow, you have that much faith in me?" Storm asked in a cautious tone.

"Sure, why not? Is there any reason why I shouldn't?" Not allowing Storm to respond, she continued, "Just keep your nose clean, do the right thing, and surround yourself with people of substance." She made sure Storm saw her glance DuBoy's way when she said that last sentence. "Everything will be cool. Besides, it's what Dutch would have wanted," she said.

"And you? Is this what you want, sis?" Storm searched the eyes of her sister for the truth. There was a moment of silence before

Skylar told her, "Yes, this is my wish, too. Okay, so look, we'll talk more about it tomorrow. Like I told you earlier, tonight just sit back and enjoy the evening because next week, you'll be on duty." With that Skylar excused herself and made her way back to Sidney, leaving Storm standing alone.

In a weird sort of way, watching her sister walk away from her saddened Storm, who for the first time in a long time realized that she had missed her. She even thought of reaching out and hugging her.

An impatient DuBoy called out for her to come join him. He'd moved over to Torch's table. They'd ordered a bottle of champagne and awaited her arrival with raised glasses for a toast.

Flynn determinedly took a seat at the bar within eyesight of this troublesome scene. Nettie, witnessing this from her perch, frowned disapprovingly.

"So, what you thinking, Nettie?" Flynn asked without taking his eyes off Torch's table.

"About Sky and Storm? Oh, they're gonna be fine as soon as they realize that no matter what they do or say, at the end of the day they are still sisters, sharing the same blood. It'll take some time, but I'm hopeful things are going to be fine," Nettie said while fixing him a club soda with lemon.

Taking a sip of his drink, he asked, "What about DuBoy?"

"Can't stand that chile!" she spat out. "He ain't never been no good. Mamma wasn't good either. Nor his daddy. So I guess he got it honest. Same thing with Torch. I'm surprised that boy ain't dead yet with all the mess he's been involved with."

"I heard he had a few girls on the street now, too," Flynn offered.

"Probably!" Nettie shook her head.

Looking at Cleet, she continued her rant. "And Cleet, with his ol' dumb self, will do anything Torch says to. Just a *show monkey.* Once she gets settled I am going to have a talk with Storm."

< TEN >

You Are Not Alone

Skylar and Sidney almost completed their ride home in silence until Sidney turned on the radio. It was set, as always, on the Quiet Storm station of WDAS-FM. The Michael Jackson classic "You Are Not Alone" played softly. Resting against the soft leather headrest of Sidney's black-on-black BMW 750, Skylar closed her eyes and lightly smiled. Sensing her melancholy mood, Sidney tenderly took her hand in his own. The unexpected, comforting gesture seemed to relax her tense state.

"I was very proud of you tonight, baby, you know that?" he said softly.

"Really? Why?" Skylar asked in a whisper.

"Just the way you handled your sister and the whole situation. I know it wasn't easy. Especially after seeing her with that dude DuBoy."

"Don't remind me," she said. "I just couldn't believe that someone could be so stupid as to hook back up with a jerk like that after all he had taken her through. She hasn't been home a good forty-eight hours and who's the first person she calls? DuBoy!" Skylar's body grew more tense as she released her hand from Sidney's calming grasp. His immediate reaction was to envelop it once more.

"How long were they together before she went in?" Sidney inquired.

"I don't know. They were always off and on. Storm has so much to offer, you'd think that her choices in men would be better. But as long as I can remember she's always gone for these no-good thugs."

"Well, baby, you like who you like, right? I mean, evidently there is still some kind of spark left between the two of them. Especially the way they were carrying on in the booth tonight," he said, starting to laugh. Skylar threw him a look.

"Disgusting, that's what it was. Did you see how he was all over her?" Skylar sat up and folded her arms across her chest. "And there's nothing funny about it, Sid!"

"I know, baby, I know." He remained playful. He always knew how to make her smile. "But actually it was more your sister on the brotha man, than him on her." Sidney saw that Skylar was not in a playful mood so he attempted to smooth things over.

"You've done your part, baby. Storm is going to have to step up to the plate and do what she needs to do to make things happen in her life," he said.

"I'm proud of you, too, honey." She leaned her head on his shoulder.

"Me? What did I do?" His facial expression indicated that he didn't have a clue as to what she meant.

"Helping that young couple the way you did tonight. Baby, you made their night." She reached up to kiss him on the cheek.

"Hey, hey, don't start nothing you can't finish," he teased.

"Seriously, neither one of them will ever forget tonight," Skylar said.

"He was the most qualified candidate I interviewed. Know what impressed me the most? He didn't spend a whole lot of time trying to impress me with a bunch a bull. My man came in there, answered all my questions and concerns honestly, and convinced me that although he didn't know everything, he was still eager to grow. That's the kind of employee you want by your side, baby. You get someone who thinks they already know everything, I promise you there won't be any growth." Sidney's voice took a serious tone. "I need to have someone I can mold into the kind of person I need to help me run my business. So if I need to take some time off, my clients won't panic. This person needs to be an extension of who I am toward my clients. I believe that's Mike."

"You're right, babe. Just from our brief meeting tonight I'd say you made the right choice," Skylar said. "Not so sure *I* did." She sighed heavily.

"Give your sister a chance, babe. When I talked to her the last few times she called, I got a sense that she knew where she went wrong in her life. If prison taught her nothing else, it gave her time to think about her life and the choices she made," Sidney said as he pulled into their driveway.

"I hope you're right, baby, but I know Storm. I know her very well and I need to keep my eye on her," she warned.

"Just don't go looking for anything, Sky." He looked at her while getting out of the car.

"I am," she replied. He gave her a look. "I *am,*" she said louder. "I'm giving her a chance."

Walking hand in hand up the driveway, he suddenly turned and, facing her, lightly stroked the tip of her nose with his index finger. "Yeah, but when will you give *you two* a chance?"

Looking up at Sidney, she paused as she gazed into the eyes of the man who brought her so much happiness. The man who made her feel like, no matter what, everything would be all right.

"I love you, Sidney Francis." Tears of joy formed in her eyes.

He pulled her closer and whispered, "And I love you, Skylar Morrison." He kissed her passionately, until she collapsed into the security of his embrace. They got lost in their lust and love, forgetting for a moment where they were. As a warm breeze brushed against their heated bodies, Sidney carefully pulled down each strap of her dress and Skylar's fingers delicately unbuckled his pants. It was evident that she wanted him just as much as he wanted her—right there. Inching away from their deep kisses, Sidney used his tongue to paint light strokes of passion on Skylar's neck. She tilted her head back ever so gently, the scent of his cologne intoxicating her with memories of their first meeting. She closed her eyes and enjoyed the sensual motions of his wet pink brush. The lovers' moans of ecstasy joined with the melodic sounds of restless crickets echoing in the midnight air.

"Excuse mc. *Excuse me!*" A loud voice startled both Sky and Sid. They turned to face the direction it was coming from. "I'm assuming you two are locked out?" It was their seventy-two-year-old neighbor, white-haired Mrs. Reed, walking her pit bull, Doug.

Flustered, Skylar immediately lifted up both straps of her dress while Sidney pulled his buttoned-down shirt out of his pants so it could fall over his embarrassing bulge.

"We're fine, Mrs. Reed. Sidney seems to have misplaced our door keys." Skylar tried to refrain from laughing as she made up this ridiculous story.

Pretending to search for them, Sidney joined in by adding, "They must be somewhere around here, honey."

"Did you try looking in your front pants pocket, Sidney? Looks like something is in there," Mrs. Reed suggested while she and Doug planted themselves in the street directly facing Sidney.

Locating the keys on the shelf by the front door, Sidney smiled and shook them in her direction.

"Got 'em, Mrs. Reed. Good night," he said. Skylar quickly scooped them out of his hand and opened the door. Abandoning him at the entrance she darted up the stairs, leaving behind only the faint sound of her laughter. With one last farewell to his neighbor, Sidney flashed a nervous smile and waved good-bye.

He quickly closed the door, intending to follow Skylar upstairs, but shortly thereafter, he heard a knock at the door.

"Who is it?" he asked.

"Mrs. Reed and Doug."

What in the hell is wrong with this woman? he thought to himself. "Yes, Mrs. Reed?"

"Can you open the door for a minute? I got something I want to show you."

She has something to show me? What the hell? Sidney didn't know what to do.

"C'mon, baby, it's cold out here," Mrs. Reed whispered. Getting closer to the door and shaking his head, Sidney took a deep breath and slowly opened the door.

"You left your keys in the door." She dangled them and handed them over. "You never know who might come in and surprise you one night. You got any protection?" She gazed into his eyes.

"Excuse me?" Sidney asked, confused.

"Protection, you know—like I have old Doug here." She gently began to pet her dog and looked up at Sidney.

"Oh, that kind of protection." Relief momentarily washed over him as he laughed. "No, no, there's never any trouble around here. We're fine, Mrs. Reed. And thanks again."

"You sure you don't have a big ol' nightstick that you carry around with you?" Speaking softly and biting her bottom lip, she shifted her eyes downward.

"Good night, Mrs. Reed!" he said in a stern voice. "Tell *Mister* Reed I said hello."

"Have a good night yourself, Sid," a smiling Mrs. Reed seductively whispered back at him while loosening the belt around her floor-length house robe just enough for it to conveniently open and reveal that she was nude. Closing the door behind him, Sidney couldn't believe what just happened. Turning the downstairs light off, he rushed upstairs to the woman who would soon be his wife.

< ELEVEN >

Sexual Healing

The noise from apartment 3A awakened Barbara Bowman from a sound sleep. Lying next to Jessie, her husband of thirty years, the sixty-seven-year-old woman lay quietly still, trying to decipher the noise. Sounds of furniture being turned over and heavy thumping dominated the air, and sudden vocal outbursts and screams could be heard. Sitting straight up in her bed, she reached for her glasses.

"Jessie, Jessie!" she called out in a whisper as she nudged him. "Wake up! Wake up!" Jessie stirred a little and moved over to the edge of the bed. Looking at him she wondered how this man could sleep with all of this going on: a repetitive banging followed by sounds of someone apparently being tortured. Grasping the collar of her nightgown, she grew more and more concerned that someone was in trouble in the apartment above her. Reaching for the lamp on her nightstand, she turned it on. Jessie was in a deep slumber and snoring even louder than before.

Barbara began dialing 911 when she heard a deafening crash. Putting the receiver on the bed she paused long enough to try to wake up Jessie again.

"Jessie, wake *UP!*" She began punching him on his side. After a few more stirs and grunts, Jessie half-opened his eyes and turned to her.

"Barbara, what the hell is wrong with you!?"

"Shut up! Listen—I believe somebody is being hurt upstairs in that boy's apartment."

"What goes on in that apartment ain't none of our business, woman. Now I don't want no trouble from that boy or anybody he knows, so lay your ass back down and go to sleep!" the irritated seventy-two-year-old said.

"You don't think we should call the police?" she asked.

"No, I don't think we should call anybody. Now go back to sleep! Damn!" He then lay back down, turning his back to her and yanking the covers around his neck. Reluctantly, a dissatisfied Barbara hung the phone up and cut off the light as she gingerly lay back down. After several moments of silence, she decided that Jessie was probably right. There wasn't anyone in danger. But what was all that noise? Maybe that boy wasn't home and somebody had broken into his place. She didn't care that much for the street thug and wished he didn't live above them, but she'd hate if a crime was being committed in his place and she did nothing about it. Suddenly, several loud screams of a woman, clearly in distress, filled the air.

"I knew it!" she said. Sitting up once again, she turned on the light and demanded that Jessie wake up. "See, I told you. Listen, Jessie. Listen!" she cried.

Jessie, fully awake by now, turned over to face her and listened intently. The screaming sounds continued, and then the thumping returned. Realizing that he now heard it himself, she pointed her finger at him and whispered, "Didn't I tell you I heard something?"

"*Shhh!*" he hushed her as his ears pricked up, straining to hear more. The sounds continued, and a frightened, wide-eyed Barbara covered her mouth in fear.

"Told you!" she whispered. "Somebody is getting beat up in there!"

Realizing what was going on, Jessie frowned at Barbara. "Barbara, ain't nothing getting beat up but some girl's *stuff*."

"What?"

"They making love, Barbara. The boy is just getting him a li'l late-night trim, that's all."

"You sound ridiculous, Jessie!" she spat out. "Don't nobody sound like that when they making love!"

"Yeah they do, sweetie. You just don't remember." With that he started laughing. Annoyed, Barbara rolled her eyes at him before turning off the light and lying back down. Pulling the covers back to her side of the bed, she turned away from him and, without saying a word, closed her eyes. Jessie continued to chuckle as he moved closer to her and put his arm around her waist.

"Get away from me, man! And get dem cold-ass feet off me, Jessie!" she demanded. "And cut dem toenails of yours before I bleed to death."

They both broke out into youthful laughter. She took his arm and returned it around her waist. "You ol' fool. You make me sick!" she said, still laughing. "Go on to sleep!"

• • •

Exhausted from their marathon sexual escapade in apartment 3A, DuBoy and Storm collapsed onto the sweat-soaked mattress. Both out of breath and panting like they had just run a sixty-yard dash, they lay next to each other, staring up at the ceiling in a postclimax haze. After a few minutes, DuBoy said, "Dayum girl, that shit was sick fo' sho. You a bad bitch, you know that?" he laughed.

"You didn't do so bad yourself," she told him as she reached over and grabbed a towel to dry herself off. "I just wanted you to get a little of what you've been missing for the last three years," Storm playfully added.

"Well, you brought back a nigga's memory with that shit. Damn! Whew!" he said, grabbing hold of the same towel. "And your body is sick girl. You ain't lost nothing while you was on lock!" he stated. Knowing that he still desired her the way he did before brought a tear to Storm's eyes. She had to admit she worried about that shit, worried that DuBoy might have found another bitch to take her place. She knew he hadn't just been sitting around waiting for her while he was out here, but her purpose was not only to claim what was rightfully hers when she got out, but to make his ass forget any bitch he might've laid with while she was gone.

"Shorti, I swear before God, ain't nobody ever put it on me like that!" he assured her. "Hell, I'm scared to look around my crib at the shit we done caused in here." They both laughed. "And the way you was screaming ma'—I'm surprised one of my neighbors didn't call the fuckin' cops. Especially that old nosy bitch downstairs. She ought to have that old man of hers touch her up every once in a while and she'd be aight."

"Shut up! You weren't that quiet either, you know," Storm said, and laughed. "All those sounds wasn't coming just from me."

"Yo, I ain't even gonna front. Man, you had me hollering like a li'l bitch!" DuBoy jumped up and sprinted across the floor toward the bathroom. As her eyes adjusted to the darkness of the room, Storm marveled at DuBoy's muscular physique. *Body fat don't have a home on this brotha's body. Forget a six pack, he's rocking an eight.*

Lying there in the quiet, Storm thought about what had gone on earlier at the club. She knew bringing DuBoy to Legends was going to fuck with Skylar, but that wasn't really her intent. Sky didn't like DuBoy and she didn't need to. He was *her* man, not Sky's. Besides, she didn't like being told what to do, how to live, or who her friends should be. Just because she needed Skylar's temporary assistance didn't mean that her sister owned her. *Hell no. I've always been my own woman. And that is not going to change just because I'm on Skylar's payroll.*

Besides, DuBoy was one of the few who readily talked to her while she was down, accepting collect calls weekly. Especially the last few months. He had even come up to see her once. So she owed him some special time. When she asked him to accompany her tonight, he reminded her that not only did her sister not like him, she had made it known that he was not welcome in her club.

"You are my guest, so you can go in with me!" Storm told him. She didn't expect to encounter such a gracious Skylar. Her sister's giving Storm the position of assistant house manager had come as a total shock. She thought that, if anything, she'd be offered a waitress or bar back job. She almost felt bad about her plan.

On his way back to the bed, DuBoy turned on the bedroom light. Immediately, Storm grabbed a pillow to shield her eyes from the light.

"Dayum! You see this shit?" he said to Storm, looking around at the mess they'd caused. Taking the pillow away from her face, Storm got a look at what he was talking about.

"Wow! Looks like a tsunami done hit this bitch!" she remarked, standing up to meet DuBoy in front of the bed.

"You know I love you, right?" he said softly, brushing the loose strands of hair away from her face as their naked bodies touched.

She nodded her head and grabbed hold of him like her very existence depended upon it. Tears softly trickled from her eyes, falling on the muscular slope of his chest.

"What up, Boo?" he asked as tenderly as he could. "You crying and shit."

"I've just missed you so much, baby. I . . . I've been so lonely." She buried her face under his neck.

"Yo, ain't no need to be feeling like that. I ain't going nowhere," he assured her. "It's just me and you, girl." Wiping her tearstained face, Storm wanted to believe him, but she knew deep down how DuBoy could be.

He led her back over to the bed and she rested her head on his shoulder. Nestling under the covers, he faced her and began to tell her how much he had missed her. She wanted to believe him.

"Shorti, you still cool on what we talked about a while ago?" he asked, planting delicate kisses on her neck. Storm did not answer right away. This caused DuBoy to stop and lean back to get a good look at her.

"Is there somethin' wrong? Yo, you ain't flaking out on me, is you?" His voice became stern.

"No, no, baby, I'm not. But I just got home. I need to take this slow with Skylar, you know that. Me trying to convince her of some shit like what you're talking about is not going to be easy," she said in a calming voice.

"I knew it! I thought we was clear on this shit, Storm!" he said, raising his voice.

"We were!" She turned his face toward her. "Nothing has changed. I know the plan."

"You sure 'bout that?" he said, arching his eyebrows.

"Yes, I just need some time to work on it. It's only been a few days since I've been home, DuBoy. Can I get my life back first? Damn!" Storm was annoyed.

"I thought that's what I was doing here, right now wit' you, helping you get your life back!" He sat up on the side of the bed, reached over, and started to light a blunt. Not wanting him to be upset with her, Storm assured him that he *was* helping, but all she was asking for was a little time. With that she leaned over and started to gently massage his neck and shoulders. Every so often she'd stop and give him light kisses in the middle part of his back. Her actions seemed to calm him down. She even convinced him that he didn't need a joint right then either.

"Yeah, well, you stressing my ass out, girl! You know me and Torch been working on this idea for some time now. He's expecting me to come through with this shit!"

"Everything is going to be fine, Boo. Don't worry." Storm tried to sound convincing. "Neither one of us needs any stress, baby, you know that." He allowed his head to fall back, but not before taking a drag off the blunt. He passed it to Storm but she declined. DuBoy knew that smoking weed wasn't Storm's thing. He started to laugh.

"I thought maybe you changed yo shit up a little by being in there, bay. You mean none of dem hos ain't try and get you to wild out wit' dem for a minute?"

Storm did not find this funny at all. "I don't want to talk about Muncy. That shit is in my past," Storm said as she lay back down, covering her body with the sheet.

DuBoy decided to join her. It was not long before they were in a sensual embrace and began another round of lovemaking. This time, they were careful, gentle lovers, taking time to enjoy every touch, kiss, caress, stroke, and embrace. Just as their bodies became one DuBoy asked, "Are you ready for all that we about to do?"

"Yes," she said softly, pulling him closer.

< TWELVE >

Tomorrow

Lovely was dreading this call but she had to talk to someone. Someone that might understand what she was going through. Usually, she'd call her mother when she felt like this. But not this time. She couldn't call her this time.

"Hello, yo dime, my time, make it quick!" The voice on the receiving end said.

"Nettie?" Lovely said softly.

"Yeah . . . Who is this?" Nettie responded with something of an attitude.

"Hi, it's Lovely."

"Lovely? Hey, girl, it didn't sound like you. I could barely hear you. How are things? You feeling better?" Nettie asked.

"I'm coming along," she lied. "Listen, I was wondering if you had some time in the next day or so. I'd like to come by and have a talk with you," Lovely asked.

"Sure, sure . . . Hmm, how about tomorrow around three or four in the afternoon? You want to come by the club? Ain't nobody gonna be there but—"

Lovely interrupted her. "No, if you don't mind, could it be somewhere else?"

"Okay, okay," Nettie said. "We could either meet at Miss Tootsie's on South Street or Ginger's Coffee House on Second and Walnut." After deciding on Ginger's at three-thirty, Nettie asked Lovely again if she was all right.

"I'm okay, Nettie, I just need some advice, that's all," Lovely assured her.

"Everything's all right with my baby, ain't it?" Nettie asked, referring to Lovely's son. "Put him on the phone so I can holla at him for a minute."

"Oh, I would, Nettie, but he's in the bathtub right now," Lovely lied.

"Okay, no worries. Maybe you'll bring him by to see me soon."

Lovely said she would do just that. "Nettie, could you keep all this between us?"

"Sure, baby, my lips are sealed tighter than a casket!" They both giggled. Lovely asked how the other dancers were doing and who had taken her spot for the last few weeks.

"Well, Miss Princess finally done gave Gidget a chance to shine. You know, with your solo spots," Nettie offered.

"I'm so happy about that. I know she was doing her thing." Lovely was sincere about this.

"But I'm worried about you!" Nettie let her know. "And look, don't worry about your job either. I don't care how good li'l Paula Abdul is, your spot is here whenever you come back, you hear me?"

"I do, Nettie. And thanks again." Just hearing Nettie's comforting words let Lovely know she had done the right thing by calling her.

"All right, baby. See ya tomorrow," Nettie said before hanging up. Lost in thought about what could be wrong with Lovely, she didn't notice that June had come in the room.

"Hello! Hello! Anybody *home*!?" June called out.

"Hey, sweetie, I'm sorry. I didn't hear you come in." Nettie got up and planted a gentle kiss on June's lips. Pulling her close, June noticed something was wrong.

"You okay?" she asked, relaxing their embrace.

"I just got a call from Lovely. She wanted to know if I'd meet her tomorrow to talk."

"Does it involve Tony Jr.?" June asked.

Nettie shook her head. "I don't think so, but whatever it is, I know it's got something to do with her requesting a leave from the club."

"Maybe she got some flack from her bosses at the hospital about moonlighting as a dancer, ma'."

"That couldn't be it. Hell, several of the doctors and her fellow nurses go to Legends on the weekends. Besides, she can do what she wants on her own time," Nettie pointed out.

"Whatever it is, I'm sure she'll tell you mañana, baby." June rubbed the center of Nettie's back and asked her if she'd like to go out for dinner. Nettie declined, saying she'd rather just stay home, maybe order Chinese, watch a movie, and just chill for the evening. Besides, she told June, they'd had so little time to enjoy their new place. "Hey, maybe I'll come back once you're settled and give you that promised massage from a week ago." June agreed and promised Nettie that she would give her that much-needed rubdown she had been begging for last week.

"Seriously?" she asked June. "Man, that would be great. I have been mad stressed," she told June, while tossing back her head with closed eyes and massaging her own neck. "Let me take a nice bath, you order the food and pick up a movie, okay?" With a sudden burst of energy, Nettie trekked off to the bathroom. She was happy that she and June had not been fighting for almost a month now. She wasn't sure which of them had grown up the most—instead of arguing over the smallest little things they now talked things over. Maybe it was also the move to a larger place. June had been sharing Nettie's small one-bedroom apartment on Twelfth and Locust Street for the last year and a half, but for the last month they'd been spreading out in a two-bedroom apartment on Eighteenth and Pine Street. The building, reminiscent of a Brooklyn brownstone, housed four apartments; they occupied the largest one, on the third floor. As her body slipped deeper into the relaxing water, Nettie leaned back and tried to forget any and every thing that was on her mind.

Taking long baths was something she did all the time. It worked for a while, until the nagging feeling of what could possibly be wrong with Lovely crept its way back into her brain. She released it. For now she wanted to enjoy her bath, her Chinese food, and her woman. Tomorrow would take care of itself.

< THIRTEEN >

My Baby Just Cares for Me

Lovely felt awful for lying to Nettie about little Tony. He was not taking a bath. In fact he had been spending the last few days with her mother. She hated being away from her son more than anything but she needed some time to figure things out. In addition to taking a leave from her job as a dancer at Legends, she had also spoken with Hertha James, nursing supervisor at Jefferson Hospital. Considering the circumstances, Hertha granted the leave from her position at the hospital that Lovely had requested, too. Hertha had to admit to herself that Lovely's was the strangest story she'd ever heard in all her twenty-five years in nursing.

As a registered nurse, Lovely dealt with a large number of organ transplant patients. As much as she tried not to get emotionally involved with any of the patients, sometimes she'd find herself taking a lot of their personal stories home with her. After losing Anthony, *life* meant so much more to her.

Over a month ago, Felix Murphy, a sixty-five-year-old, had been admitted to the coronary care unit in need of a heart transplant. Although Lovely was not his primary nurse she was very familiar with all the patients on the ward and there were times when she did attend to Mr. Murphy. Felix was one of the nicest men she had ever met. He never complained about anything and always seemed grateful for everything the nurses or doctors did for him. He was such a pleasure to be around, she thought. No matter what kind of stressful day she had at the hospital, after walking into Mr. Murphy's room she'd feel better in a matter of minutes. During one of her visits, Lovely asked Mr. Murphy why he'd never married or had any children. He told her that at one time he thought about it but felt he wasn't deserving of a family. Seeing how his mood changed once he said this, Lovely felt it was best for her to leave it alone. However, Felix wanted to talk more and went on to tell her that he wasn't always the nice guy he was now.

"What, Mr. Murphy? You cheated on an old girlfriend or something?" Lovely teased.

"I wish it were something as small as that," he told her.

Lovely could hear the serious tone in Felix's voice. He asked her to sit down. Pulling a chair close to his bedside, Lovely could not imagine what he was about to tell her. "I've never talked to anyone about this before now," Felix spoke softly. "Lovely, about thirty years ago I did something to a woman I cared deeply for. I . . . I forced myself on her and raped her," he said, bowing his head.

"What!" Lovely was shocked. "Why?"

He paused for a few moments before continuing. "I was an alcoholic, still am, because no matter whether you drink anymore or not, once an alcoholic, always one," he said. "Anyway, she told me if I did not stop drinking she was going to leave me. Of course I promised her a million times that I would. Well, one day I believe she just got fed up 'cause she called me and told me we were through. I figured that she just needed some time to cool off. You know, because she always took me back." Felix looked at Lovely as tears formed in his eyes. "Anyway, I had made up my mind this time that I was going to get some help. And I did, too, Lovely. I hadn't touched a drop in over two months. Anyway, after being clean for a period of time, I went by her place one evening, just to talk to her. When I got there I saw her getting out of another man's car. Before he pulled off they were hugging up all over each other. I was crushed. I couldn't believe this. She was my girl and now she all over some other man. Instead of just going home, I . . . I went by the bar. . . ."

"Oh, Mr. Murphy, you didn't." Lovely took his hand in hers.

"I got drunk. If that wasn't enough, I didn't go home, I went back to her place to confront her," he said.

Lovely held her breath, expecting the worst. *Oh, God,* she thought, *did he hurt her?*

"She didn't want to talk to me, especially seeing that I was blasted. She could see through the chained door that I was. When she went to close it I pushed it open and I . . . I forced myself on her," Felix said as he began to weep uncontrollably. "I raped her." He sounded ashamed at this admission.

He went on to tell Lovely that he was arrested but received probation. His court-appointed attorney convinced the jury that it was her word against his. "Everyone knew that we were an on-and-off couple in the neighborhood, so there were witnesses on both sides." After it was all over, Felix said he moved back down South with his family and did not come back to Philly for years. He had no idea what became of the girl.

"It feels good finally getting this all out. Even if it took thirty years and a stranger to admit it to," he said as he wiped his eyes.

Although his story repulsed Lovely, she did not want to judge this man who seemed so kind and gentle. She certainly did not condone what he had done, but judging by the pain on his face, she could see he was suffering. She patted his hand gently and told him to get some rest and she'd see him tomorrow.

A few days passed and Lovely had not gone back to see him. However, she had been checking his charts and noticed that his hemoglobin levels had decreased and the doctor had ordered a blood transfusion immediately. They were looking through all possible resources because Mr. Murphy's blood type was so rare. Because of how everyone felt about Mr. Murphy, any one of the nurses would have donated, but it was Lovely who was called into the nurse supervisor's office. She was told that out of all the employees, only she was a match. Her supervisor asked if she would be willing to donate a unit of blood. "Sure," Lovely said.

Lovely went into the laboratory, wondering what if she and Mr. Murphy had the same DNA? Lovely suddenly felt as if she were going to faint. Her mind started to race a mile a minute. *No, it couldn't be.* She tried to reason with herself. Lovely thought of her parents. Her mother had always been overprotective of her, as was her stepfather. She'd had a wonderful childhood. But as any inquisitive child would do, she'd often ask about her biological father. Especially as she got older.

"Your father passed on before you were born, sweetie," her mother would say. "It's too difficult to talk about, baby." Seeing this obviously pained her mother, Lovely stopped asking. Her stepfather was the best daddy any girl could have so she left things alone.

Lovely still had to find out if Felix Murphy was truly her father. If so, not only had he raped her mother, but he'd also had a child he had never known.

On another visit to his room, she asked him about the woman. Did he remember her name? She braced herself for the answer. "Theresa Waters," he spoke painfully. *My mother's name,* Lovely thought.

Not able to cope with the news, Lovely became withdrawn and detached from everyone. She had to get away for a while. Her mother knew something was wrong because they talked about everything but suddenly Lovely clammed up. Lovely didn't know what to do. But she knew she had to make a decision soon enough. A man's life, her father's life, was hanging in the balance.

< FOURTEEN >

In da Club

It was hip-hop night at Legends and the crowd was much younger than usual. Skylar wanted to make sure that, unlike most other clubs in Philly, Legends highlighted all genres of music. The sounds of Nas, Lil Wayne, Trey Songz, Kanye, and T.I. dominated the air as the crowd of twentysomethings took to the floor with the latest dance moves, eagerly anticipating a special midnight performance by Philly's own Cassidy. Normally Skylar would hold off on booking a hard-core artist like Cassidy, but he promised her that the show would be tamed down, and the two of them had been friendly since he started in the business, back when they met at an open mike event at Phoenix Dance Club down on Arch Street years before.

Flynn made his way through the crowd over to the bar, where Nettie was checking a young man's ID, looking up at him and then back down at the ID several times before pouring his drink. Even then, she still gave him a look of uncertainty. He left a dollar tip on the bar and took his drink away. Nettie watched as he walked away, wondering if he'd just got over. Noticing Flynn, she shouted out, "Aw shit now! Look at Mr. Flynn. Sharp as Dick was when Hattie died!"

Flynn, dressed in a tailored single-button suit, spun around with both arms spread open.

"You like?" he asked.

"Yes, I do, baby. I don't think I've ever seen you look so handsome. And who are those flowers for, like I don't already know." They both laughed.

Looking around, Flynn asked if Alexia had come in yet. Nettie pointed out Alexia where she was already working. "Aw, Flynn, you really like that girl!"

"Yeah, I do, but she hasn't really given me a chance," he said. "I mean, I've been asking her out for more than three weeks, and she always turns me down. I've tried everything."

"Well, let me tell you a little secret, but swear you didn't hear this from me."

"I swear, Nettie. Scout's honor."

"Boy, you ain't never been no kind of boy scout. But I think you get it, so here go. That chile's confessed that she likes you, too, but she's just not ready to date again. I can't put my finger on it, but that girl got a lot on her mind. She's got some secrets," Nettie stated matter-of-factly. "But just give her some time, I believe she'll come around." Nettie smiled.

Noticing Alexia making her way through the crowd with a raised serving tray, Nettie told Flynn here was his chance to be alone with her for a few minutes, because she had to go to the restroom.

"Watch the bar for me, baby, while I go pay my water bill," Nettie teased as she scurried off. Watching her as she left, Flynn shook his head. *I can't believe Nettie is letting all that go to waste. As fine as she is at her age, she won't let a man touch her. She really don't know what she's missing.*

A surprised Alexia did a double take at the stylishly dressed Flynn,who usually wore black slacks and the standard Legends logo T-shirt.

"Flynn? I almost didn't know who you were. You look so handsome." She stood back and looked him up and down.

"Thank you. These are for you," he said and handed her the bouquet of flowers.

"For me? Why? It's not my birthday or anything." She took the flowers from him and brought them to her nose, allowing her nostrils to fill with the sweet scent of the fresh tulips.

"Mmm . . . tulips. How did you know tulips were my favorite flower?"

"A little birdie told me," Flynn said, a bit shocked that such a corny line was coming out of his generally very cool mouth.

"I see, so what else did this *little birdie* tell you?" She sweetly looked at him.

"That a certain young lady named Alexia Adams would finally see that a certain guy named Flynn Wilson isn't such a bad guy and allow him to take her out sometime . . . like maybe after she gets off tonight?"

"Oh really now." Alexia giggled. "Do me a favor, tell that *birdie* it was right. You're not a bad guy at all. Thank you for these. I'll put them in some water until I go home later." She walked behind the bar and got a clear crystal vase. Filling it up with water she arranged the flowers nicely as Flynn watched her every move.

"So what do you say?" he asked.

"About? Oh, a date? Flynn, I feel so bad. You have asked me out about four times—"

"Five times," he interrupted.

"My bad. Five times. Please understand it has nothing to do with you. I'm just not ready to date anyone right now."

"Look, I'm not trying to get married or get matching tattoos. Just have one innocent little date."

Alexia laughed heartily, and looking up at him for a moment, she appeared to be thinking. "Okay, Flynn, I will go out with you," she said, letting out a sigh.

"Seriously?" Flynn was glowing.

"You heard right. But it will have to be tomorrow when I have off. I'll be whipped after we close tonight. I like hip-hop, but these kids have been working my nerves," she laughed. "Let me put my drink order in for Cassidy's table. Where's Nettie?" she asked, looking around.

"Oh, she went to drop the kids off at the pool," Flynn playfully remarked, waiting for a reaction from Alexia.

"What?" Alexia didn't quite understand.

Flynn told her that Nettie had gone to the restroom to do her business.

"You are so silly, man. You make me laugh a lot. And it's been a long time since I really felt like laughing." Looking at him she smiled, and they both knew there was an attraction. Nettie returned and Alexia put in her order. Flynn went to mingle with some familiar faces, but not before mouthing the word "tomorrow" to Alexia. Nettie could tell that Alexia had finally accepted a date from Flynn.

"Thank you, Jesus!" she said, throwing up her hands. "I take it you are going out with that boy? That chile was about to worry me to death about you." Nettie waved her hand.

"I just hope he doesn't get his hopes too high, Nettie. You know, like it's going to be something serious."

"Just let nature take its course, girl. That's all you gotta do. Don't fight the feeling. If y'all feeling each other, it'll happen, if not, it won't. You feel me?" Nettie stopped what she was doing and looked up at Alexia.

"Yes, I do, Nettie." She grinned.

Just before Flynn introduced the dance segment of the show, he told Skylar that an intoxicated Storm had just arrived. Skylar looked toward the entrance and saw Storm laughing it up with a couple seated by the back. Looking at her watch, she saw that Storm was late again, this time by nearly an hour. Skylar would be glad when Ruta Lee returned to the club. She decided that she and Storm had to talk, soon. For now, she'd do what she had been doing for the last few weeks, keeping quiet. She desperately wanted to give her sister a chance, like Sid and Nettie had asked her to, but she knew in her heart that nothing had really changed with Storm. Not even after being locked up for three years.

At that moment Flynn took to the stage to introduce Gidget, who would be doing a solo hip-hop dance to one of Beanie Sigel's classics. Quince cranked up the music, dimmed the lights, and the audience gave their undivided attention to the stage. Princess stood off to the side, ready to critique Gidget's every move. DuBoy, who was sitting with Torch and Cleet, nudged Torch and let him know that this was the bitch he'd been telling him about.

"She's bad, dawg," DuBoy bragged. "Man, I done run through that ho a coupla times. That bitch was down for whatever," he laughed.

"Word!" Cleet said, looking up at Gidget.

"Nigga, you better not let Storm find out about that shit! I'ma tell you that!" Torch threw a sharp look at DuBoy. Cleet laughed.

"Dude, Storm don't know shit, man. I got that ho on lock! She feenin' over this dick like a crack ho on a new pipe!" he laughed. "Nigga, all I got to do was lay the pipe right and that bitch became a muthafuckin' Stepford Wife."

Everyone laughed except Torch, who knew that if Storm reneged on the agreement she had with DuBoy, his plan would be null and void.

Gidget was doing her thing, and by the reaction from the crowd they were loving it, especially Torch, who for a moment had forgotten about Storm. He had other fish to fry and Gidget would be his next *catch*. The attention he was giving her had not gone unnoticed by Gidget, who flirted with Torch during her entire routine. Completing her dance, she stepped down from the podium. As she passed Torch's table, he slipped her a hundred-dollar bill. Beaming, she gladly accepted it and pranced toward the dressing room. Unbeknownst to her, Princess was watching this whole exchange.

"Good routine, Gidget," Princess commented.

"Thanks," Gidget said proudly. Princess then warned her not to play to just one table. Everyone was here to see the show, not any particular person.

"He was a big tipper. I didn't want to be disrespectful," Gidget innocently offered.

"I feel you, but Legends is not a strip joint. We pay our dancers very well so there is no need to hustle for a dollar," Princess stated in a stern voice.

Gidget told her she was sorry and that she understood. Secretly, she didn't like being reprimanded by Princess. As she walked away, Princess stopped her again.

"Gidget!" Princess called out her name above the music.

"Yes," she answered without turning around.

"I mean it. Don't let it happen again."

Skylar made her way over to the bar where a pensive-looking Nettie seemed to be just going through the motions. Skylar tried to chitchat, but noticed right away that something was a little different. She immediately thought that Nettie and June were fighting again. Nettie assured her that things couldn't be better between the two. In fact, she told her that Deana's, the lesbian bar in town, was honoring June for all the work she had done for AIDS awareness in Philly.

"I know she'd like you to be there, Skylar. You think you could make it?" she asked her.

"Sure, just let me know when it is and I'll roll through with you," she said, smiling.

"But you gotta stay close to me when we go in the place," Nettie told her. " 'Cause those biker dykes will be salivating when they see you step in the spot."

They both laughed, and Skylar told her she was not worried about anything like that, that she would be there to support June. The conversation ended abruptly though, as Skylar realized she had not gone by Cassidy's table to ask if he and his crew needed anything. She was very happy that things were cool with Nettie and June and knew that they had a genuine love for each other. Frankly, she never really understood the whole lesbian thing, but she didn't judge Nettie or anyone else. She believed that love was possible between any two people. When it came to intimacy for her, well, *sex,* there was no substitution for having a man. But her security in herself allowed her to go into a club like Deana's and have a great time regardless. She knew women would try and hit on her. Hell, that had happened right here in Legends on occasion, but she always handled it with grace. She couldn't get her mind off Nettie. Something else was bothering her, but Skylar didn't know what. Nettie was mum on the subject.

Watching Skylar walk away, Nettie looked at her and beamed. She loved her some Skylar. Skylar had always accepted her for who she was. Not just the fact that she was a lesbian, but everything else, shortcomings and all. She then directed her attention to Storm, who was standing on the opposite side of the club. *My two girls,* she thought to herself. *They's like night and day.* She loved them both the same. She longed for the day when they would get things right and be the sisters that Dutch always wanted them to be. In fact, she looked at all these girls as her children, even Lovely and the new girl Alexia. Thinking about the conversation she'd had with Lovely earlier still had her a little mystified.

When Lovely first told her about the rape, Nettie had felt like saying to her, "Let the muthafucka die for what he did." But she knew that was not the right thing to say. Instead she told her that since she had uncovered the truth she had a moral obligation to act.

"I know this is a very painful time in your life, baby," Nettie said. "But ease your mind and soul by doing the right thing and forgive the man. You don't have to forget what he did to your mother, but you not giving him the blood . . . no one wins."

She continued: "Sometimes in life you gotta be the bigger bitch, baby. If your momma is strong enough, you can discuss it with her and give her the option. If not, then don't tell her. Now, I'm not saying you should all of a sudden start kissing and embracing the nigga like he was there when you came out the womb, 'cause I'm not," she pointed out. "You met him in a strange way, but it was for a reason. Shit, I never knew my daddy, and I had a momma that didn't care to know me." Her tone grew slightly more serious, but she lightened it up, saying, "You don't want *blood* on your hands, girl! No pun intended." They both laughed.

"See, it's about saving somebody's life. Whatever he did, he gotta take that shit up with God! That ain't none of your business. Besides, if shit was different, you wouldn't be here and that would just kill my ass!" She hugged Lovely, who thanked her for the advice, telling Nettie that she'd think it over more and make her decision, but that what she'd said had really helped. They embraced once more before leaving the coffee shop.

That was just this afternoon, and now that a few hours had passed, Nettie counted herself lucky that Lovely did not ask her what she'd do, because she would have had to lie. Nettie told Lovely what she thought *she* should do. But Nettie knew damn well how she really felt about the situation. She would have let the nigga die right there in that bed for the shit he did. Matter of fact, she would have unhooked the bastard's lifeline in the hospital room and watched him die a slow and painful death. Yeah, she would have wanted her face to be the last thing he saw before descending into hell! *Men. Hmph. Most of them are fucked up—that's why I don't deal with them.*

"Let me get a Heineken," a female voice said to Nettie. To Nettie's surprise it was Pia Scott, an old nemesis of Storm's.

"What pimp drug you in off the street?" she asked sarcastically.

"Wow, you funny, you know that? I mean, I know you're *funny,* but I mean in a comical way," Pia spat while laughing.

"Bitch, don't try me. Now, is a Heineken all you wanted?" Nettie glared at her with a hand on her hip.

"For now," Pia smirked. "Heard Storm was out. She here?" she asked while looking around.

"Why you worried about Storm? You ain't never liked that girl and you know it. You one of the reasons she got into the trouble she did in the first place!" Nettie stated.

"What are you talking about? I ain't got no beef with Storm. We cool." She took a long sip of beer.

"Yeah, right! Why all of a sudden you just pop up in here, Pia, huh? 'Cause this club been open for two years and I think maybe yo ass was here one time. Why now? Huh?"

"I heard Cassidy was here doing a little concert. So I came by. This is a public place, ain't it?" She rolled her eyes and finished off the beer.

Nettie told her that since she had missed the show she should probably leave because there wasn't any other reason for her to be there. Pia then saw DuBoy sitting over at Torch's table and her mood changed.

"Yo, I see a few old friends in the house." She didn't take her eyes off DuBoy.

Nettie saw this and offered, "Well in that case, why *don't* you go over and get him, and you both ride off into the muthafuckin' sunset."

"Oh, DuBoy don't want me, girl. And I don't want DuBoy. Been there, done that," she reminded Nettie.

"Yeah, I forgot, there ain't too many you ain't been with, right, Pia?" Nettie spat viciously.

"Now, I know you ain't talking, when you was known for giving niggas head for five dollars in the old days." Pia threw back her head in laughter.

Not missing a beat, Nettie retorted, "True, but I could never get ahead in the game 'cause I was always splitting my take with yo momma! Remember, that ho ran them same streets with me till she got a hold of something that made her lose her fucking mind! Got everybody thinking she's bipolar. Ha! The bitch was born crazy. And she birthed a crazy bitch!" Nettie stated emphatically.

This affected Pia more than anything else. Attacks on her she could handle, but those about her mother crossed the line. She slowly put down the beer bottle and walked away, saying nothing else to Nettie. Not getting more than five feet from the bar, she turned back to face Nettie one last time with a hate-filled glare and then quickly exited the club.

Whatever Pia's plan had been for the visit, it was quickly scratched after the encounter with Nettie. Outside the club, she walked toward her car in tears. She hated Nettie. In fact, she *blamed* Nettie—for turning her mother out on the streets years ago. Passing Nettie's car, she thought of keying it but changed her mind after seeing a couple making out in the car behind it. Although they probably wouldn't have noticed her, she didn't want to take the chance.

She'd have another opportunity. Once she befriended Storm again, she'd be back in the club and she and Nettie could finish what had been started. *Yes, the time will come to get even.*

Inside the club, the rest of the evening went smoothly. The crowd continued to have a great time. Skylar and Storm avoided each other like the plague. Flynn, still excited over his upcoming date with Alexia, kept on flirting with her. Nettie phoned June and gave her the good news that Skylar would be at Deana's for her celebration.

Torch left the club, and when he reached his car, an unexpected guest was leaning against the driver's side, smoking a cigarette.

"You mind if I hitch a ride home with you tonight, playa?" the girl asked seductively.

"Sure, baby, where is home?" Torch smiled while opening the door for her.

"Wherever you want *home* to be," she said, dropping the cigarette in the dirt and grinding it out.

Torch asked, "Are you sure you know what you're doing, ma'?"

Not answering, she just looked at him and threw a sly smile.

"Get in the car, Gidget," Torch said as he shifted his large frame to the side, allowing her to step up into his burgundy Hummer. As the car sped off, the radio blasted a familiar Kanye West tune, "Gold Digger."

< FIFTEEN >

Monday, Monday

Skylar was not particularly looking forward to the drive into the city today. For one, it was Monday, the day she set aside as *Skylar's* day. On Skylar's day, she did whatever she wanted to do. Sometimes, she stayed in bed all day watching TV. Other times, she'd catch a midday movie in town and grab a bite to eat with a friend. Even Sidney knew not to plan anything with her on Monday. In fact, she didn't even answer her phone or check messages on Monday unless it was absolutely necessary. This was just a practice that she had been doing for years. It was something Dutch did all his life.

His day was Sunday. After church, he would perhaps take a walk in the park and sit down on a bench and think about all the blessings God had showered on him. Or take a long drive alone somewhere, way out, and just see God's land. He didn't go into the restaurant. The staff would have to handle everything from the cooking to the cleaning.

Those memories brought a smile to Skylar's face, a smile that disappeared quickly as she remembered why she was heading to the club. Storm!

She demanded that Storm meet her at the club at ten that morning for a discussion. For the first week or so, things had gone rather smoothly with Storm handling management duties. However, as the weeks went on, things were changing, and Skylar had been holding back her comments far too long.

Once inside the club, she headed for the main dining area, where the meeting would take place. Pacing the floor, trying to calm down before Storm arrived, she grabbed a bottle of water from the small refrigerator beneath the bar. The picture of Dutch that Nettie had hung on the wall caught her eye.

"I'm going to need your strength, Daddy," she said softly while looking at it.

Noticing that it was now ten-thirty and still no Storm, Skylar retrieved her cellphone from her purse. As soon as she began to make a call, the door opened and a hungover Storm entered. Storm had no intention of making eye contact with her sister until she was ready.

Dressed in an off-white designer running suit and tennis shoes, with her hair hidden under a baseball cap, she pulled out a chair from a nearby table and sat down. Skylar glared at her the entire time. There were several uneasy moments of silence.

"What's up, Sky?" Storm asked, still not making eye contact.

"That's what I should be asking you." Skylar folded her arms across her chest. Storm hated when Skylar did this.

"Listen, Skylar, I'm a little tired. I did work last night you know." For the first time she looked at her sister. "So could we have this little meeting and talk about what the hell you want to talk about so that I can go back to bed, *please*? Thank you!"

"What's wrong with you? Huh? I thought we had an understanding," Skylar said, still trying to remain calm.

"I have no idea what you're talking about." Storm started toward the bar. Skylar told her how she had been coming in late on her shift, and that customers were complaining about her attitude. She also let her know that some of the employees had mentioned that there were times when they'd smelled liquor on her breath.

Before Skylar had finished the last statement, Storm had already poured herself a drink.

"I just need you to do your job. I know all of this is new, but I need you to be more focused while you're here, Storm, that's all." Skylar seemed exhausted and threw her hands up in the air. Storm refused to comment on anything. She took a seat on one of the bar stools and nursed her drink.

"I've tried to stay out of your personal life these last few weeks. But now it's starting to affect my business, so I need to say something. I thought you had changed. The drinking, the streets, running with your old crowd. Aren't you tired of all that shit?"

Storm slammed her glass down on the bar. "Crowd? What old crowd? Say what you really mean, Sky. You're referring to DuBoy." She stood up.

"Well, I didn't think I needed to say any names," Skylar said.

"And yes, I am tired. I'm tired of you bringing up my past," Storm continued as she began to pace. "I just spent the last three years of my damn life locked up, and I'm trying to get adjusted to my life again on the outside, if you don't mind."

"I just want you to get yourself together. In fact, that's all I've ever wanted for you."

"Save that shit, Sky! You never cared for anyone but yourself. The entire time I was away, you came up to see me twice! Two damn times, *Skylar!*" she spat.

"I came when I could. You never asked for me, Storm," Skylar told her.

"Why should I have to ask my own sister to come to a fuckin' prison to see me?" Storm said, getting angrier.

Skylar defended herself by reminding Storm of all that she had had to deal with back here. "You know, keeping the business up and running and taking care of Daddy when he got ill. Dutch needed me. He could have used your help, too, but yo ass was locked up!" she shrieked.

"Fuck you!" Storm was beside herself with rage.

"No, fuck you!" Skylar returned the sentiment. She couldn't believe that Storm had gotten her to the point where she was using such language. She couldn't remember the last time she'd cursed likc this.

"You know that shit was not my fault!" Storm stressed.

"When is it ever, Storm? When is it ever your fault? When are you going to grow up and take responsibility for something for a change? You did all that time because of all the crap you were involved with," Skylar reminded her.

Storm could not believe that Skylar had said this to her. Suggesting she *deserved* to be *wrongly* locked up three years. "For *what*? All I really did was drive a car with a suspended license!"

"It was more than that and you know it!" Skylar said. "They were going to charge you with murder! You pled guilty to manslaughter, Storm!"

"I did what they forced me to do! How the hell was I supposed to know that shit? Huh? I was just driving the damn car!" Storm explained.

Skylar raised her voice."That's what you thought. It didn't matter. You were there. I've told you time and time again that Asia and Lenora were no damn good. None of the chicks you used to roll with here were any good!"

Calming down a bit, Storm retorted. "Let me remind you, sister, that I am almost thirty years old. I was twenty-six when I went upstate, okay? To handle a life more real than you've *ever* imagined. I don't need you telling me who I can and can't run with. You are not my mother and you sure as hell ain't my father, so you need to stop."

"You're right, I'm not," Skylar stated. "But Dutch tried to get through to you, too. How many times did Daddy tell the both of us that we would be judged by the company we keep? Even he knew your so-called friends would be your downfall." Skylar stood and again folded her arms across her chest.

Instead of blowing up any further, Storm sauntered back to the bar and poured another drink. Skylar got a disgusted look on her face and spoke out.

"See, there you go."

"Bitch, I am grown! And if I want to drink until I pee out yellow vodka it's my damn business!" Slamming down the bottle, she turned her back on Skylar, but could still see her in the mirror behind the bar. Softly, she began to talk.

"All I did was drive Lenora by her job before she went to the club. She called and said that her and Asia were going out, and if I didn't mind could we all go in my car because hers was being worked on. I had no idea that those two had other plans, too. On the way to the club was when she said she had to stop by her job because she'd left her wallet there.

"I asked if it could wait until Monday, I did. But she said her ID was in there and if we got all the way down to the club and she got carded that me and Asia would be pissed. She was right, so she had us pull up to this huge house in Chestnut Hill, not the office building on City Line Avenue where I thought she worked. I asked her what we were doing there and she said this was where her last assignment was. That she had been assigned as Ida Tuttle's home-care companion for the last month.

Skylar hadn't heard her sister's story before. Although she was still certain that her sister's friends were worthless and that nothing good could come of Storm still palling around with them, she knew that she had to let Storm have this moment.

"Asia went inside with her because Lenorea said she didn't want to go by herself. No one was home and that house could be scary. That's what she said." Storm walked over to a table near Skylar and continued.

"I told them to hurry up or I'd leave their asses right there. I spent the next three years, Skylar, three fucking years in a cell, regretting that I didn't leave. Lenora was going to rob this old woman's place, because she knew the old lady kept a lot of cash and jewelry just lying around in her room, and since Lenora came and went a lot during the week she not only had a key but she knew the alarm code, too.

"When they went in, they didn't turn on any lights. Lenora knew exactly which room to go to and went to work. Asia went into the office and started rummaging through Ida's desk drawers. Lenora was into Ida's bedroom dresser, grabbing all kinds of stuff, a topaz ring encrusted with diamonds, a gold pocket watch that dated back to the 1800s, diamond rings, pearls, and a money box about the size of a shoe box that was kept in the back of a drawer. That's where Ida kept loose money, like fifty- and one-hundred-dollar bills. That box had tempted Lenora every time Ida had sent her in there to grab money for groceries or medicine. But Lenora never took anything other than what she was told before, because she knew that no matter how much Ida Tuttle told her she trusted her and she was *such a nice girl and all,* she doubled-checked everything once Lenora left for the day."

Skylar just shook her head.

"But when Lenora was ready to leave, the bathroom door suddenly opened and there was frail, frightened Ida Tuttle. Without her glasses, Ida couldn't see it was Lenora, who pushed past her, knocking her to the ground as she ran down the stairs. It wouldn't have been so bad, but Ida had a heart attack right then and there and died."

Storm welled up as she remembered everything about the evening.

"I caught a rap for a damn murder that I didn't commit!" she cried.

"The tape from the closed-circuit television clearly showed your car, Storm."

"No! That's bullshit, Skylar. When they went into the house, I turned the car off, and there was no light in front of the house. Those two bitches turned me in. They had to say that it was me driving the car because how else could anyone know I was even there or think that I'd touched any of that stuff? Nothing in there had my prints on it. Dammit!"

She started to cry uncontrollably. Skylar watched her with no emotion. A few seconds passed. Skylar got up and took a few steps before speaking softly.

"I remember when Daddy got the call that the police had arrested you for murder. He literally fell down in front of the phone. He never believed that you were involved."

"You did, though," Storm said, glaring at her twin.

"What did you expect me to think, Storm? All the time you had gotten into shit!" She threw her hands up and walked away, but continued talking. "Dutch said as long as he had breath in his body, he'd fight for your freedom. Took all his savings and military pension to get the best lawyer he could for you."

"I had no other choice than to plead. At least that's what my attorney said. Even though Asia finally admitted that I really didn't know what was going down. It was too late. The damage was done," Storm admitted. "They were sentenced to fifteen to life."

"Dutch even wrote a letter to the judge begging for mercy for you. He was never the same after that," Skylar remembered.

"Oh, so now you blaming me for Dutch's death, too? You saying I had a hand in that situation, too?" Storm said.

"You know what, Storm, I'm tired of pretending. Yes, you definitely played a part in what happened to him. There was nothing Dutch wouldn't do for you. Even put up his restaurant to save your ass. Anything for his Storm."

"Oh, okay, that's it. Now we're getting to the real shit, ain't we, Sky? Yeah . . . you couldn't understand the fact that even though my shit was fucked up at times Daddy still loved and supported me. . . ." Storm was on a roll now. "Well, I'll be damned! That's it. You've always been the same since we were kids. Never able to stand it, how I wasn't half as perfect as you thought you were, but Dutch still loved me more." Heading back toward the bar, Storm started laughing. This upset Skylar, who lost it and started screaming at Storm.

"Daddy felt sorry for your ass, Storm! That shit ain't have nothing to do with love. Before he died, he told me that he had resolved in his mind that he was going to take care of your trifling ass for the rest of your life, or his, whichever came first!"

This hit Storm hard, like a blow to the gut. "Dutch would never say anything like that about me. He would never call me out my name that way. That's all you, Skylar. If he even thought something like that, it was during one of those times when he got pissed at me for not wanting to follow in his footsteps with the business."

"Wow! You have got to be kidding. Dutch knew you had no business sense," Skylar ranted. "He *never* wanted you to be a part of the family business. He told me himself that he prayed to God I would take over when he retired, because leaving it in your hands was a sure disaster!" Skylar tossed a chair to the side and walked over to the bar.

"If what you say is true, Sky, why is my name on the deed of this place as co-owner along with yours? Huh? Yeah, my dear sister, I had it all checked out!" Storm stood and folded *her* arms across her chest and gave Skylar a piercing look.

Skylar took a moment before she responded to what Storm had said. Turning toward her, she spoke softly.

"I never tried to hide anything from you, Storm. I told Dutch to put your name back on it along with mine because I did not want any trouble with you over this property. After Dutch retired, I offered to buy it from him because I wanted to keep it in the family, and because I had dreams of opening a nightclub. And you know what he said to me? He said, 'Baby, if anybody can make it work, you can. You have my blessings!' " Skylar patted her chest for emphasis, with tears in her eyes.

Storm walked toward Skylar and, when she got right in front of her, started to applaud.

"Congratulations, sister girl. Is that what you want to hear? Huh? That the good daughter came in to save the day? Well, let me tell you something, sis." She got right up in her face. "All that bullshit you talkin' don't mean shit to me, 'cause I'm just as much a part of this place as you are. Remember that shit! I'm just as responsible for this business as you are. I'm just as entitled to make decisions about it as you are. And I have an executive decision to make right now."

"What the hell are you talking about, Storm?"

"I want to collect on my inheritance. That's what this is, right? Dutch left it to both of us?"

Skylar couldn't believe what she was hearing.

Storm continued. "Yeah, you heard me. I've been down for three years, and it's time for me to collect. So I tell you what. Either you buy me out or we sell this bitch and split the money."

Stunned at what Storm had just proposed, Skylar needed a moment for all of it to sink in. "Are you crazy? I have no plans to sell Legends, nor are there any plans to buy you out. If you think that I am going to let you ruin what I've built in the last two years, you have lost your *got damn mind*!" Storm could not remember the last time she had seen her sister this angry. It actually surprised her a little. She tried reasoning with Skylar.

"Look, I see what you've done to the spot. You've made your mark all over this place. But I'm just saying sometimes you gotta look at the bigger picture. Grow bigger, expand til you blow shit up!" Storm's eyes lit up with excitement. "Just think about the possibilities of what could happen—just hear me out."

"You have lost your friggin' mind. I'm not even listening to this." Skylar started to walk away.

"Wait a minute, sis," She grabbed Skylar by the arm gently. "I just want to bend your ear about an idea DuBoy and Torch have been talking about—"

Jerking her arm away, Skylar snapped, "Don't you touch me. I am not interested in any get-rich-quick schemes involving two lowlifes like DuBoy and Torch."

"There you go, judging people. Torch made shit happen in this town and the brotha is giving us a chance to make *bank*. I'm talking serious paper, girl! Not this nickel-and-dime shit you got rolling up in here."

Skylar could literally have killed Storm at that moment. "I'm done," she said as she started walking toward the kitchen area. Storm followed right behind her. Swinging open the door leading into the kitchen, Skylar abruptly stopped and spun around to confront her sister. "I'll be damned if I'm going to allow you to downplay what I've done here. Now, if you're not happy, then you can get the hell out!" Standing toe-to-toe, Skylar shouted, "I have had enough of you—and you know what?" She stopped herself from continuing and saying something she would have regretted. Instead, hot tears streamed down down her face and she trembled with anger—and with fear. Was it possible that her sister and her thuggish clowns could ruin all that she'd worked so hard to save?

Witnessing a side of her sister that she had never seen before—and determined to make this business proposal work—Storm softened her approach and apologized.

Tears formed in her eyes—a bit less genuine than her sister's—and she said, "Look, I know I seem out of hand. It's just that I am out, sis. I'm free, and I just want a chance. That's all. I want to succeed and push forward, too." She paused for a moment before continuing. "And you're holding me back. It's almost like you wish I hadn't come home."

Skylar didn't say a word, but the expression on her face showed Storm that she'd hit the nail on the head.

"Wow, that's really fucked up that you would even think some shit like that, with all I've been through," Storm said, turning away from her sister and wiping away her tears—these as genuine as they come. She was pissed that she'd allowed Skylar to see her so weak at that moment.

"Been through? Girl, what have you been through?" Skylar came from behind her and faced her. "You had three squares, a warm bed to sleep in, and no damn bills, while I worked my ass off to keep my head above water." Skylar's voice intensified as she went on, "Sometimes I was not even able to make payroll. With all you been through? Bitch, please! You try waking the hell up every day with that *shit* on you. Not knowing what state of mind I was going to find Dutch in every day." Skylar was becoming more and more upset as she continued getting off her chest what she had obviously been feeling for quite some time.

"Having to bathe him, feeding him like some damn baby! Cleaning him up after he'd shit on himself. I didn't mind it, because that was my father, but don't you come in here with 'All I been through.' So let me say it again: You ain't been through shit! Now get the hell out of my face and let me do my work!"

Silence fell over the room. Neither sister knew what to say next. Just then Storm's cellphone went off. Taking it from the pocket of her sweats, she looked at it then shut it off. Walking up to Skylar, she softly told her that she was sorry that she wasn't there to help with their father. Sounding a bit more sincere, she admitted, "Look, I know I fucked up, more than once even, but Skylar, don't you ever say that I haven't been through shit. Talk about unfair. I think I deserve a chance to do my own thing. You got to do yours. Now it's my turn."

Skylar smirked, "It's easy to say stuff like that now, Storm, now that all the work and effort has already been put in." Thanks but no thanks was her feeling about Storm's tearful confession.

Walking away from her sister, Storm went off with her head bowed, rested both hands on the stainless steel counter for balance, and closed her eyes. Tears ran down her face in perfectly straight lines and gathered under her chin before falling onto her top. Not lifting her head she began to recount her time in prison.

"You know the first few weeks weren't so bad, before the trial. Bitches just chillin'—doing their time. I had heard that as long as you minded your own business, shit would remain cool. But after I had to turn in that plea, reality set in that this was going to be where I would spend the next few years of my life.."

They were led off the bus in pairs. Storm was handcuffed to a hardcore dyke by the name of Trae who tried talking to her the entire ride. When Storm stepped off the bus, shit just got quiet. Even in her loose-fitting jumpsuit Storm looked good. The Bulls—that's what they called the inmates—hadn't seen a bitch this bad in a long time. The whole yard suddenly became speechless. "Shit, they ain't looking at me," Trae said. "Gotta be you, Shorti. Be strong, 'cause bitches up here are ruthless."

Trying not to show any signs of fear, Storm held her head high and gave hard cold stares to the women, who looked as if they could devour her at any moment. Something trickled down her leg and she didn't know if it was pee or if her *flow* had started. She was frightened.

Storm told her story calmly, and Skylar listened, their argument forgotten for the moment. "Wasn't long before things changed.

They started fucking with me. The guards didn't say shit. And I know they saw what was going on. Bitches playfully pulling on my hair when I walked by. This one named Shane tried me and I knocked her the fuck out!

"You know I have nothing against lesbians. We both know that Nettie's one and we love her to death," Storm reminded Skylar. "But I'm not down with that shit!" She took her time before she went on with the story.

"I . . . I was finishing up my shower one day when I felt a hand around my mouth and one around my throat. Before I knew it I was being forced down on the floor. Right away I knew what was happening. It was four of them." Storm got lost in the memory of it and tearfully went on; she'd almost forgotten that Skylar was in the room. "I fought for my life as they took turns doing shit to me that . . . that made me feel like throwing up. One by one, they probed my body with fingers, hands . . . objects."

Skylar covered her mouth with her hand, frightened as she listened to her sister's story. It was hard for Storm to go on, but she did.

"One of them told me if I didn't shut up and cooperate, that I'd meet *Johnny.* The voice sounded familiar to me, and when I opened my eyes, it was Trae—the one I was handcuffed to when I came in. The one that told me to watch myself. Another one shouted that the last bitch that didn't do what they wanted was now wearing a colostomy bag. With that, Trae showed me what looked like a broomstick. Stroking it up and down like it was a dick, she let me know that this was Johnny. I closed my eyes and let them do just what they wanted. Even in the midst of what was happening to me I secretly vowed to get revenge." Tears flowed down both sisters' cheeks. Storm had no control over her words, talking even though her brain said stop, even though her heart said it was too painful. Storm steadily purged every disgusting and foul thing they had done to her.

At this point Skylar wished that she'd stop, too. It was not what she had expected to hear from her sister.

"You know what it does to a person's mind when they've been

messed with, Sky?" Storm said, looking at her sister with tears in her eyes. "And the worst part?" She fought the lump in her throat. "There ain't shit you can do about it. Who you gonna tell? Huh?"

She went on to tell Skylar that for days she pretty much stayed to herself. She didn't shower, even when the stench of her own body got to her. Not long afterward, she was moved into another cell with three other girls. They'd all heard about what had happened to her, but no one said anything until Layaway, a lifer Jamaican chick in her fifties, befriended her. Layaway got her name because she was always borrowing from the commissary and promising to pay it all back as soon as she got more money on the books.

Storm said she was leery at first because she figured that Layaway would eventually want the same thing from her as the others. But this was not the case. Layaway was actually disgusted when she heard what they did to her. Dyking might have been her thing, but rape sho the fuck wasn't. She told Storm that Trae had set the whole thing up and was boasting to everyone that she'd turned "Shortirock" out!

"Layaway told me if I wanted to get even, she had a plan. Told me to put in for laundry duty in the basement with her. Trae worked there, too. I wanted to ask what the plan was but I didn't because I didn't give a fuck. I just wanted a chance to get that dyke back. Wanted to get all four of them, but that would be impossible, especially so soon, and having a shot at the ringleader sat very well with me. But I needed to know what was in it for Layaway.

"Well, she just didn't like the bitch, that was it. They had some beef over Trae snitching about some weed or something," Storm said and let out a chuckle. "Layaway got angry just thinking about it! So we put a plan together, knowing that Trae had asthma and always needed her inhaler; she kept one in her cell and one in her prison smock that stayed in the laundry room, because it was always stifling hot down there. Shit, it was so hot the guards barely even came down there. It was usually just the three of us, me, Layaway, and Trae, who would do shit like slither her tongue in and out of her mouth and whatnot whenever I passed by. And so one day we're working, and Layaway walked by me and mouthed 'Today' and kept going. It took a moment for it to register what she meant, but seconds later my heart started pounding out of my chest. After all the anticipation, this was it.

"I still had no clue what Layaway had cooked up, but I was ready no matter what. Like clockwork, at three in the afternoon, the heat was getting to Trae and she went for her inhaler. Only this time it was not in the smock pocket. Out of the corner of my eye, I saw her going from pocket to pocket looking for it. Only it wasn't there. She asked Layaway if she saw it, and me, and we were all like, 'Nah.' But then Layaway said she'd go up to Trae's cell to get the other one, pretending to do her a favor, you know?

"I was kind of shocked when Trae agreed, but so be it. But she didn't know that inhaler was never coming. Layaway left the room and gave me a nod to follow her. Trae was so into her own breathing and shit and keeping cool that she never even noticed that I was right behind Layaway, or that we locked the door behind us.

"I was scared shitless. Layaway said she'd be right back and under no circumstances should I open that door. To make sure I did what she said, she took the key with her. After a few moments, Trae looked up and saw that I was gone and started rushing toward the door.

"She was screaming at us to open the fuckin' door! Twisting and turning the doorknob, pounding on the glass. She even tried to find something within reach to break it. But nothing could. It was too thick."

Turning to Skylar, Storm asked, "Do you know what a person looks like when they can't catch their breath, and all the while know that directly on the other side is fresh air? Staring through that glass, I never once thought of trying to help that bitch in any way. I wanted her to feel what I'd felt that horrible day on the shower floor—helpless. I wanted that dirty bitch to die. That was one of the best days of my life," Storm proudly stated to Skylar.

Storm took her time before finishing the story.

"When the warden questioned us about Trae's death, I expected

Layaway to say how she hadn't gotten back in time with the inhaler and that I hadn't come to work that day. Anything! Layaway's record was clean. All the Bulls thought she was cool and the staff trusted her. Imagine my shock when I heard her say that in fact she was the one who didn't come to work that day, and that to her knowledge, only me and Trae were down there.

"I started screaming at her to tell the truth. She didn't budge, and I was led away to the hole, awaiting further investigation," Storm told Skylar.

Thrown into the dark room, Storm had stayed in a fetal position for the next eight hours. She wondered why all of this was happening to her. Had she really been that bad of a person? Where was God? Where was Dutch? No one was there to help her. No one cared.

When they took her out of the hole, they brought her back up to the warden's office, where he told her that, although there was no clear evidence that she had anything to do with Trae's death, he was recommending that she serve out her entire sentence. Too many other cellies knew she had gone to work that day. Therefore, she was most likely present when Trae needed help but chose to stand around and watch her suffer.

"I couldn't believe that shit," she continued. "I thought about calling Clara Bow, that attorney, but I knew I'd pissed her off last time. I just went back to my cell, and who's there but Layaway, just chillin', reading a magazine.

"I straight up asked her, 'Why would you do this to me? Why didn't you tell them the truth? My eighteen months was almost up and now I have to finish my entire sentence. I thought you were my friend.'

"Well, she just looked at me like, 'Would I rather her tell the Bulls what really happened, so they could keep fucking with me verbally and sexually and all that, or would I rather her say I wasn't to be messed with? You know, that fucking with me could result in what happened to Trae.' She was straight up, 'cause she ain't have nothing to lose. She was like, 'They taking me out in a body bag, so it ain't shit for me to admit to what I did.' That was real. Nothing was gonna change her situation, but she said, 'You, well you are a li'l different.' This way I looked like a cold-hearted bitch who had had enough, and no one would dare mess with me."

Turning to her sister, Storm walked closer to her. "Yeah, sis, I done seen a lot, done a lot. So don't you ever tell me I ain't been through shit!" Walking toward the kitchen doors leading back into the main club area, she turned to Skylar one last time. "Now give me my muthafuckin' cut or we selling this bitch!" With that, she burst through the door, leaving it swinging back and forth, a visibly distraught Skylar standing in her own solitude.

< SIXTEEN >

The Storm Was Passing Over

A few days after pouring her heart out to Nettie about the discovery of her biological father, Lovely decided to donate blood to Felix Murphy. It had not been an easy decision. She was shocked, angry, sad, and confused, but surprisingly a little happy. Happy because at least the unanswered question of who her father was had been answered. She'd never believed the story that her mother told her about him dying before she was born. Whenever she asked about her father as a child growing up, her mother would become angry. "I told you he died before you were born, didn't I?" her mother would say. One time she had even made the mistake of asking her mother if she missed her father. She was sent to her room and told to go to bed. Seconds later she heard her mother softly crying in her room. That moment, she decided never to ask about him again.

Now she was on her way to the hospital to do the *right thing.* She made it clear to Hertha James that although she had agreed to do this, in no way did she want any communication with Mr. Murphy. Even after he inquired about the "pretty brown girl" who used to come and see him. She was not going back to see him. She couldn't. She didn't love him. How could she possibly love the man who had raped her mother and put her through the mental anguish she'd obviously been going through for so many years? Besides, he never knew about her. It was too painful. But as a nurse, she had pledged to help anyone with a medical crisis, and if that meant getting personally involved by donating blood for a person to live, then so be it.

As she pulled into the hospital employee lot, her cellphone rang. It was her son, Tony Jr. "Mommy, when are you coming to get me?"

"Soon, baby. Mommy's coming to get you soon," she said. There was a moment of silence on the phone. "Tony, are you okay? What's the matter?" She knew that whenever her son got quiet, something was bothering him.

"I'm sad, Mommy," he said softly.

"Sad, why? Aren't you having a good time with Grammy?"

"Yes," he said, even softer.

"Then why are you sad, Booby?"

"Because I miss you," Tony said in between his sniffles.

"Aw, baby, Mommy's right here. You know that." Lovely sounded sad herself.

"I don't want you to go away like Daddy," Tony said before getting quiet.

"I'm not going anywhere, baby. I'll come and get you today," she said. After hanging up with her son, Lovely broke down. She could not believe that her son felt abandoned. She honestly thought she was doing the right thing by sending him to his grandmother's while she tried to figure out everything that was going on in her life.

None of this stopped the guilt from taking over. Maybe it was selfish sending him away. No one meant more to her than her son, and his thinking any differently killed her inside. She knew what she had to do. As soon as she left the hospital she was going to get her son, take him home with her, where he belonged, and never leave again.

Entering Jefferson, Lovely was hoping not to see many coworkers—she didn't feel like any conversation. In fact, she instructed Hertha not to mention that she was coming in. She just wanted to go directly to the lab, do her duty, and leave. Before she got there, though, she ran into Hertha. "Hey, Lovely, could I have a word with you in the office?" Hertha asked.

Lovely assumed that Hertha was going to try again to persuade her to see Felix. But her mind was made up and there was no changing it. After today, she never wanted to think about Felix Murphy again.

"Hertha, I know what you're going to say and the answer is still no. I—"

Hertha cut her off and asked her to sit down. "I'm afraid I have some bad news, Lovely. Mr. Murphy died this morning."

"What? How? When?"

"Less than an hour ago. He took a turn for the worse and suffered a massive heart attack. I tried calling your cell but it went directly to voice mail. I'm sorry, Lovely."

"What happens now? I mean, has his family been notified?" Lovely asked.

"Unfortunately, Mr. Murphy did not have any next of kin listed in his records. He resided at the Simpson House in Bala Cynwyd. They are sending someone to claim the body."

Simpson House was an adult-care facility, a rest home for the elderly. Lovely had visited it several times while in nursing school and volunteered there during the Christmas holiday.

Hertha thanked Lovely for coming in and asked how she was doing.

"I'm coming alone fine, thanks," Lovely said, forcing a smile.

"Well, you're very much missed around here. We look forward to you returning when you're able. Just take as much time as you need. You're one of the best nurses this hospital has, and your job is secure with us." Hertha got up and hugged Lovely.

After leaving Hertha's office, Lovely walked down the hall in a daze, full of mixed emotions. Why was Felix Murphy's death affecting her? It couldn't have been losing a father, because to her knowledge *her father* had been dead for years. Was this her fault? Would he have survived had she donated the blood days ago? In order to avoid a group of nurses waiting for the public elevator, Lovely went down a side corridor to the service elevator, which actually went down closer to the employee parking lot anyway. On the way down, the elevator stopped on the sixth floor. Kareem, an orderly, got in with a gurney holding a covered, deceased patient. He was happy to see Lovely.

"Hey, Lovely, you're back, huh?" he said, smiling at her.

"Hi, Kareem. No, I'm not back yet. I just had to come in to take care of some things." Before the door closed, Kareem stopped it midway.

"Shoot, I forgot my radio. Lovely, you can go on down, Rob is waiting in the back to transport this body to the holding area. He'll meet the elevator when it stops. Thank you!" Kareem leapt off, leaving the gurney, with his clipboard flat on the top sheet.

"Okay, Kareem." Lovely managed a chuckle. She always liked Kareem and thought that he was a great kid. He planned on being a doctor: He worked at the hospital during the summer and was a full-time student at Temple during the rest of the year.

A sudden jolt of the elevator stopped it between floors.

"Damn!" Lovely said out loud. She had forgotten that this particular elevator periodically got stuck between floors. Something caught her eye on the paperwork Kareem had left on the clipboard. At the bottom right corner in red block letters the word "unknown" was stamped. Lovely knew that it meant the person was a vagrant or homeless with no family or next of kin. She looked toward the top of the page and to her stunned horror, she saw the name "Felix Murphy." Dropping her purse and closing her eyes, she backed up against the wall of the elevator and clutched her chest. She frantically started pushing the lobby button on the elevator panel. But then Lovely was suddenly overcome by a sense of calm. She slowly turned toward the body on the gurney and began to speak through her tears.

"I'm sorry that your life has ended this way. I truly am. These last few weeks you have caused me a lot of heartache, but not nearly as much as the lifetime of pain you caused my mother. However, somehow, I don't hate you. I pity you. I feel pity for what must have been a trying life you led. May God bless your soul, and may you rest in peace." Wiping away tears, she stepped a bit farther back from the gurney. The elevator started moving and continued its descent. As the doors opened, she turned toward the body. "Good-bye, Father."

< SEVENTEEN >

If Loving You Is Wrong, I Don't Wanna Be Right

Sitting on the side of his bed, DuBoy lit up a blunt and took a long drag. It had been more than two weeks since he last brought up the issue of the club to Storm, and Torch was sweating him now more than ever. Storm was going to have to act on this shit! Hell, he was tired of pretending that he loved her. How could he? They spent damn near three years apart. To be frank, he wasn't even feeling her that much sexually anymore. Sure, the first few days were off the chain, but Storm was falling off her game. She was spending more and more of her time at Legends, which would have been a good thing if she had been working on her sister about the buyout. But he knew for a fact she hadn't been saying too much of anything to Skylar. In fact, Gidget told Torch that Skylar and Storm hardly ever spoke.

Thinking about Gidget made him laugh. That girl came to Legends like she was a little innocent white farm girl wanting to dance, when that was far from the truth. DuBoy knew the kind of freak Gidget was. The shit the two of them did sexually would've been banned from a porn flick. Thinking about it made him want to lie back across the bed and pleasure himself, but he decided against it. He had plenty of freaks on speed dial. Picking up his cellphone he made a call.

"Yo, 'sup? What you doing? Why don't you come through the spot? When? Now, bitch! I'm hittin' you up now, ain't I?" he raised his voice.

"Aight, I'm sorry, Shorti. I ain't mean to holla at you. It's just I'm here all by myself wanting some company, you know, so I thought I'd hit my girl up." He took another drag on the blunt.

"Don't worry about her. This is my spot. She ain't here no way. Yo, look, you coming through or not?" A smile crept across his face and he lay back down across the bed. "Yo, you miss me?" he said in a low sexy voice.

"Hurry up!" DuBoy shouted out playfully before hanging up. Feeling the buzz from his high, he headed to the shower, but not before calling Torch and telling him he was going to come by and holla at him later.

On the other side of town, Flynn and Alexia stopped by Ben and Jerry's while taking a summer night's stroll down South Street. South Street was a very popular, trendy ten-block strip of quaint little restaurants, shops, and boutiques. If Philadelphia was known as the city of neighborhoods and cultures, then South Street was a sure indication that this was true.

Flynn and Alexia had been spending a lot of time together the past couple weeks, just getting to know each other. Flynn was ready to take it to the next level, but he didn't want to push her. Alexia was very guarded about her feelings, which Flynn chalked up to a past relationship gone bad. But Flynn was willing to be patient. It had been a long time since he'd actually met someone he felt this way about.

Even though Flynn was pretty open about his story, Alexia offered little about her background except that she was an only child and that, except for her cousin, she didn't really stay in touch with many of her relatives. "Have you ever been married?" he asked in between spoonfuls of ice cream.

"Nah . . . I don't think a committed relationship has to have a piece of paper from City Hall," Alexia replied.

"True. But I thought most girls wanted the fantasy-type wedding. The long white dress, bridesmaids, the church. You know, the whole nine yards," Flynn said, chuckling.

"Not all girls," Alexia offered. "If I am ready to settle down with anyone again, a small intimate commitment ceremony is fine with me. I don't need all that pomp and circumstance."

"You are a rare one, Miss Alexia Adams. I'm definitely not letting you go." They both laughed.

"Oh really, now. Who said you *have* me to let go?" Alexia teased.

"It's like that, huh? Well, I thought by now that I was doing a pretty good job of winning you over." Flynn stopped walking and turned to look in Alexia's eyes. He wanted to kiss her but just wasn't sure if it was where Alexia wanted to go. She looked away momentarily.

"What's the matter?" Flynn asked.

Looking at him for a moment, Alexia smiled and said, "Nothing is wrong, Flynn. You've done nothing wrong. In fact, you've been doing everything right. It's just that . . . well. Look, I like you very much Flynn, I really do. But I'm not ready, okay?" Alexia teared up.

Taking her face in his hands Flynn pulled her closer. Her body stiffened initially, but after looking into his eyes she relaxed a bit.

"Who hurt you?" Flynn asked in a low voice while searching her eyes for an answer.

"Excuse me!" a female voice bellowed over the various street sounds.

"Y'all need to get a room—dang!" said a member of a group of teenage girls trying to pass the couple, whose romantic embrace was blocking the thoroughfare.

"Oops, we're sorry," Alexia said, taking Flynn's hand and moving off to the side. She was relieved: The girls' interruption gave her a chance to change the subject.

"Hey, why don't we walk down to Penn's Landing and sit by the water? I love it down there."

Flynn agreed and they started toward the landing. After a few steps, Flynn took Alexia's hand in his. She didn't object. He smiled and they walked the next few moments in silence, taking in the night.

"I'll wait, Alexia," Flynn said, still keeping his eyes straight ahead. Alexia didn't respond. There was no need for her to do so. She knew exactly what Flynn meant. Instead, she exhaled and tightened her grip on his hand. They passed the same group of girls, who paraphrased a line from a Beyoncé tune: "If you like it like that, put a ring on it!" and broke out into girlish giggles. The happy couple joined in and laughed themselves.

In apartment 3A, the piercing sound of the bell jolted DuBoy from a sound sleep. Stumbling over to the front door he shouted out, "Who is it?" Leaning in to the peephole, he recognized who it was and slowly opened the door.

"What the fuck took you so long, ma'?" a sluggish, half-dressed DuBoy questioned the scantily dressed young woman.

"You gonna let me in or not?" she asked him with both hands on her hips.

"What you got for me, Shorti?" DuBoy asked while biting his bottom lip.

Pushing past him, she headed directly into the bedroom and started taking off her clothes.

"Y'all got any beer in there," she shouted out.

"Girl, you come here to drink or get busy?" DuBoy said, sticking his head in the refrigerator. All he saw was Storm's last Heineken. She had warned him not to drink it. Pausing for a moment, he almost decided against giving it to his guest but reasoned that he wasn't the one who was going to drink it.

It was only a matter of seconds before the two were entwined in a steamy sex session that seemed to last forever. Both exhausted, they lay still as DuBoy lit up another blunt. As he passed it to her, she asked, "So, how was it?"

"The blunt? Shit, good as always," he said and took another drag.

"You know damn well what I mean, DuBoy!" she said as she

turned her nude body away to rest on her side. He softly stroked the lower part of her back.

"Girl, you know I'm just kidding. You know yo shit be good or I wouldn't still be hollering at you," DuBoy said. But his words fell on deaf ears.

"Stop playin', girl . . . You hear me? . . . Pia?"

Pulling her hair away from her face, Pia turned and faced DuBoy.

"DuBoy, how much longer we gonna go through this shit? You know I don't even like the fact that bitch be over here with you," Pia said.

"Relax, ma', you know I gotta do what I gotta do. I need Storm to make this shit work and you know it," DuBoy whispered as his lips brushed up against hers.

"I know, but why she gotta stay here? She got a sister—shit, let her stay with her. And don't think I'm stupid enough to believe that ya'll ain't doing shit in this bed, either."

"Look, like I said, a nigga gotta do what a nigga gotta do." He paused before continuing, "You know it don't mean nuthin'. Shit, I just be going through the motions."

"Yeah, but how do I know you ain't feenin' for her ass like you used to before she went down?"

"'Cause I *told* you I ain't," he said, raising his voice. "Now look, I gotta get ready and bounce. Torch wanna see me tonight."

"I'm sorry, Boo, I just want things to go back to the way they were before you-know-who came home," Pia said, softening her tone.

"It will. You just gotta stop trippin' and let me handle my business, you feel me?"

"Okay," Pia said.

DuBoy took another hit. "Yo, have you linked up with her yet?"

"Nah, not yet, but I have gone by the club. But you know I got into it with that bitch Nettie. Pissed me off so bad I just up and left. I ain't got time for her shit."

"Well, you might wanna fix that shit 'cause ya'll used to run together. You need to get back in Storm's good graces. You know, for old times' sake." DuBoy got up and started toward the bathroom.

"Yeah, I know, but I might have to kill that old dyke first!" Pia spat.

DuBoy laughed as he peed. "I hear laughter in the rain," he hummed, chuckling a little harder. Once he came out, Pia used the bathroom, and he got to work ripping all the sheets and pillowcases off the bed and tossing them in the washer.

The sound of a door closing in the apartment above her indicated to Barbara Bowman that she could finally put down her *JET* magazine and attempt to fall asleep. The familiar noise coming from her neighbor had once again awakened her. Instead of lying there, hearing the *live* sex show, she'd decided to turn on her night-light and read. She was glad that Whitney Houston was making a comeback. *That girl could sing her ass off,* she thought to herself. For the life of her, she couldn't understand why anybody that talented and beautiful would ever get mixed up in all that mess. Then she remembered that bout of alcoholism her thirty-three-year-old son, Rodney, went through a few years back and the pain it caused her and the family. Closing *JET* and putting the light out, she said a silent prayer for Whitney and her son.

< EIGHTEEN >

Sometimes I Feel Like a Motherless Child

Skylar was sitting in her office at Legends going over the books. Legends was enjoying its best quarter since it opened two years ago. Normally, it took restaurants and clubs a few years to turn a profit. The attention and success her club was enjoying had been overwhelming, to say the least. But she knew the club deserved every accolade it was given. The road to success hadn't been easy—not at all—but she was happy. Sidney had been away from home more than ever, because his business continued to grow, too. Hiring Mike Chin was supposed to ease his workload, but the two worked so well together that the number of projects keeping them busy during the day—and clients keeping them awake at night—kept increasing. At times Skylar felt as if she and Sidney were like two ships passing in the night, they saw so little of each other. She missed him; since Dutch died, Sidney had become her rock.

Skylar was glad they had decided to take a trip to Rio once the summer was over, just to enjoy each other, to enjoy life. A dose of paradise was what they both needed right now.

Closing her eyes, she pictured her and Sidney lying out on the deck of a beachside villa sipping piña coladas and sunrise daiquiris. They would make love every day. That was going to be Sidney's only job. He'd have no complaints about that. No cellphones, intruders, or business decisions. Just the two of them and the ocean.

"Skylar."

"Hmm, hmm," Skylar answered, still smiling with her eyes closed.

"Girl, I don't know where you are right now, but wherever it is, you're having you a good ol' time," Nettie teased.

"Oh, Nettie. I'm sorry. Just closing my eyes for a minute. What are you doing here?" Coming out of her temporary state of tranquillity and serenity, Skylar sat upright in her office chair.

"I called the house, and Sid said you were still over here at the club," Nettie said.

"Yeah, just going over the books from last quarter."

"No problem, was there?" Nettie looked concerned.

"No, no. Things are good. Couldn't be better . . . businesswise." Skylar smiled. "So, what's on your mind, Nettie?" Skylar leaned forward with her hands folded under her chin.

Nettie sat in a chair directly across from Skylar's medium-size oak wood desk. Nettie seemed a little uneasy, taking some time before she spoke.

"Skylar, you know I don't get in you and your sister's business . . ."

"Now, how did I know that this was what you wanted to talk about?" Skylar folded her arms across her chest.

"Because you know me, that's why," Nettie said. They both laughed. "Like I said, I haven't said much. In fact, I've kept quiet about it 'cause I was hoping that things would work themselves out without my interference." The words seemed to flow a little easier for Nettie now. "But it is straight up *killing* me the way you two have been acting. Like y'all aren't even sisters! In fact," she said, "I am glad that Dutch isn't around to see all of this discord."

"You think I want to fight with Storm, Nettie? I don't. But my hands are tied," Skylar said, throwing up her hands. "I wish Daddy were here. Then I'd let him handle her, because even though she'd still do what she wanted, he'd have a better chance of getting through to her."

"I'm sure if your father could be here, he would, Skylar. But you know how he started to forget things. Toward the end, he didn't even know who you were. That was hard for him," Nettie said.

"That's crap, and you know it, Nettie!" Skylar said as she snatched a tissue from the small floral box planted on the edge of her desk.

"Skylar!" Nettie said in a sharp tone.

"Nettie, Dutch gave up on himself, me, and everyone else. He was selfish."

"There was no cure for what your father had. He knew it would have gotten to the point where me, you, and Sidney would have had to take care of him, and he didn't want that."

"I would never have put my father away!" Skylar raised her voice. "I had already discussed it with Sidney. He was fine with whatever I wanted to do, Nettie!"

"His health was already failing with the diabetes, and when the diagnosis of Alzheimer's hit him, he got beside himself. I remember him telling me that he didn't want to be a burden—"

Skylar interrupted. "A burden! Do you hear yourself, Nettie? It's like you agreed with him. Dutch was never a burden. We would have made it all work!" Skylar's voice escalated, *"Taking his own life was not the answer!"* Skylar banged her fist on the desk.

Silence overtook the small office momentarily as both women tried to calm down.

"As hard as it may be for us to accept what your father did, it was his choice," Nettie said very softly. "I remember him sitting up one night on his front porch and telling me how no one knew what it felt like to lay your head down at night and not know how you're going to wake up."

"He said that to you? What did you say, Nettie? Why didn't you tell me?" Skylar asked.

"Baby, don't you know if I thought your daddy planned on harming himself that I would've told you or tried to stop him?"

"I'm sorry for yelling at you, Nettie," Skylar said as she walked from behind the desk and sat in a chair adjacent to Nettie's. Looking at a framed portrait of herself with a smiling Dutch on the wall, she told Nettie how the most difficult day of her life had been when she had to bury Dutch. "Watching them lower him in the ground literally took the breath out of me." Nettie took her hand. "And Storm was no help," Skylar continued. "I couldn't count on her for any support if I wanted to."

"What did you expect her to do, Sky? She was locked up! You know that she loved your daddy as much as you did." Nettie rubbed Skylar's hand and continued, "She's all the family you got. Dutch didn't raise either one of you to be like that."

"To this day, Storm has you wrapped around her finger, just like she did Daddy. She was a disaster! She was in jail because she got herself in some more trouble. She put herself in that predicament. She was—"

"Now you stop it right now, Skylar!" Nettie jumped straight up. "You don't think your daddy and I know your sister? Stop being so self-righteous!"

"You know what, Nettie, it's getting a little too warm in here," Skylar said, and got up and walked out into the main area of the club. Nettie was right behind her.

"Dutch loves both of you girls the same, Skylar."

Swiftly turning around, Skylar scolded her. "The word is *loved*. Remember? Dutch is dead. He made the choice to check out."

"Love is eternal," Nettie said.

"Let me ask you something, Nettie. Do you think Dutch was a Christian?"

"What kind of question is that? You know your daddy was close to the Lord."

"Really?" Skylar asked sarcastically. "Because, see, Daddy committed the worst sin of them all. He took his own life! I wonder how God felt about that one. Huh? You think he just welcomed him in with open arms?"

"That ain't got nothing to do with me or you, Skylar Morrison. That's between your daddy and his maker!" Nettie yelled.

Skylar went to the bar and poured herself a drink, something she rarely did.

Nettie took a moment before walking over to her. "Look, Skylar, I know you are a strong young woman, and you never gave your father any trouble. In fact, when you were a little girl I could tell that you were going to make something special of yourself. We all could. And look at you now, girl. Everything in your life is going well. You know I ain't never been that religious, but God is truly blessing you."

"Funny, I don't feel that way," Skylar said, sitting down at the bar and sipping her drink. "Sometimes I think God has left me, too. Just like Dutch." She became misty eyed.

Looking right at her, Nettie told her, "God never left you. He is always around and so is Dutch."

"Was God around when Dutch killed himself?"

Again there was silence. "Nettie, I'm sorry," Skylar said. "I don't know where that came from. Let's go back to the original subject: What am I going to do about Storm? She came to me a while ago talking some crap about selling the place or I'd have to buy her out. Can you believe that?"

"Storm was just running off at the mouth. You more than anyone else should know that the girl changes her mind more than a traffic light. She'll be onto something else tomorrow," Nettie chuckled.

"How can she come back here after being locked up for three years and just think she has some claim on things?" Skylar asked.

"Your father left the property to the both of you," Nettie reminded her.

"Because I made him! It was the right thing to do! It was supposed to be in name only! She never wanted anything to do with it!"

Nettie sat on the bar stool next to Skylar. "You know, as long as I've been working here, I've never sat on this side of the bar," she said, looking around and giggling. Rubbing the middle part of Skylar's back, Nettie told her, "Regardless of how Storm was, Dutch had two daughters, and he wanted nothing but the best for the both of you."

"I know, Nettie, but I just wish Daddy would have been more strict with her, instead of babying her and letting her have her way all the time. Growing up, there were times when I thought he loved her more," Skylar tearfully said.

"Girl, now you know your ass is crazy! He may have given your sister more attention than you at times, but *love,* you're mistaken. I ain't gonna accept that one. And the attention was because he knew that she needed more. He could see that, despite raising you two the same, you girls were going down two completely different paths in life. No, Storm was not as ambitious as you. Whereas you worked for everything you had, Storm felt the world owed her something. What, I don't know. But he didn't love you no less. Hell, I feel that same way. I love both of y'all like you were my own girls, and yes, your sister gets on my damn nerves at times. Shit, she's disappointed me, too, but I still love her, like I love you. Dutch never worried about you. He knew you were going to be okay." Skylar rested her head on Nettie's shoulder.

"You were always Dutch's little adult," Nettie said, patting Sky's head gently.

"I know that, Nettie. But did he ever think that maybe, just maybe, I didn't want to be his little adult, but just be his little girl?" Skylar said. She took a moment to regain her composure. Wiping her eyes, she stood up and moved over to the edge of the bar where the mail had been placed in a stack. One letter stood out. She could tell by the envelope that it was the check from the attorney for the balance of Dutch's estate.

"I never gave my father any trouble. Nor was I ever locked up!" Skylar said.

This made Nettie lose her cool. "But that don't make you no better than her, Skylar!" she screamed at her. "Instead of judging every little thing Storm does, why don't you try loving her more, supporting her more? Love goes a long way, baby. Sometimes you don't have to understand a person to love them, because that's all they really ever need, is love. I should know. I grew up without it. Not loving myself was the reason I couldn't love anybody else. That man right there"—she pointed to Dutch's photo on the wall—"showed me more love and care than my own family. And I miss him." Nettie started to cry. "And Storm misses him, too, but most of all, she misses your stubborn ass!"

"Yeah, well, Nettie, Storm should have thought more about that before she went to prison. Even if that screwup wasn't her fault. Storm went to jail for everything that she *didn't* get caught for in the past. How about the many times she made Dad cry, getting him all sick? If it wasn't for her, Dutch would still be alive! She was going to have to pay for all of that at some point."

"Everything you say is true, but nothing . . . nothing . . . hurt Dutch more than . . . when you turned your sister in." Immediately Nettie covered her mouth in regret. She had given Dutch her word that she would never let Skylar know that he knew this.

Skylar was stunned. She could not move or speak. It was as if a ton of bricks had fallen on her. She wanted to get up, leave, and pretend that she hadn't heard what Nettie said.

"What?" she said softly, turning toward Nettie.

"I . . . I told Dutch that I would never tell you that," Nettie said as she began to pace, wringing her hands together and looking away. Looking up at the heavens, she mouthed *I'm sorry.* But she had come too far down to stop here.

"It wasn't Lenora or Asia who turned your sister in. It was your call to the police tip line that told them the car outside the house belonged to Storm," Nettie said.

A few words managed to stumble out of Skylar's mouth: "Daddy knew? You knew?"

"Yes, Dutch knew and it hurt him to his very core. He knew that Storm was not involved in that murder. Storm's attorney didn't even know how to tell him that the records revealed that the call came from your cellphone. It was in the records, Sky," Nettie told her. "Dutch begged the attorney not to bring it up during the trial. It wouldn't have helped the case any, just cause more division between his girls at a time when the family needed to pull together more than ever."

Skylar wanted to disappear but she knew she had to face what she'd done.

"Nettie, please understand: I thought I was doing the right thing. I thought that saving my sister from her own self-destruction was a priority. I didn't want her to hurt Dutch anymore or end up dead in some back alley. And more important, I didn't want her to be able to hurt herself. It was all just to scare her. I had no idea . . ."

"But that was not your place!" Nettie said. "Who put you in charge of your sister's journey or her destiny? Huh?" Nettie was raging now. She continued to lash out as she walked around the club. "You don't own nothing but this club! And even that's only half yours! What you did was worse than anything *she* has ever done! Now that ain't coming from your father, but from me, dammit! You should be ashamed. That's the reason why you stopped going to the jailhouse to see her. Wasn't 'cause of all you were dealing with here. No, that shit was guilt! And guilt is a muthafucka!"

Nettie was so upset now that she could have slapped the shit out of Skylar, not because she wanted to hurt her but to knock some sense into her. Instead, she went over to the bar and poured herself a stiff drink. Before she put the glass to her lips, she said, "And I ain't on duty yet, so I can have a drink! And I'll make sure I pay for it!"

"Not a day has gone by that I haven't agonized over the choice I made. I know it was wrong," Skylar said. "I thought the worst that would happen was that maybe the judge would put her on probation. I never thought Storm would be forced to take a plea."

"You're an entrepreneur, not a lawyer, in case you forgot that," Nettie said. Then she raised her glass in a toasting manner, and consumed the drink in one swig.

"Does Storm know? Will you forgive me?"

"I had to forgive you long ago. So did Dutch. He felt forgiveness was a part of the healing process. But what I wants to know is do you forgive yourself?"

"Will Storm forgive me? Does she know?"

"No, Storm doesn't know. I done fucked up one too many times today by running my mouth to you. I ain't saying shit to your sister. Matter of fact, I'ma superglue my damn lips together!"

"Thank you for not saying anything, Nettie. You don't know how much I love and appreciate you. I agree with most of what you've said, and I've tried reaching out to Storm by giving her employment, offering her a room in my home. But she chose to stay with that loser, DuBoy, instead. And it doesn't help that Torch has given her some ridiculous idea about a far-fetched business venture. I'm at a loss here." Skylar searched Nettie's face for answers.

"Why not start by letting your sister be her own woman and work through all her shit!" Gathering up her things, Nettie said, "Just like you're working through yours.

"Remember that tonight is June's affair at Deana's place, so I will see you later at the club. Get there around nine—before the bulldaggers and silly queens take up all the seats," she said lovingly. Skylar couldn't help but laugh at Nettie.

Skylar knew that Nettie was right. Her eyes fell upon the smiling portrait of Dutch on the wall. Lightly touching his photo, she said, "Dutch, I'll make things better with Storm, I promise."

< NINETEEN >

Last Dance

Princess called all the dancers together for a rehearsal. Two of the regular girls, Rainey and Vanessa, were already there; they were waiting for Gidget.

"Okay, y'all. We've got a hot new number for y'all to perform for the seventies-eighties flashback night. For this number, you're gonna have to channel your inner Vanity 6." Rainey looked a little perplexed. *Probably wasn't even born yet, youngin'*, Princess thought, before continuing, "You know. . . . Prince's sexy trio that he produced back in the day? That Vanity 6? So, we're going to use their biggest record, 'Nasty Girl,' as our song for this."

Princess was more than annoyed with Gidget. She had been calling out sick more and more frequently, and when she did come in, she wasn't as on point as the other girls. In fact, her routines had gotten a little sloppy lately. Princess didn't know what was going on with Lovely, but she'd be happy when she returned. But Lovely or not, she'd made up her mind that if Gidget didn't straighten up her act in a hurry she'd be placing another ad for dancers in the papers.

As Princess prepared to show the girls the routine, a disheveled, haggard-looking Gidget pushed open the door and apologized for being late. Already dressed for rehearsal, Gidget tossed her dirty gym bag to the side. Rainey and Vanessa exchanged looks as Gidget said, "What's up, y'all?"

"Okay, ladies, let's make it happen!" Princess shouted as she pushed the Play button on the nearby boombox.

For the next hour and a half, Princess led the girls through a rigorous routine with complex choreography. Afterward all the dancers slapped five and collapsed on chairs and the floor. Princess was very pleased at how the rehearsal went. Surprisingly, Gidget kept up with the rest of the girls. "Okay, ladies, see everyone tonight. Don't be late!" Princess said.

As the girls bid each other good-bye, Gidget lingered. "Hey, Princess, can I have a word with you?" Princess was too busy toweling herself off to notice that Gidget had stayed behind or to hear what she'd stayed behind to say.

Gidget repeated herself. "Excuse me, Princess," she began again, but still no response. Not one for being ignored, she figured maybe a direct approach would be better, so she started again, this time in her "outside voice." "Yo, you and the other chicks aren't feeling me, are you?"

Princess was startled. "Excuse me?" she said. "I have no idea what you're talking about." She put the towel around her neck and sat down at one of the tables.

"Ever since I walked in that door it was obvious you didn't like me," Gidget told her.

"Maybe I should remind you that, um, I *hired* you. Why would I hire someone I didn't like?"

"Yeah, you hired me, but that was because I was damn good. That's why."

"Don't flatter yourself. You did all right Gidget. You weren't the worst, but you weren't the best, either.

"Really, then why didn't you go for someone else? Why settle?" Gidget waited for an answer.

"Well, you know, we believe in not discriminating here. I happen to have a boss who felt that we needed to hire some minorities. To show the community that we are *one* here at Legends," she said cynically. "But listen, Gidget, my personal opinion of you doesn't matter. As long as you perform well, my issues are limited."

"I beg to differ. I think a person's work environment is very important to what kind of performance they give."

"Speaking of performance, although you did surprisingly well today, frankly you haven't been up to par lately. You've been late a few too many times, and you've been looking more tired than usual onstage."

"Wow, the jealous angry black woman rears her ugly head," Gidget said under her breath.

"What did you say?" Princess walked toward her in a defensive mode.

"Your problem is twofold," Gidget said. "One, it's obvious how you're a little jealous of the attention the customers give me when I dance, because all my solo numbers have been cut. Trust me, I do not want your job. And two, I think you're scared I'm here to steal someone's black man."

Princess thought to herself that she could jump this bitch right here and now and beat the shit out of her but decided to whip her with her tongue instead.

"You have it all wrong, Miss Thing. Princess is not jealous of anything. Especially of another girl's dancing. Please! You must know that I don't have to be at Legends. It's a career move for you, not me. Offers come to me all the time, from New York, L.A., Vegas, *and* Europe," she boasted.

"Yeah, I heard all of that. But then why? Why ain't you going on this global escapade, being one of the world's dancing divas? Wait, don't answer that. Let me. You're afraid. Yeah, see at Legends, you're Queen Bee, you're the *one*! No matter how small the crowds are, they come to see you. Outside of here, you'd be just another decent dancer," Gidget said, letting her have it. "And you can't take being second. Not *Princess,*" Gidget laughed.

"Let me tell you something, little girl," Princess came back. "I am here because of my respect for a *sista* who owns and operates a top-notch spot and my wanting to be a part of her dream. You don't know my journey—"

Gidget cut her off in mid-sentence, "And you don't know mine!"

There was a moment of silence before Princess continued.

"As far as the whole *black man* thing, I couldn't care less about who you fuck. And if your choice of a nigga is Torch and you really think you're stealing one of *our* men, bitch, *please,* don't flatter yourself. Now I think we have come to the end of our little conversation. If you're not happy with the way I run the dancers here, leave. Other than that, I'll see you when you report to work tonight—*on time.*"

Princess retrieved the boombox and CD and prepared to leave. But Gidget was not ready to be dismissed.

"You know, I think you have a few more issues and problems in your life than you want to deal with, so maybe it's best that I put in my resignation. Effective now. That'll be one less bit of stress on you," she said. Reaching the door, she turned back to Princess. "You need to be less judgmental. Sistas shouldn't fear that every white chick that comes around wants their black man. That shit is tired and played out. Torch just so happens to be black and we're doing our thing. If I can give you some advice, I'd stop worrying 'bout white chicks, we ain't the problem. It's those Asian bitches you better be worried about. They're the ones that got a lot of brothas on *lock.* Hell, we ain't even in style no more. You know what I'm talking about? You are biracial aren't you?" Gidget quipped as she reached for the doorknob.

With her back to Princess, Gigdet cracked a killer smile that showed just how much she'd relished this opportunity to tell homegirl off. But before she got a chance to feel the midday breeze outside, the door had been slammed shut and she was being dragged by her hair back into the club.

Princess proceeded to beat the shit out of her, ripping off her blouse and slapping Gidget around like a rag doll. Gidget got in a few good licks, but nothing compared to the sista-girl beat-down Princess gave her. Princess only stopped after she was out of breath, her arms worn out from throwing so many solid blows. Dragging an exhausted Gidget by her hair toward the front door, Princess said, "I just wanted to thank you for your resignation. I hope this was something you can remember us by," she laughed. "And oh, yeah, I am biracial. But don't worry about that. If anybody asks you what happened to you, just tell them that a *jealous, angry black woman* whooped yo ass." Princess pushed Gidget outside and tossed her dirty gym bag out behind her. "And I'll make sure last weekend's check is mailed to you." She slammed the door shut and began to pick up chairs and overturned tables, returning them to their rightful places.

< TWENTY >

Used to Be My Girl

After spending the entire afternoon shopping, Storm decided to have an early dinner before going in to work. She was back in her element. Visiting shop after shop on Walnut Street, she felt like her old self. Although she hadn't been able to get any credit cards, she had plenty of cash. Not from her salary at Legends—to her surprise, Skylar had presented her with a check for thirty thousand dollars the other day. It was her half of the money Dutch had left his daughters in his will. Her inheritance! He'd also left fifteen thousand to Nettie. Skylar hadn't told Storm about this when she first came home, fearing that she'd run right through the money as fast as she got it. But after the talk with Nettie, she decided giving her sister the money was the right thing to do.

Storm applied for a one-bedroom apartment in the Society Hill Townhouses that she was sure she'd get. Dressed in a pair of white Guess jeans that clung to her like Saran Wrap and a flowing cotton three-button blouse, she stood out among the passersby. Her three-inch white summer sandals accentuated her beautifully done pedicure, finished off with her favorite light pink polish. Her swagger was back. She stepped easily into her trademark walk, her stroll—one that made passing brothas turn around to check out the back shot and sistas cut their eyes at her. She even went into a new salon, called Justine's—she'd decided against Zenora's because she knew that's where Skylar went—and got her hair done. She was lucky to even get the time in a chair, being a walk-in and all. But she did and she was happy. Turning the corner of Eighteenth and Walnut, she swore she saw DuBoy's jeep, but it pulled off so fast and merged into the traffic that she couldn't tell. If it was him, she was glad that he didn't see her, because she hadn't told him about the thirty thousand. Seeing her with all these bags would have piqued his interest for sure. After she had a bite to eat, she planned on dropping the bags off at Nettie's place.

Storm was covering for Nettie at the club tonight so Nettie could make it to June's celebration. Storm had only met Nettie's lover once, and felt she was okay, but after what she had been through in prison, June made her a little uneasy. Storm was cool keeping her distance, she didn't need to be at the ceremony. Besides, she knew that Skylar would be there and she didn't want to socialize with her. She saw her enough at work—she didn't need to see her in her free time, too. And she especially didn't need everybody commenting on the fact that they were twins. How annoying was that?

"Hey, Miss Girl," a voice said behind Storm's ear.

Swiftly turning around, she saw who it was. "Pia! Hey, girl, how you doing?"

Before she knew it, Pia was hugging her. "I'm good. I heard you were home and I've been meaning to come back to the club to see you," she said.

"Back? You were there before? No one told me."

"Yeah, it was a couple of weeks ago. I told Nettie to tell you," Pia lied.

"I'm sorry, she must have forgotten. Everybody is so busy over there." Storm knew that Nettie did not like Pia. Truth be told, Storm wasn't that crazy about her either.

Storm and Pia were known for their battles. Both were beautiful sistas with bangin' bodies and attitudes to match. Perhaps that's why they had often clashed. Storm felt Pia always had to try and one-up her on everything. Whether it was money, men, homes, or cars, she knew Pia would try and compete. And she couldn't be trusted. She remembered Lenora telling her that.

"If that's the way you feel about her, why do you have her hanging around you all the time?" Storm remembered asking Lenora.

"Ever heard the saying, 'Keep your friends close but your enemies closer'? Well, that's what I'm talking about," Lenora had said. The thought of Lenora brought a frown to Storm's face. Still, Storm had to admit, looking at Pia, it was good seeing one of the old gang.

"I see you still holding it down," Storm told her. "You look good."

"Thanks, it's a struggle every day, you know that, but I'm still in the game," Pia giggled.

After an uneasy moment of silence, Storm told her that she had to leave, she wanted to grab a bite to eat before heading over to the club. Perhaps they would run into each other again. Pia told her that she pretty much had the afternoon and evening free—if she didn't mind, she'd join her. It would give them a little time to catch up. Storm's uneasiness about this offer was apparent from the expression on her face, which did not go unnoticed by Pia.

"Okay," Storm reluctantly said. "I'm thinking about Rouge," she said, pointing to the quaint five-star restaurant next door to her old residence at the Rittenhouse Claridge. Once they were seated, the maître d' offered to take Storm's bags and put them away for her, to free up room at the table. She agreed and thanked him. Storm had planned for this to be a quick dinner, and then she'd leave. There was only so much of Pia she could take in one sitting.

But forty-five minutes later, there they were, still cackling about any- and everything. The wine started to loosen them both up. Storm asked, "So, girl, are you dating anyone special?"

"Not really. I mean, got me a regular and all, but nothing serious," she laughed, taking another sip. *If she only knew,* Pia thought to herself. "What about you? Seeing anyone special?" She held her glass up to her lips and sipped.

"Me and DuBoy still together, girl," she told her.

"For real? Get out of here. I thought maybe since you were—"

Storm cut her off. "Locked up? Yeah, well, you would have thought it, but, yeah, we sorta picked up right where we left off three years ago. Now, I ain't no dumb bitch, I know he has probably messed with a few chickenheads, because that shit was going to happen." The pinot grigio was doing a number on her now, for sure.

Being indirectly referred to as a chickenhead didn't sit well with Pia. She wanted so bad to tell Storm that DuBoy was in fact with her, but she knew he would kick her ass. Besides, he had promised that everything would be straight in due time. Pia would get her opportunity eventually to see the look on Storm's face when she found out that DuBoy was her man. She listened as Storm went on and on about him, how *good* he was in bed.

Ha! You don't know the half of it, girlfriend, Pia thought to herself. She couldn't imagine why Storm was sharing all this with her anyway. It *must* be the wine. She decided to put a stop to Storm's bragging. *Nothing has changed. She's still a bitch!* Pia thought.

"So, girl, tell me what the hell did you do all that time you was locked up? You know, doing without?" she asked Storm. "I mean, didn't none of them women get to you, did they?"

"Hell no!" Storm lied. "I let it be known from day one, mother was strictly dickly." They both laughed. "And that strap-on shit don't do nothing for me!" she protested.

They proceeded into a lively discussion that would normally have been overheard by others in the restaurant, but luckily the combination of music and the chatter from the other tables was masking their conversation.

Storm confided, "I don't care how real-like they are, they don't do the trick!"

Pia laughed but agreed.

The whole thing reminded Storm of a story that she wanted to share with Pia, but she could hardly get it out because she was laughing so much.

"Girl, what? What is it?"

She told Pia about a guy she'd dated named Purvis. "A coffee-brown-complexioned brotha who was a dead ringer for Taye Diggs. One night we were lying in bed, and he said to me that he'd like to try something a little new."

Pia was already laughing but not enough to be distracted; she was hanging on to every word Storm said.

"That was cool with me, 'cause I'm always up for some new freaky skit," Storm said, laughing herself. "I figured maybe he was gonna *ring my bell* a different way, you feel me? In the heat of passion, nigga pulled out what musta been a twelve-inch dildo and wanted me to mount him! I was speechless."

"No he didn't, girl!" Pia shouted.

"Yeah he did. Talking about, 'I ain't gay or anything like that. . . . I just want to keep our lovemaking exciting.'

"Okay, so once I got myself together, I thought about whooping his ass, but then thought, what the hell. So I strapped the shit on!" Storm leaned in to tell Pia.

Pia's mouth was wide open. She couldn't believe the story, but she had to admit, she was loving it.

"I had no idea how he was gonna take all of this. Girl, that shit went in so easy, you woulda thought his ass had been sprayed with Pam. I knew right then that this wasn't the first time he had done some shit like this. I wore his ass out! Literally and figuratively." She gave Pia a high five and went on, "Girl, you would have thought I was ridin' a mechanical bull! And the power I felt, whew, let me tell you." Pia was practically on the floor now, holding her stomach and begging Storm to stop.

"But mother held on," Storm told her. "Get it, ma'! Get that shit! Purvis started screaming like a bitch in heat. I just could not *believe* that this six-foot-five, two-hundred-and-thirty-pound man was actually enjoying this shit. For a split second, I found myself getting jealous. Shit, he was having more fun than me!" Storm shouted.

Pia was hysterical at this point, but she found out that Storm was not through yet.

"But wait, then out of nowhere he started screaming at the top of his lungs, *'Mother Popcorn, ride it! Mother Popcorn! Pop it! Pop it!'* "

Pia spat out her drink and quickly apologized, grabbing her cloth napkin and wiping herself off.

"I didn't know whether to laugh or start crying, girl. This confused queen was screamin' like he had just won a million dollars on *Deal or No Deal.* I thought any minute Howie Mandel and one of those skinny bitches was gonna come in our bedroom and open a suitcase." Storm was on a roll now. "When it was over, we were so wet, it looked like we had been swimming. The sheets were so soaked I thought he peed on them. And here this brotha was, laid out on his back, breathing all hard like he just ran a marathon. So I stumble into the bathroom, you know, trying to get my shit together, 'cause this nigga done knocked my ass off balance. When I look in the mirror, though, how pissed was I? I was like, 'Aw, hell naw!' That bastard made me sweat my one-hundred-and-twenty-five-dollar perm out!"

"Girl, don't you hate when that shit happens?" Pia high-fived Storm. Storm's increasingly inebriated state caused her to miss Pia's hand.

"So, pissed as all hell, I go back to the bedroom and find the dude in bed eating popcorn! Now I've heard of people wanting a cigarette or getting the munchies, but he actually got up and popped popcorn! I don't know what the connection was with sex and popcorn, but I refuse to eat popcorn to this day. As a matter of fact, whenever I go to the movies, I close my eyes while passing the concession stand."

Finally managing to get themselves together, Pia and Storm decided that they'd end the night on this happy note. Actually, Storm couldn't believe how much fun she'd had with Pia. She invited Pia to come by the club if she felt like it tonight.

"I will," Pia said, before hugging Storm and saying her final goodbyes. They headed in opposite directions leaving the restaurant. Walking down Walnut Street, Pia texted DuBoy asking if he could pick her up. He told her he couldn't, that he was still with Torch and

Cleet, so she took a cab home. During the ride, Pia thought heavily about Storm. *I must confess, that was enjoyable. Could I actually be starting to like Storm Morrison?* A smile crept across her face until she remembered what Storm had revealed to her about still being with DuBoy. A saying that her mom used came to mind: "A smile ain't nothing but a frown upside down."

< TWENTY-ONE >

Where Do Broken Hearts GO?

Skylar was thrilled that Sidney was joining her for June's celebration at Deana's. She knew that Nettie was going to be surprised, too. Riding with him in the BMW, she grabbed his free hand and just held on.

"You okay, baby?" Sidney asked, quickly glancing at her while still trying to keep his eyes on the road.

"I'm fine. Just so happy that you are with me tonight," she said, and squeezed his hand tenderly.

"Same here, baby. Anytime I'm with you it's a treat, and you know it." He kissed her hand. "Listen, I know the office has kept me away from home and away from the club a lot more than usual, but the workload will ease up soon and I promise I'll make up for it, okay?" He looked at her again with *that* smile. Skylar couldn't help but feel comforted by his words.

"You know I understand, baby. Your business is growing so fast. I know this is your dream. You deserve success, and I'm so proud of you." Skylar knew all the hard work that Sidney had put into his business since striking out on his own several months ago. She also knew that, even with that, he had been there one hundred percent in support of what she was attempting to do at Legends. However, something else was on her mind, and she wanted to talk with him about it.

"Baby, you know I told you what Storm wanted to do with her share of Legends?" Skylar asked him.

"Yeah, but we're not going to let that happen. If we have to, we'll buy her out," Sidney said. "What did your attorney say?"

"She said that, because I didn't officially buy the property from Dad, no matter what business was operated on the land, both Storm and I are the equal owners. I wanted to buy it from Dutch but he said he wasn't going to sell anything that he owned to his own daughter. That I could just do what I wanted to do with it since he was retiring. Besides, when he passed it would be mine anyway, so why would he sell it to me? I never thought I would have problems with Storm about it. She wanted nothing to do with the family business. 'That isn't my thing,' as she would say."

"So what does she suggest?" Sidney asked.

"Who, Storm?"

"No, your lawyer."

"Either I buy her out, or like Storm said, we sell the place," Skylar said, and frowned.

"Selling isn't an option, baby. Legends is you. So what's the damage?"

"The property has been assessed at four hundred thousand, which means I have to give her half of that."

"Damn! Hey, well, look, between the two of us if that is what we gotta do, we will. I mean we're not Will and Jada Smith, but we can handle our business. You know I got you, babe."

"Okay, baby, thank you for that. But seriously—I wouldn't dare want you to put any of your own money up."

"Baby, we're getting married next year. Anything I have, you have," Sidney said.

"I know, and I'd feel the same way if the situation was reversed. But I gotta do this on my own. I already told the attorney to draw up all the papers. She's going to meet Storm and me next week in the office. It'll wipe me out financially for a while, but I want to get it over with," Skylar sighed. "It is literally all of my savings."

"Have you told Storm yet?" Sidney asked.

"I planned on it tonight, when we get to the club. I'm just tired of all the fighting. She had the nerve to tell me that she spoke with a lawyer about the whole thing and, although she didn't want to go that route, she'd sue me. Can you believe that?" Skylar said, raising her voice.

"Don't get yourself all worked up, baby. Things happen for a reason. Who knows, maybe when all of this is over you and your sister can begin to rebuild your relationship," Sidney said, trying to comfort Skylar. "Storm is operating with a broken heart. She's gonna need you one day, baby. I believe that. You just be there for her. Let her make all the mistakes she needs to. If that means using her part of the money to fund some ridiculous scheme of DuBoy's, that's her right. I know you feel that your father worked really hard to even own property, and that what Storm is doing is a waste, but she's got to see that for herself. You'll be free from all of it."

Skylar didn't respond to what Sidney said, but she knew that everything he was saying was true. She turned the radio to WDAS-FM. The Quiet Storm format was on, and Whitney's Houston's "Where Do Broken Hearts Go" played softly. "Where do broken hearts go? Can they find their way home? . . ."

Sing, Whitney! Skylar thought.

< TWENTY-TWO >

All About the Benjamins

Torch had been waiting for DuBoy for the past two hours. He was excited about moving forward with his plans for TorchLight, his proposed dance club down at Penn's Landing. The state-of-the-art night spot was to be housed in an abandoned ship that at one time was a restaurant called Dock's Seaside Port.

Lounging back in a soft brown leather chair, he was smoking a cigar and watching ESPN. Sitting at his feet was Gidget, who was giving him a pedicure and foot massage. Every so often he glanced down at her. She was unaware that he was watching her.

"I've been thinking about putting you on the stroll for a while," he said, then waited for a reaction.

It threw her off for a second. She briefly stopped drying his left foot, but then, saying nothing, she moved on to his right.

"I know I told you when we hooked up that I had enough fresh bait on the street, but there's a sports convention coming in next week and I may need you to do some housework over at the Doubletree on Broad Street."

Gidget knew that *housework* was Torch's term for his girls who didn't usually walk the street but were placed in hotels when conventions came through Philly. The convention clients were more discreet and preferred to do business in their hotel rooms. They usually wanted women who didn't look like typical working girls, but would be able to blend in to the environment. Torch preferred these arrangements because they were more lucrative. However, there were only a few conventions that hit Philly during the summer, and fewer still where the majority of the attendees were men.

When Torch and Gidget got together, he bought her clothes, took her to the casinos in A.C., wined and dined her in fine restaurants, and moved her in with him. Sure, she had done a few select dates for him since they'd met, but other than that she was free from being one of his stable of girls. She thought he felt she was special. Torch promised her that she would be the headline dancer at TorchLight. It would make that "little shit" she did while at Legends look like slum work. He also told her that she was his *bitch*. And for a while, all of that was true. No other girls were allowed to stay at the house or drive any of his cars but Gidget.

What she failed to realize was that she was being groomed for Torch's true intention.

"How many days are we talking next week?" Gidget asked.

"Most likely Wednesday night thru Sunday. I'll get you a room in the hotel for the week, get you all set up, and have all your supplies in place for each assignment," Torch said between puffs on a knockoff Cuban cigar that stunk up the entire room.

"Why can't you send a car to pick me up every night so I can come home to you?"

"Because I need you on call twenty-four. Whenever dem muthafuckas get an urge, I need you to be there, young, willing, and able. What I don't want is for a john who got that *right now* urge to be unable to get to you, and he hits the street for one of dem forty-dollar hos."

"I thought Shirley houseworked. You can't send her?" Gidget asked.

"Bitch, I'll send who I fuckin' want to send!" Torch screamed, kicking her in the mouth with his wet foot and causing her to fall backward. She was shocked—Torch had never hit her before.

"Now, like I said, I'ma set you up next week, aight?" He rose from the chair, staring at her. "And yeah, Shirley gonna be working, too. The redneck cracker boys gonna wanna buck with her, but dem country-ass, suga-coated coons be feelin' you white bitches. You the muthafuckin' American dream for dem sports niggas. I need to think about getting Julie up in that bitch, too, next week," Torch thought out loud.

Julie was a beautiful Asian chick that Torch had found down in Chinatown working in her uncle's Chinese restaurant, Peking Wok. He could tell by her face the first time he saw her that she wanted out. During their conversation he found out that her New York grandmother had sent her to Philly to live with her uncle and pay her way through school. At first, Torch made a point of frequenting the restaurant at least three or four times a week, so Julie would warm up to him. He made sure she was his server and always gave her a fifty- or hundred-dollar tip. He also gave her his phone number and told her to call him anytime she needed anything.

It wasn't long before he was picking her up from classes at Temple and she was staying over at his house, telling her uncle she was studying at a friend's dorm. Shortly afterward, a mysterious fire claimed Peking Wok, and Julie's uncle told her he had to send her back to New York. She called Torch.

"Ouch! Damn, girl. What's wrong with you?" Torch screamed as he jerked back his foot. Gidget had cut the nail too close on one of his toes.

"I'm sorry," she said and started to laugh. "I was trying to clip a hangnail but the clipper must be too sharp. . . . I'm sorry." She laughed again.

"Well, bite it off with your teeth then!"

"What?" She looked up at him like he was joking, but his expression indicated otherwise.

Cupping his foot by the heel, she used one hand to steady it and wrapped the other around his toes as she proceeded to put the toe in her mouth. Nipping gently she was able to remove the hangnail with little pain to Torch. Taking a towel and wiping off her mouth she got up to go to the bathroom.

Torch watched her intently, and for a moment he felt bad about the way he had spoken to her.

"Find you something nice and sexy to put on, we going out later," he shouted back toward the bathroom.

"Okay," she faintly said.

A knock at the door brought a wide grin to Torch's face. He knew it was DuBoy. Jumping up, he kicked the basin of water, causing a large portion of it to splash onto the floor.

"Nigga, what took you so long?" he said to DuBoy as soon as he swung open the door.

"Yo, you getting you a foot bath and shit?" DuBoy said, laughing and pointing to Torch's feet.

Entering the living room, DuBoy's eyes became fixed on the large flat-screen, where the Sixers were playing the Lakers.

"What's the score?" he asked Torch.

"Nigga, fuck that! What the fuck was going on? Where we at?" Torch clicked the remote off and threw it on the sofa.

"You got this bitch washing your feet now, nigga? Dat's what's up!" DuBoy laughed as he reared back his hand to give Torch a high five. Torch was not amused.

"It's been almost two months now. What's up with your lady, man?" Torch motioned for DuBoy to have a seat on the sofa and shot a stare at Gidget to get lost. She quietly excused herself and headed toward the kitchen.

"She's coming along. I been staying on Storm about what she needs to do," DuBoy said. "But it's her fucking sister man; Skylar isn't budging. So Storm got a lawyer and shit, and she'll sue her if she has to."

"Damn! That's just gonna hold up shit for a while. We don't have a lot of time. I was hoping for a different outcome." He stood up and started pacing. "Skylar needs to get the fuck out the way!" Torch lit up another cigar. DuBoy didn't even want to imagine what Torch meant. He tried to soften things up.

"Yeah, the papers are going to be served first thing Monday morning, demanding Skylar sell Legends altogether or buy Storm out of her share. Either way, Storm gonna git the money and she's down with what we doing."

"Nigga, she better be! Shit, I done dropped thirty Gs on the spot for a *hold* now. But I'ma need the eighty Gs from you before next month. Now she got her a good muthafuckin' Jew lawyer, or what?" Torch looked at him for an answer.

"Man, I don't know all that shit! I just know the bitch said everything was straight. So look, yo, I gotta believe that shit," DuBoy said, standing his ground. "She was feeling a li'l bad about the shit for a minute. Saying she felt like she was doin' her sister wrong 'cause she knew how hard Skylar had worked to make the spot successful. But we clever, dude. Damn!"

"I don't give a fuck! I know yo bitch ain't getting soft on us now! Look, we had a deal, nigga. You said you'd come through with the cash. I could've brought some other muthafucka in on this. But you my nigga, so I was like, cool. Me and DuBoy got this. Now you talking sideways, nigga? Yo. Get that bitch back in line like she used to be or some shit gonna get fucked up around this muthafucka, you feel me?" Torch's anger frightened DuBoy, who knew oh so well that you didn't fuck with Torch. He almost wished that he had kept his mouth shut and never involved himself with this deal. In fact, he wished he had never mentioned to Torch that he and Storm had been communicating while she was locked down. Telling him that he could get her to do whatever he wanted to do probably wasn't a good idea. Storm was hooked on his johnson, true, but she still was a smart bitch.

"I'ma hit the head, man," DuBoy said, starting upstairs to the bathroom. Approaching it, he passed Gidget in the hall. He noticed right away that the fun-spirited spark she used to have was now gone.

"Hey, girl, what's up?" he said softly, nodding his head as he closed the bathroom door. Gidget barely spoke and headed back downstairs. She had changed into a canary-yellow bare-midriff top, white miniskirt, and white patent leather boots. Sizing up her outfit, Torch liked what he saw.

"That's bangin'," he said, moving his head up and down and smiling. "That's just the kind of shit I want you in next week at the hotel." Gidget didn't respond to his comments and went into the kitchen.

DuBoy turned on the faucet and splashed cold water on his face. He was a nervous wreck. Holding onto both sides of the sink, he caught a glimpse of himself in the mirror. *Man, what the fuck you done got yo'self into, dude?* His frightened reflection told the whole story. Sitting down on the closed toilet, DuBoy pulled out his cellphone and called Storm. It went directly to her voice mail.

"Yo, Storm, it's me. Check this, ma', I need you to make sure we get that situation taken care of wit' your sista, ummm, as soon as possible. Yeah, we gotta do this, Shorti. Call me back." DuBoy sounded scared. After making the call, he took a moment to get himself together before returning downstairs.

"Damn, nigga, I thought you fell in, you took so long," Torch said, laughing. He stood on the landing at the bottom of the stairs in his robe, his cigar in his mouth and a nickel-plated .357 magnum revolver in his hand.

Seeing the gun, DuBoy stopped dead in his tracks.

"Nice ain't it?" Torch waved it in DuBoy's direction and then jokingly pointed it at him.

"C'mon, dude, turn that shit away from me fo' you slip up and that shit go off," DuBoy said, trying not to sound afraid.

Torch let out a hearty laugh as DuBoy descended the stairs. When they were side by side Torch encouraged DuBoy to hold it and examine it.

"Pretty, ain't it? Just got it yesterday. Can't wait to try this bitch out." He took it back from DuBoy and laid it on the coffee table. "Man, once we get TorchLight open, it's gonna be on, brotha!" Torch put his arm around DuBoy's neck and pulled him in to a playful chokehold. "You gonna be glad that you were down with this shit!" he said when he released the hold.

"Aight, dude. I'ma roll out. Catch you later," DuBoy said, pounding him and heading toward the door.

"Cool. Yo, DuBoy, that new bitch Alexia, she still working over there at Legends, ain't she?" he asked.

"Huh? Ah, yeah, she there. But I don't say shit to her, though. She just work at the spot. Why?"

Torch began laughing. "I figured out where I knew her from. Me and Cleet are gonna stop by Legends later tonight to pay the ho a visit. And nigga, you might wanna stop by 'cause it's gon' be wild up in there." He continued laughing as he said good-bye.

DuBoy could still hear Torch laughing halfway out of the building. DuBoy was sweating like crazy. *Where the hell are you, Storm?* Checking the time on his phone, he assumed she must be at work by now. He planned to stop by Legends on his way home, before Torch arrived. What the fuck was that shit about Alexia, the chick at the club? *If it involves Torch, it ain't gonna be good, no matter what it is, that's for sure.*

< TWENTY-THREE >

All Night Long

By the time Skylar and Sidney arrived at Deana's the dance club was packed and the celebration was in full swing. Inside, sweating and pulsating bodies moved about in a frenzied state to the throbbing high-intensity dance music. At first glance, Skylar and Sidney probably looked like they had stumbled into the wrong place. Although chic, they were casually but conservatively dressed, quite different from some of the other fashions present. A flamboyant heavyset young man, CeCe, stood behind the encased partition collecting money and checking in V.I.P.'s. Skylar told him they were on June Alvarado's list.

"I see a Skylar Morrison but there ain't no plus one," he said, still looking down at the list.

"That's fine, we'll pay for the other ticket. How much is it?" She started to pull out her wallet, but Sidney stopped her and told her he had it.

"Twenty dollars, but he gonna be in a different section of the club than you 'cause they got you in V.I.P.," CeCe told her.

"Oh, well, I'm not sure what to do here," Skylar said looking at Sidney.

"Look, baby, you go in. Just text me when you're ready and I'll come back to get you," Sidney said.

"No, I can just go in whatever section you're in," Skylar said. Before Sidney could respond someone behind them in line loudly started clapping.

"Okay, okay, let's move it, y'all. I'm trying to see the show, thank you!" an effeminate male voice shouted. "Ah, Miss CeCe, girl, can you either let these children in or put 'em to the side so we can move on? *Thank you.*"

CeCe asked Skylar and Sidney to excuse him and stepped to the side for a minute. He then lashed out at the voice in line. "Easy, Hoe Cake! Bitch relax yo neck and settle yo queen-ass down! You have little to do! Now, *thank you!*" CeCe drew out the words "thank you" in the same fashion as "Hoe Cake," drawing laughter from the others in line, including Sidney and Skylar.

"Girl, I'm sorry, look, I'ma let y'all both in the V.I.P. section, don't worry about it," CeCe said, eyeing Sidney.

Skylar and Sidney both thanked him and received neon-green wristbands notifying security they were to go to the V.I.P. area.

"Y'all together, or ya'll just girlfriends?" CeCe asked Skylar while lustfully ogling Sidney. Sidney was not quite sure what CeCe meant by this remark, but the quick laughter from Skylar indicated that it was a harmless comment, so he relaxed.

"Ah, we're together, man, thanks," Sidney said, smiling and pulling Skylar close.

"Ohhh, and a pretty-ass smile, too? Miss Skylar, girl, I'd say you hit the jackpot. You better stay close to him in there 'cause some of dem cha-cha queens gonna be trying to holla at him." CeCe was serious, but laughed. "And you better watch her, too, Mr. Fine-Ass, 'cause dem Diesels gonna be on this fine bitch you got with you," he said, looking Skylar up and down.

When they entered the main part of the club, one of the security guys noticed the green bands and beckoned for them to follow him. Maneuvering through the dancing crowd, they had a hard time really getting a look at where they were going. The flashing lights, sirens, and smoke machines made it difficult to do anything but dance. Skylar held Sidney's hand as they were led by security—it was the only way she could guarantee that they wouldn't get separated.

Sidney was getting an eyeful. As secure as he was as a heterosexual male, and knowing beforehand where they were going, he was amazed at what he was seeing. As they reached the roped-off V.I.P. area, a screaming Nettie rushed toward them, arms wide open for an embrace. She was *loud*—it was easy to tell that she'd had a few too many.

"Aw, shit! Here comes family!" she screamed, grabbing them both and throwing her arms around them. Nettie led them over to where she was seated. She was shocked to see Sidney and teared up. The fact that he had come to support June meant the world to her. June stood up and gave them both hugs. Also seated in the V.I.P. section were the evening's two speakers, Mayor Michael Nutter and television personality Ananda Lewis. June introduced Skylar and Sidney first to Patrick Willis and Beverly Knight, the two other honorees of the evening, and then took them over to the mayor and Ananda. Skylar had met Mayor Nutter several times before: She had been a big supporter of his when he became the city's third African American mayor. Ananda complimented her on her earrings and the two briefly discussed where Skylar had purchased them. Sidney chatted with the mayor about business, but it was clear he was mesmerized by Ananda. Skylar noticed how smitten Sidney was.

"Close your mouth, baby!" she teased.

"Huh? What?" he asked.

"Baby, I see the way you came undone when you saw Ananda," she giggled.

"What are you talking about? I'm good, I mean, she's a nice-looking sista," he said while stealing a glance at her again.

Skylar laughed. "Sidney, it's perfectly fine. Ananda is a beautiful, smart, and classy woman. I don't blame you for being attracted to her. If Eric Benet came up in here, you know I would be acting the same way!"

"Eric Benet? Please!" Sidney dismissed the singer with a wave of his hand.

"Don't get jealous!" Skylar shouted over the sound of the music. She playfully slapped his thigh.

"Jealous? Girl, what are you talking about? I'm just saying, Eric Benet? I mean if you gonna leave me, let it be for some real competition. Eric Benet?" He reared back and looked at her, baffled.

Skylar laughed with him and told him she'd heard Ananda was dating somebody, so he'd have to select another girl to leave her for.

"She's hot. I'd date her, but I wouldn't leave you for her, baby," Sidney said. He reached over and gave her a peck on the forehead. Skylar smiled.

"Now, if it were Gabrielle Union, I might have to think twice!" Again, she slapped his thigh. Just as the music stopped and people were asked to leave the dance floor, Skylar leaned over and reminded Nettie that she and Sidney were going to leave immediately after June got her award, because she had to get to the club. Nettie nodded.

A zany, campy female impersonator named Pepper, who dressed like Patti LaBelle, opened the show with a few off-color jokes, ending one with a litany of profanity. She then remembered the mayor was in attendance.

"Ohh, chile, Mayor Nutter, I hear you're in the house. Where you at, baby? I mean yo' Honor." A spotlight shone on the area where he was seated and he stood and waved to the audience. You could tell by the positive response that he was well liked.

"I just love saying your last name, Mayor," she said, camping it up. "Let me ask the audience what their favorite cookie is." Some shouted "Oreos," others "Chips Ahoy," and, way in the back, a lesbian shouted out "Girl Scout Cookies, any flavor!" The audience howled.

"Well," Pepper said, "my favorite cookie is Nutter Butter peanut sandwich cookies." The crowd erupted into laughter.

"Okay, it's my job to introduce the host for the evening. Now, this bitch is gorgeous!"

The full-capacity crowd stood to hoot and holler again with shouts of approval. "She's classy, intelligent, and no nonsense. Kind of a girl, you know, like me. Everybody, put your hands together for one of the few, and I did say *few,* black sistas in Hollywood not wearing a weave, Miss Ananda Lewis! Y'all, give it up!"

The statuesque caramel-skinned beauty made her way to the stage in a pair of hip-hugging jeans and a leopard-print top with spaghetti straps. Her silky jet-black hair flowed long down her back. Leopard-skin ankle boots lent even more height to her lean but shapely figure. The mostly gay female crowd whistled and punched their fists in the air like they were at a pep rally. The queens screamed and snapped their fingers in unity, voicing their approval. At least a third of the crowd was straight, and they clapped appropriately—but they seemed more mesmerized by the show offstage.

Before introducing each of the honorees, Ananda spoke about how, in America, HIV / AIDS continues to affect more African American and Latino women than any other group. She said that none of what she was telling them should be news to anyone there, but that it was important they continue not only the fight against HIV, but the dialogue about it, as well. "The alarming reality is that the devastating effects of HIV / AIDS in our community are nothing short of shocking. Media propaganda would love for you to believe that we are just dealing with 'uneducated, impoverished women of color,' or a 'promiscuous' gay community, but I'm here to tell you this is not the case." There was a sudden hush over the crowd as Ananda continued. "Speaking at many college campuses and before professional women's empowerment groups throughout the country, I often hear stories of women who are in what they assume are monogamous relationships. So they forgo protective measures, only to find out that their mates are bisexual men or on the down-low. Or at gay teenage support groups, where I hear about kids who often look for 'love' in all the wrong places when they are shunned by their families. I can't say enough how this is not a gay disease, or a white man's disease, but a 'people's disease.' " This drew thunderous applause from the crowd, and Ananda stepped aside, making way for Pepper to proceed with the show.

All three honorees were led onstage as a large projector screen descended from the ceiling so the audience could be treated to a mini-montage of their individual lives and the accomplishments they'd made in the community dealing with the illness. They were touching, funny, and poignant. When the film clips were over, Mayor Nutter came forward and presented each honoree with a Certificate of Merit from City Hall and the City of Philadelphia. Each had a few moments to address the crowd and community and to pose for pictures.

When June stepped forward, Nettie became the loudest person in the audience. June's door-to-door awareness crusade in the community had signed up over one thousand teenagers and young adults to be tested for HIV. Because of her tireless efforts, over seventy-five HIV-infected people were being treated. Although June knew that Nettie was proud of her, she wished that she would take it down a notch. After they all left the stage, Ananda reemerged and introduced the talent segment of the show. The music started and three female impersonators came onstage who were dead ringers for Destiny's Child. They did renditions of "Independent Women" and "Survivor" that had the crowd going wild. Even Sidney couldn't get over how, with makeup, lights, and choreography, the three had mastered the personas of Beyoncé, Kelly, and Michelle. Afterward, Pepper took over the hosting duties again, thanked everyone for coming, and told the crowd to enjoy the rest of the evening.

Mayor Nutter, followed by his security, exited the club with Ananda Lewis and her publicist not far behind. June rejoined Nettie, Skylar, and Sidney back in the V.I.P. section. They each told her how proud they were of her. Skylar and Sidney shared a quick conversation with the two and then got up to leave.

Streams of well-wishers congratulated June while Nettie was downing her fifth drink, which did not go unnoticed by Skylar, who asked Nettie if she was going to be okay. Nettie said yes, hugged and thanked them for coming.

Skylar and Sidney made their way through the crowd on the dance floor until they reached the side exit that led to the street.

"Well, that certainly was interesting," Sidney said to Skylar as they walked hand in hand toward their car.

"A little different, huh?" Skylar lay her head on his shoulder.

"I'd say so. It's like a whole different subculture in there," Sidney stated. "Don't get me wrong, I thought I was prepared for what I was going to see tonight. I knew there were going to be a lot of guys like CeCe and Pepper, you know, real over-the-top personalities, but, babe, there were some thugged-out brothas in there. I swear, if I saw any of those cats on the street or at a Sixers game, I wouldn't know shit. And some of the sistas? Whew, man, I was like—what the hell?" He shook his head.

Skylar laughed. "Tonight we got a crash course in reality."

"You're so right about that. This was a night to remember."

"Thanks, baby, for coming with me. It meant a lot to Nettie, and it meant even more to me," she said and kissed him passionately.

"Damn, I get all of that? Just for going out with you? Man, what I gotta do next for a little more than a kiss?" he playfully asked.

"Well, I don't know. I mean, are you sure that I'm the one to give you *more*? Because your eyes were burning holes in Ananda's butt when she walked offstage."

Sidney couldn't tell whether Skylar was seriously jealous or just teasing. He didn't care which, he liked it.

They joked for the rest of the ride. When they reached home and got out of the car, they lingered in an embrace on the street before Skylar got in the driver's seat and Sidney went into the house. Looking at her watch, Skylar figured that by then most of the Friday night crowd had assembled at Legends. She wondered if Storm had arrived on time and how things were. At least she had Flynn and Princess overseeing things until she got there.

Back at Deana's, a strikingly beautiful light-complexioned girl was next in line to give June a congratulatory hug. Her presence caught June off guard. It was her ex-lover Candice. She stood and hugged her, and asked how she'd been. It was immediately obvious to Nettie that this was not just some old friend. In a split second, her whole energy changed.

"Babe, this is Candice. Candice, this is my girl, Nettie." June was uneasy about the introduction but played it off.

"Nice to meet you," Candice said as she offered her hand to Nettie, who did not take it but nodded her head while offering a slurred hello.

Candice and June played catch-up, keeping the conversation light while Nettie quietly continued stirring her drink. Candice told June that she had just moved back to Philly from Miami because her mom was sick. June asked for her mother's number. She wanted to call her and say hello. They both took out cellphones and exchanged numbers. Afterward, Candice excused herself and went over to the bar, but not before addressing Nettie.

"Nice meeting you, Neda," she said.

"It's Nettie. Nice meeting you, too," Nettie said and then raised her glass to her lips and took a sip. Watching Candice walk away, she didn't waste time asking about her.

"So, when did ya'll break up? And don't tell me some shit, like, ya'll just friends, 'cause I can tell that shit right there. That wasn't no friend hug. That was an 'I used to be your *piece'* hug." Nettie looked at June.

"Mami, don't start, okay? That was somebody I dealt with a long time ago. I ain't even seen that girl in years," June told her. But this didn't satisfy Nettie.

"How long ago?" Nettie wanted to know.

June already knew where this was going, so she came out with it.

"Since high school. Candice was my first." June offered.

"First what? Ass? Friend? Lover? First what, June?" Nettie snapped at her.

Seeing that Nettie was completely smashed, June suggested that they get ready to leave.

Nettie told her that she wasn't ready, and for her not to run off just 'cause her *first* came in. June rolled her eyes and shook her head.

"I'ma head to the bathroom and when I come back we going home, ma'." She attempted to plant a kiss on Nettie's lips but was pushed away.

A waitress came around and asked if she could get anyone a drink. Nettie ordered another Ciroc straight up with a twist of lime.

While sitting there alone Nettie noticed a female watching her. Once the woman realized that Nettie saw her, she disappeared into the crowd on the dance floor.

June came out of the restroom, to see Candice standing by the entrance.

"So, I see you're hag-tagging now?" She hurled the insult at June, who didn't appreciate it.

"I don't like talk like that, Candy, and you know it!" June warned her.

"I'd apologize, but I just didn't think I'd ever see you with a chick that old," Candice said and laughed. "You always liked them around our age, right?"

Realizing that Candice was only going to become more and more sarcastic, June tried to excuse herself and leave.

"That's right, walk away. Just like you walked away from me years ago," Candice said, getting loud. Even though the music was blaring, her voice could be heard within earshot of several patrons, who assumed it was a lovers' quarrel.

"I never walked away from you. You cheated on me, remember? How dare you say that shit to me, ma'!" June barked. Candice moved her to the side wall of the club to calm her down and avoid all the attention they were now getting. Once against the wall, Candice managed to calm June down.

"I'm sorry for causing a scene, but seeing you again brought up so many memories."

"It's cool, ma'. That's understandable. But look, I'm finally happy now. In these past three years with Nettie, I've seen some trying times, I won't front. But I'm in love."

"That's not easy to hear," Candice said, forcing a smile. "Did you ever love me?" she asked.

"Of course I did, girl," she told her. "Still do. You never stop loving your first. I'm just in a different place now."

Nettie wondered what was taking June so long to come back. She was ready to go home now. Her festive party mood was now over. Standing up, she looked over the crowd to try and spot June, but knowing how short June was, she figured that this was impossible. Amusing herself with that thought, she headed out into the crowd to find her.

"Let me get back over there to Nettie. Take care of yourself, Candice. It was good seeing you—and tell your mom I'm going to holla at her, okay Mami?" She started to leave when Candice asked if she could at least get a good-bye hug.

"No prob', ma'." June reached out and gave Candice a heartfelt hug. Candice held on for dear life and June could tell she was crying. Comforting her, June closed her eyes and patted her gently on the back. Memories of what could have been entered her mind.

"What the fuck is this?" an out-of-control Nettie shouted, and crashed a beer bottle down on Candice's head. "Bitch, I knew when I met you that you had bitch eyes!" She started grabbing Candice by the neck to choke her. June tried to pry her off Candice, who was bleeding, and screamed for Nettie to stop and let go. By now the music had stopped, the lights had been turned on, and surprised spectators were looking on. Even though her head was bleeding, Candice refused to go down in flames. She managed to grab hold of Nettie's wig, tossing it in the air while slapping her in the face. It took a while for security to break them up. The women were finally separated, but continued kicking and screaming as they were being led away.

The bouncers took Candice to a back office to attend to her bleeding head, while another security guy hurriedly took Nettie to the exit with June. As they were escorting Nettie out, somebody handed June her award. She looked back but couldn't make out who it was. But she could hear the sound of Candice's voice, screaming, "I'm going to kill that old hag!"

< TWENTY-FOUR >

Who Is He (And What Is He to You)?

By the time Storm arrived at Legends, it was packed. Thank goodness that Flynn had been handling things until she arrived. After her impromptu encounter with Pia, which had lasted longer than she'd anticipated, she had little time to go home to freshen up before getting to the club. She wondered how June's celebration at Deana's went. She felt bad that she hadn't been there to support Nettie, but all those dykes would just bring back memories of her time upstate. Besides, since Skylar was going to the celebration, there needed to be someone in management at the club. Walking through she greeted the waitresses and made sure they were all on their game. She saw Alexia near the bar talking with Flynn. She liked Flynn and hoped for his sake that the situation between him and Alexia worked out. Alexia seemed cool. They hadn't really had a lot of time to get to know each other, but whenever they did interact it was pleasant. Flynn noticed Storm and walked toward her.

"Hey, Storm. What's happening?" He couldn't help but notice that she had been drinking.

"I'm good. Everything all right here tonight?" she asked as she looked around.

"Yeah, cool. Everyone's having a good time, so we're good."

"What time did Skylar say she was getting back tonight? You know?" Storm asked.

"I have no idea, but she said as soon as June received her award she and Sidney were leaving." Looking at his watch, he said, "I figure she should be here soon. Everything all right?" he asked.

"Yeah, I just need to talk to her about something," Storm answered.

"Oh, okay, cool. You know, Storm, can I have a word with you on the personal tip?" He pointed to one of the back tables on the side not far from the bar, away from most of the crowd and nowhere near the speakers.

"Yeah, sure," she replied.

"I know it ain't none of my business. I know you and I don't really know each other that much, but I do know and respect your sister. It's obvious that ya'll ain't feeling each other. But I know, too, that your sister is hurting inside about it," he said sincerely.

"Listen, Flynn, you're right, it isn't any of your business. I know you mean well and I don't have any beef with you. You're a pretty cool cat. But what me and my sister are going through didn't happen yesterday or before I was locked up."

Flynn looked surprised.

"Oh, so you telling me you didn't know I was in jail?" Storm said, surprised.

"No, I never knew. I mean, I knew Skylar had a sister, but just assumed you were away," Flynn told her.

Storm was shocked. She assumed, surely Skylar would have relished telling anyone that wanted to listen that her loser sister was in jail. Well, on second thought, maybe not. It might have embarrassed her, now that she thought about it. In either case, she wasn't about to rehash her life story for Flynn.

"Yes, Flynn, I was locked up for a while, but I'm out now and ready to claim what's rightfully mine," she said.

"That's what I wanted to talk to you about, Storm. Some of the staff have been talking and everybody kinda heard that you wanted

Sky to sell the place so you can get, I guess, your half. We guess that's what you want." Flynn was cautious but continued speaking: "But let me say, this place *is* Skylar. She worked so hard to get this place to where it is, and we're all proud of her. Closing it down will kill her. Like I said, I don't know what kind of bad blood you two got running through your veins, but ya'll is family, and it just seems that something should be done to work it all out," Flynn said and shook his head.

"It can. She can either sell it or buy me out. That's all I'm saying, Flynn. Now, I know you're trying to be helpful, but let's end this conversation, now. This is about much more than this property. Skylar and I have issues that go way back, my brotha. If she didn't tell you I was in jail, then I know damn well she didn't tell you what they are," Storm said.

"Like I said, I just want you two to work things out because I don't have any family. I lost my brother to street violence. We weren't on the best of terms. As a matter of fact, the day he was killed we weren't speaking. It was over some petty shit that we should have squashed long before then." Flynn paused to collect himself. "When my grandmom called me and said that I should come home because something happened to my brother, I played it off. I thought he just got jumped or something because he ran with that kind of crowd. So, I took my time getting home.

"When I finally got there, my brother was gone. Shot twice in the chest, the second bullet piercing his heart. When my grandmother called me, he hadn't died yet. Once he was pronounced dead, she suffered a heart attack. 'Momma' died, too." Flynn's eyes welled up, as did Storm's.

"Now it's just me, Storm. I probably couldn't have prevented those two events from occurring in my life, but I could have controlled my stubbornness and selfishness. You know what's funny? They say that most comedians are sad and unhappy, which is why they select comedy as a way of dealing with shit. That can't be far from the truth. But I'll tell you, ain't nothing *funny* 'bout what I went through!"

Storm honestly felt sorry for him, but like she said, he didn't know Skylar's and her history.

Flynn wiped his face with his hand and said, "Look, Storm, I'm sorry for getting in your business, but you can see why I had to say something. I don't want to see you two sisters make the same kinds of mistakes me and my brother made. And Legends is like my new family. It would *kill* me to see it torn apart, too."

Storm stood, unsure of what to do or what to say.

"Look, it's about time for me to start the show, so I'll see you out there." He started toward the main club room. "By the way," Flynn said, "your boy DuBoy came by looking for you. Said he had been trying to call you and for you to call him as soon and you got in." Flynn shook his body like a boxer entering the ring, and took the stage.

Storm was still standing where Flynn had left her, the echoes of his family drama now replaced by his antics as he pumped up the crowd with his opening. Everyone was laughing at his routine, and Storm finally moved from her spot, making her way over to her purse. She needed to call DuBoy and tell him that she had all the paperwork for Skylar and everything was on target. Searching through her purse, she realized she couldn't find her phone. Maybe it was on the bar. She asked Jose, the bar back, if he'd seen it in the area. He hadn't. Thinking for a moment, she looked around the club.

Alexia walked over to the bar to get a drink order, and Storm asked her if she had seen her phone. She hadn't seen it either, but told Storm that on her way to a table she'd double-check for it in the office. Storm thanked her.

Watching Alexia walk away she was happy that she and Flynn had found each other. She didn't know much about Alexia—and she hadn't known much about Flynn before tonight—but it seemed like a pretty cool match. And if Flynn could find happiness, where was hers?

In jail, she thought happiness was going to be getting out. But now she was out and not feeling joyous at all. Discord with her sister, dealing with a man who really wasn't right for her: the opposite of happiness. Why was she even with DuBoy? That was the million-dollar question these days. Who needed to put up with his shit? Yeah, the sex was the bomb, but obviously it took more than dick to be happy. Was it because fooling with DuBoy really fucked with Skylar? Would leaving him mean that Skylar had won again? Not one for all the introspective shit—and definitely not in the mood—Storm shrugged it off and reached for the bar phone to call DuBoy. For the life of her, she couldn't remember his number. Damn cellphones. Who really knew anybody's number anymore when all you had to do was push a button? She chuckled at the thought. Then she remembered that her cell was at DuBoy's. She called it, hoping DuBoy would pick it up, but it went directly to voice mail.

"Damn!" she said out loud. She forgot that she hadn't turned it back on. It didn't matter, she thought. DuBoy probably wasn't home anyway. She decided that as soon as Flynn completed his routine, she'd run back home to get it. Skylar would be here shortly. . . .

Her attention went directly to the front door, where she saw Torch and Cleet arriving. They sat themselves at their regular table; at least tonight they didn't have to kick an unsuspecting couple out. Flynn noticed the two and decided to include them in the finale of his act.

"Hey, everyone, give it up for Suge Knight and Djimon Hounsou." He pointed toward the two as a light came up over their table. The audience howled. Cleet didn't react, but Torch displayed a sinister smile and waved his pointer finger at Flynn.

"Aw, shit, I've done it now. If y'all hear about anyone being hanged from a balcony by their ankles, it's my ass!" Flynn joked to a very pleased audience. His act complete, Flynn exited the stage and Quince immediately started the music. Some patrons headed to the floor to get their groove on, while others enjoyed drinks and conversation. Flynn, a little nervous about the Suge joke, went over to Torch to make nice.

"'Sup, man," he said as he smiled and pounded Torch and then Cleet. "Thanks for playing along, dude." He directed this to Torch although he was including both.

"It's aight, nigga. It's a *funny* night. And you a *funny* dude," Torch said sarcastically as he glanced at Cleet, who nodded his head.

"Cool . . . Y'all need anything? I'll send one of the girls over," he said, relieved that things seemed okay with Torch.

"Send over your girl, Alexia. She's good at what she does," Torch said. Cleet couldn't stop himself from laughing. Flynn didn't know what he meant, but headed over to Alexia. Storm stopped him.

"Hey, Flynn, look, I gotta run out for a minute. I'll be back in less than thirty minutes," Storm said as she rushed by him. As she reached the door, Skylar entered. They almost ran into each other.

"Storm, hey, I need to talk to you for a minute," Skylar said, her hand on Storm's arm.

"I'm done talking, sis. It is what it is," Storm told her as she removed Skylar's hand.

"I think we really need to talk," Skylar said.

"About?"

"Whatever you want to talk about, Storm. I'm open to listen." She looked at her sister.

Storm couldn't believe what she was hearing. "Wow, Skylar. I don't think you've ever been open to anything from me before. The mere thought that you want to hear what I have to say is stunning to me." Storm crossed her arms and glared at her sister. Skylar was fully aware that Storm was mocking her with this stance, but refused to go tit for tat at this point. Taking a moment to relax herself, she closed her eyes momentarily and sighed softly.

"I deserve that. So, if you wouldn't mind sticking around a little while after we close we can sit and talk." Skylar said and waited for an answer.

Storm agreed. "But I need to run out for a few minutes. I'll be right back."

Skylar nodded and watched her sister disappear out the door. She had no idea what was up with Storm but assumed it had to do with DuBoy. *It always has to do with DuBoy.*

Quince lowered the music, and Flynn got back on the microphone to continue the show. Alexia had suddenly disappeared so he sent another waitress over to Torch's table. He assumed she was in the restroom or something. He prepared to introduce the dancers for the evening.

"Okay, okay, people, let's give it up to the best DJ in the city, DJ Quince!" he screamed, while pointing up to the booth. A light shined on Quince and he waved to the crowd. The audience applauded.

"All right, enough of that. Don't pump up a brotha's head too much!" he said, laughing. Changing the subject, he announced the night's featured act.

"Ladies and gentlemen, I'm about to bring to the stage three of the hottest sistas you've ever seen! I'm talking Danity Kane hot. I'm talking Pussycat Dolls hot. Fellas, you're going to love this. Put your hands together for three of our very own sexy, beautiful girls. Doing their thing to the classic Vanity 6 'Nasty Girl.' Give it up for the Black Baby Dolls."

The lights dimmed, and "Nasty Girl" started playing. Clouds of smoke billowed into the air as an extravagant light show complete with strobes and sirens illuminated the silhouettes of the three sensually clad dancers. As spotlights shined on each girl, the men in the audience erupted—first for Rainey, next for Princess. But when the third light came up, you could hear a collective gasp rise from the crowd. The third was Alexia! Skylar's mouth flew open, and Flynn appeared to be in shock. During the routine, each girl took a turn stepping forward and lip-synching the words to the song while the other two danced in the background. The routine was steaming hot! Everyone enjoyed it immensely. Torch, however, had a look of shock on his face, and didn't take his eyes off Alexia. Cleet just stared with glassy-eyed lust at each girl, periodically licking and biting his bottom lip.

The club regulars were stunned beyond belief with delight. Miss Shoes stood and started stomping her five-inch black patent-leather pumps on the floor like she was attempting to kill a roach or perform a mariachi dance. The dancers stepped down off the stage onto the floor among the crowd and did sensual but tasteful romps at tables where men were seated. From the way she moved, it was clear that this was definitely not Alexia's first time dancing. All three worked themselves back onstage and ended in the same pose that had started the routine. The song ended as the three joined hands and bowed to a wild standing ovation. They disappeared backstage and the house music resumed as the crowd attempted to settle down.

Flynn waited impatiently for Alexia to emerge from backstage. He couldn't believe she'd never told him that she was dancing tonight—or that she'd ever even danced at all. His attention was drawn to the entrance, where he saw Head talking with a girl. Because of Head's massive build and height he couldn't make out who the girl was. Once he moved, though, Flynn saw that it was a very provocatively dressed Gidget. *Look at this bitch. She's out here with everything showing but her birth date.*

Blinged-out, she went directly to Torch's table. Flynn shook his head. Skylar, preoccupied with a couple at one of the side tables, didn't notice her.

• • •

DuBoy couldn't understand why Storm hadn't turned her phone back on. He tried a dozen times to reach her, even going by the club. All this shit was making him way too nervous. Something was wrong. To calm himself down, he lit up a blunt. His doorbell rang. Grabbing his piece from under the bed, he went to the door. *Please don't let it be Torch or Cleet.* Looking through the peephole he saw that it was Pia. He jerked the door open, his attitude showing he was not happy to see her.

"Well, damn, is that any way to greet somebody?" she asked as she walked in.

"What you want, Pia?" He didn't move from the door.

"It's about what you want," she said as she unbuttoned her blouse.

"I ain't in the mood, girl. Where the fuck is Storm?" He started pacing the floor.

"Relax, she's cool. When we finished dinner she said she had to make a stop and then she was headed to the club," Pia said as she got close enough to DuBoy to smell the weed on his breath.

DuBoy didn't hear her and continued ranting. "Why the bitch ain't answering the phone? I been trying to holla at her for over two hours. And I went by the club—she wasn't there."

"I know she was running late 'cause we hooked up longer than I thought we would," Pia said, trying to calm him down.

"Wait, wait, wait. Yo, you talked to her?" DuBoy asked.

"Yeah. That's what I was trying to say. Baby, now will you relax? Storm is going to do whatever you want her to do. That bitch is so sprung for you, you tell her to jump off Ben Franklin Bridge, she'll do it," Pia said with a smirk.

"Aight, I'm just saying I don't need no shit." He wiped the sweat off his forehead with the butt of the gun.

"What you got that shit for?" Pia said at the sight of it, as she stepped back.

"Bitch, I ain't know who was at the fuckin' door!" he screamed as he locked it and headed toward the bedroom. She followed him.

"Let me hit that," Pia said, pointing to the blunt. DuBoy passed it to her and sat on the edge of the bed. Checking the chamber for bullets, he spun it several times. Pia took another puff and passed the blunt back to him. It wasn't too long before DuBoy started to relax. Maybe he was overreacting. Storm knew what was up. She was doing the right thing. Besides, Pia was right, Storm didn't want to disappoint him. She was hooked on his one-eyed snake. The more Pia massaged his neck, the more relaxed he became. It wasn't long before the two were stripped of their clothes and immersed in a hot sex session. With pillows and sheets tossed aside, they engaged in familiar positions, again soiling the bed that DuBoy and Storm had occupied earlier that morning.

Pia could smell the Vera Wang perfume that lingered on the sheets. She recognized it from the hug that she and Storm had shared earlier that day. Closing her eyes, she told herself that this would be the last time she would have to worry about this smell or

Storm. As she got ready to climax, Pia's body feverishly jerked about and her legs kicked wildly around, knocking her purse off the edge of the bed. A slight thump was heard hitting the hardwood floor. It was a phone. Storm's phone.

• • •

Gidget excused herself from the table, telling Torch that she needed to go to the restroom. On her way, Flynn stopped her.

"So that's who you running with now? Torch? Wow, a real step up," he said.

"Nigga, I know you ain't talkin'," Gidget said with an attitude. Flynn couldn't believe that this white girl had just called him a nigga, but before he could say anything, Gidget continued, "Look at you, still hanging around Legends every weekend doin' yo tired-ass stand-up act. Thinkin' you gonna be Chris Rock or somebody." She laughed. "Ain't nothing funny about you but the way you look. And for your information, Gidget don't run with nobody, niggas run with Gidget." She turned to leave.

Flynn, flabbergasted, shouted behind her, "You know, you used to be so sweet. What in the world happened to you?"

Gidget shifted her weight to one leg, leaning back with a hand on her hip to give him one more dressing-down. "Naw, punk. I used to be so *broke,* like yo ass. Know what? I take back what I said. You are funny . . . yeah, a real joke." Tossing back her blond hair, she went into the restroom.

In his entire life, Flynn had never entertained the notion of hitting a woman . . . before now. But as that thought started to take over, Alexia appeared, dressed back in her club uniform, all smiles, and she immediately calmed him down.

"Girl—what the—! I had no idea. I mean, you danced your ass off!" Flynn was excited. He took her hands in his and marveled at what he saw.

"You liked it? I didn't want to say anything because I wasn't sure I was going to do it," Alexia said, beaming.

"Well, you did your thing, that's for sure," Flynn said.

"Thank you again, Flynn. Now, you know I have to get back to work. You and I can talk later." It was obvious from the batting of her eyes and her wide smile that Alexia was flirting with him.

"Sounds good. Are we still hooking up after the club closes?"

"Most definitely."

As she headed over to the bar, customers continued to congratulate her. She thanked her relief waitress and did the rounds checking on her customers. She noticed Torch sitting with Cleet. She would prefer not to go to his table—she'd done a great job avoiding it during her set—*Note to self: Thank Rainey for that lookout*—but this was her job. "Can I get you guys anything?" she asked.

"We good, Miss Alexia," Cleet sarcastically said, looking straight at her. "By the way, good routine. I had no idea you could shake your ass like that. You surprised me."

"Alexia is full of surprises, ain't that right, baby?" Torch said.

Torch's smile and the look on his face made Alexia a little uneasy, but she wasn't sure why. Her intuition told her that there was something else behind that statement. A cold chill crept up her spine and she had the sudden urge to leave the club. She didn't ask if they would like to place an order.

Feverishly trying to locate Skylar, Alexia found it difficult not to panic. Finally, seeing Skylar at the bar in conversation with Princess, she dashed toward them.

"Skylar, can I speak to you for a minute?"

"Sure, what's up? By the way, you were great out there. I had no idea—"

"I was wondering if you wouldn't mind if I left a little early tonight?" she said, wringing her hands.

"Sure, you okay?" Skylar excused herself from Princess. She and Alexia walked off to one side, and Alexia told her that she was feeling a little faint and might need to lie down. Skylar offered to call a doctor for her. Cutting her off, Alexia assured her that it was probably just exhaustion— "You know, after all the lights and smoke and moves. I'll be fine by Monday."

"Well, let me get one of the guys to drive you home," Skylar said, concerned.

"Thanks, Skylar. Really I'll be fine. Besides, my car is here."

"Okay, if you're sure. I'll get someone to cover your shift tomorrow. Take care of yourself." Skylar sensed that there was something else wrong with Alexia but she didn't want to push the issue. Flynn rushed over to see what was wrong.

"Hey, hey, what's the matter?" he said, grabbing Alexia's arm as she tried to rush by.

"I'm sorry, Flynn. I'm not feeling well. I don't think I'm staying around tonight."

Flynn could see the fear in Alexia's eyes. "Well, I'll take you home then."

"Not now, Flynn. Please!" she pleaded. "I'll call you tomorrow."

Flynn nodded. She grabbed her purse from under the bar, quickly said good-bye, and started toward the exit.

"You can't run forever," a loud voice boomed from across the room. "Shit was bound to catch up with you sooner or later," Torch yelled.

The room suddenly became silent. Cleet stood and started to clap wildly.

"Bravo! Bravo, bitch! You gave the performance of your life." Cleet started toward Alexia, who stood paralyzed in fear.

Skylar immediately stepped forward and said, "Cleet, that's enough. I'm not sure what this is all about but it doesn't seem good. Maybe you and Torch should leave. We don't want your kind in here. Just leave and there won't be any trouble."

"Our kind? You hear that, Cleet? They don't want *our kind* in here." Torch stood as well but didn't move away from his table. Instead, he lifted his glass to his lips and slowly sipped before continuing: "And what kind are we, Skylar? Huh? I mean we patronize your spot. Bring in our peeps. Spend dough up in here. So, what *kind* are you talking about? Surely you're not discriminating, are you? Naw, not golden girl Skylar who loves everybody."

Torch knew he had the attention of the entire club at this point.

"You don't want me and Cleet in here, but you'll open your door to every other freak that walks in."

"What the hell are you talking about?" Skylar challenged him.

"Freaks, my sista. You know, like ah . . . ol' girl over there," he said and pointed at Alexia.

Everyone looked in the direction that Torch was pointing. There stood Alexia. She slowly turned around and stared at Torch, who by this time had walked to the center of the dance floor.

"She knows what I mean. Ain't that right, *Alexander*?"

Gasps could be heard throughout the club.

"You know, you almost got away with it. The first day I laid eyes on you, I knew that I knew you from somewhere. And that shit bothered the hell out of me. Then one night Gidget mentioned that you were from Newark." Torch walked around like he was before a jury in a courtroom. "I still wasn't sure if it was really you. So I called a buddy of mine who used to hang out at Fat Larry's, a tight little strip joint on Beechmont Street. Everybody kinda hung out there when you ain't had shit to do.

"I asked him about you, and when he gave a description of the person I was referring to, he described Alexia to a *T*. The only difference," Torch said, "was when I told my friend that Alexia had blond hair, he was like, 'Naw, this freak has long black hair.' He asked me if you danced, but I told him that you were a waitress here. But I was still about eighty percent sure that you were the same person." He paused for dramatic effect. He knew he had the crowd in the palm of his hand. "And then you come out here tonight and start shaking yo ass!" He slapped his hands together purely for effect. "That's when I told Cleet, 'Damnit! I got the right bitch.' You are the tranny that had everybody fooled in Fat Larry's, including my buddy Larry. They even said the dude fell in love with yo ass."

At this point no one knew what to do or say. Flynn fell back against a bar stool. It was almost as if people were afraid to speak, move, or make any kind of sudden gesture, for fear they may disrupt Torch's incredible scene.

"All hell broke loose when the shit came out he was messing with a freak—his wife broke out, his business went to hell. But the worst shit was—he lost his manhood," Torch said glaring at Alexia. "And then, on top of all that, after *all* that, my dude's fourteen-year-old son went by the club after school one day and saw his father hanging from a pipe in the basement. That dumb ass took his own life over that shit."

Looking directly at Alexia, he asked, "Do you have any idea what that kind of shit does to a kid?"

"A chick with a dick!" someone shouted. Isolated chuckles and gasps were heard around the club. Skylar looked at Flynn and then at Alexia. No one knew what to think.

"Oh, I'm sorry, my bad. You already took care of shit like that, huh?" He got close enough to touch her, but didn't. Alexia's eyes filled with tears but they remained focused on him.

"Yeah, bought you some titties, got your li'l hormone shots, kept your weight down. You even went as far as to have your name legally changed. All that to become a real bitch!" He started to laugh, then took on a serious tone. "But you see, a real bitch bleeds every month. So, you don't want our kind in here, Sky? Huh? But you'll allow this trash to work here? She even got that nigga buying her flowers and shit!" he said, pointing at Flynn. "Didn't know you rolled like that, playboy." Torch let out a hearty laugh as did a few others.

Flynn lost his cool and lunged at Torch, and folks started screaming. Head stopped Flynn well before he connected with Torch, who stood stoically, not flinching at all. He simply pulled back his suit jacket to reveal the .357 stuck in the waistband of his pants.

"Relax, nigga. I don't knock nobody, man." Torch laughed and then turned to address Alexia. "Yo, A-man, you ever tell Flynn that you used to pee standing up, nigga?"

Head, not sure what Flynn would do next, kept him subdued in a hold. Flynn relaxed his body and calmed down so Head released him, although he kept a close eye on him.

Flynn made his way over to Alexia. He wanted so badly for her to say that this was all a mistake, and that what Torch had been saying was a lie.

"Tell me that this bastard is lying," he said softly. Alexia said nothing. "Is he telling the truth? *Answer me!*" he screamed. The anger and hurt in his voice startled Alexia, who closed her eyes tight as tears started to fall.

In his rage, Flynn tossed a bar stool across the room and then bolted out.

The bar was so quiet you could have heard a mouse peeing on cotton. Skylar stood with her hand covering her mouth. She wished that Sidney were here right now. Or Nettie. Someone. Anyone. She wanted to go to Alexia, but wasn't sure if it was a good idea.

Suddenly, Cleet's harsh footsteps could be heard echoing throughout the club as he approached Alexia.

"And to think, I was trying to holla at you on your first night here." He spat on the floor. "You ain't good enough to speak my name. Tell you what. Why don't you go home and wash off all that ho paint, take off that dress and high heels, put you on some slacks and a pair of Stacy Adams. Then you bring yo man-ass back here and let me buy you a drink. You know, hang with the fellas for a while." Cleet twirled a toothpick around in his mouth and then flashed his pearly whites.

Alexia felt like her feet were submerged in cement. She wondered why she hadn't left before now. Why did she subject herself to this? Maybe it was because she was tired. Tired of running. She walked up to Skylar and without a word took her hands in hers, to thank Skylar for everything that she had done for her. This was what she wanted to say, but she couldn't find the words. Releasing Skylar's hands, she turned and started toward the exit. But not before giving the coldest stare she could to Torch.

• • •

Storm raced through the streets of Philly toward DuBoy's place to get her phone. She imagined that he must really be tripping since she had not been able to touch base with him since she'd left the apartment that morning. She knew that he wanted to know the outcome with Skylar. But if she was really honest with herself, she'd admit that she was having second thoughts about everything. Aside from the fact that her attorney hadn't gotten back to her yet, what Flynn had said to her earlier about not "waiting until it was too late" was hitting home. What if Skylar was sincere about wanting to listen to her? What if things really could be different?

How could she forgive all that Skylar had done to her over the years. Yes, she knew it was something Dutch would have wanted. There wasn't any doubt in her mind that he loved both of his girls. She parked a few doors from the apartment and sprinted up the street. She'd grab her phone, turn it on, call DuBoy, and then hurry back to the club. Glancing at her watch, she couldn't believe that it had taken her over thirty minutes to get home.

She passed DuBoy's parked jeep on her way to the building. Looking up at the front window of their apartment, she noticed the lights were out. This usually meant that he was knocked out. *He probably stressed hisself out after not being able to reach me and lit up a blunt and went to bed.* That was something—one of a host of things—that bothered her. She didn't like it. She had never indulged in any type of illegal drugs, not even during her turbulent teen years, not even in Muncy. But hey, she was at his spot—at least for now. In a few days she would be moving into her own place. Freedom and happiness were right around the corner. That brought a smile to her face.

Not wanting to wake DuBoy up, she was careful turning the key in the lock. Once the door was open, she decided not to put on any lights. She'd simply go to the bedroom and get her phone. It was probably in full view, but she wondered why DuBoy hadn't seen it.

Opening the bedroom door, she made her way over to the dresser.

"Shit," she said as she kicked something. Reaching over to pick it up, she saw that it was her phone. Finding this odd, she looked closer at the bed, where a sound asleep, nude DuBoy lay on his side. She wanted to wake him and ask him about her phone but decided against it. Picking up the bedsheet off the floor, she covered him back up. She had thought that he only kicked off the covers when they were in bed together.

Turning to walk out, she noticed a faint light shining under the bathroom door. Obviously, DuBoy had left it on, she thought. How many times had she told him about leaving lights on when they weren't in use? Hey, she didn't pay his bills, so fuck it! She decided to leave it on.

But just as she stepped into the living room, she heard running water. Stopping for a moment, she tried to locate the sound. It felt as though her heart had stopped. Stepping back into the darkness of the room, she saw the bathroom door inching open and what appeared to be a woman's nude body going toward the bed.

"What the fuck?" Storm clicked on the light, and simultaneously DuBoy sprang straight up as Pia grabbed the sheet and tried to cover herself.

"Storm!" Pia cried out.

"Oh, shit!" DuBoy said as he grabbed a pair of shorts.

Without hesitation, Storm lashed out at DuBoy, attacking his face with the phone. He lost his balance and fell to the floor, but she pounded on him relentlessly, even getting in a few solid kicks. DuBoy couldn't get his bearings, and he couldn't restrain Storm. She was too out of control.

Pia was flitting about the perimeter of the room, feverishly trying to locate her clothes. She thought to herself, *Just let me find my panties and a top, and I'll grab my purse and leave. Fuck the other stuff.*

As she struggled with DuBoy, Storm peeped his gun on the nightstand. She grabbed it and pistol-whipped him on the head. DuBoy threw his hands up for protection but Storm continued beating him with the butt of the gun. Out of the corner of her eye, she noticed Pia heading for the door. With one giant leap, she put the revolver to the back of Pia's head and cocked it.

"Bitch, you move one more inch, and I'll blow your fucking brains out." Frozen, Pia started to urinate on herself.

• • •

An inebriated Nettie sank into a hot bath and tried to relax. June had pissed her off. Flaunting some ex in front of her face and then having the nerve to embrace the bitch in public? "Fuck that!" Nettie said out loud. "I don't give a shit if it was innocent. How she gonna defend that bitch against me?" Nettie's speech was slurred and she had started to cry. "Same way she can pack her shit and leave. Like that shit gonna bother me. I don't give a flying fuck!" Nettie rambled on as she took her washcloth and wiped her face. "I'ma change the damn lock on her ass, that's what I'ma do. Shit!"

Suddenly, there was the faint sound of the apartment door opening and closing. Nettie knew it was June coming back to beg for forgiveness.

"I knew she'd be back. Well, she ain't staying!" Nettie said quietly. "As soon as she tells me she's sorry, she can get her fat ass out." Hearing the footsteps coming toward the bathroom, Nettie took her wet, hot cloth and draped it across her face. She didn't even want to look at June. *I'll just let her say her piece, then she can get the fuck out.*

Nettie could feel June was closer to the tub now because she heard her breathing. *What, is this bitch on her knees getting ready to apologize?*

Nettie felt a sharp pain in her neck. Pulling the cloth off her face, her eyes widened. Just as she tried to speak, another sharp pain went directly down her face. Slash!

Looking at her attacker, she could not believe she was doing this to her. She tried to get out of the tub but was pushed back down while the slashing continued. Blood gushed from everywhere. Her attacker was relentless.

Nettie put up as fierce a fight as she could. Kicking and splashing, she tried to climb out of the tub. "Get outta my house, bitch!" she tried to scream, but the sound of her voice was barely audible. Her throat had been slashed and she was gagging on her own blood. Her attacker was strong and knocked her back down. Nettie kept trying, even getting hold of the hand holding the knife. But her attacker one-upped her, gouging out Nettie's right eye with her long fingernails.

Nettie raised her hands to protect her eyes from further assault, and then the attacker pressed her down into the water. She refused to give up without a fight, but Nettie could feel herself weakening. Somehow, she managed to spring loose once again as she gasped for air, but she was losing so much blood, so much blood. She tried pulling on the shower curtain in one last effort to lift herself up and out of the water, but the curtain rod broke and fell.

Nettie knew it was about to be over. Submerged underwater, just before closing her eyes one more time, she saw so much red. Everything was now still and quiet. The only remaining sound was the front door opening and slowly closing.

< TWENTY-FIVE >

There's Got to Be a Morning After

After what had happened in the club the night before, Skylar considered not opening the club tonight. However, Sidney convinced her otherwise. The Bebashi HIV / AIDS fundraiser, one of the many planned AIDS functions throughout the Philadelphia area that summer, was scheduled to take place that night at Legends. Several dignitaries had pledged their attendance, as well as their financial support. The month of August had been chosen as HIV / AIDS awareness month by the City, so everyone was doing their part, including businesses, churches, social groups, and schools. She knew that Sidney was right, and she was not about to let the organization down by postponing the event and risk them losing much-needed donations. So she knew that she must go on, despite her concerns—most especially about the lack of staff. She doubted very seriously that Alexia would ever come back to the club. And she knew that Flynn would need some time to sort things out.

She hurt for Flynn, the brother she never had, and it bothered her to know he was so wounded. *I'll reach out to him a little later to see how he's doing.* The whole Alexia thing had Skylar in a state of shock. *Why wasn't Alexia just honest with him? And how far did they go?* More than anything, Skylar wished she could stay in bed all day.

And where was Storm? She'd never made it back to the club.

Skylar had tried several times to reach her on her cellphone last evening but the call went straight to voice mail.

Skylar thought of calling Nettie, but assumed that she and June had celebrated late into the evening and didn't want to disturb them. Although Nettie had gotten a little wasted last night, Skylar could scc how proud she was of June and how happy she felt when she and Sidney came in.

Rolling out of bed, she noticed Sidney's gym bag was gone, which meant, as was his usual Saturday morning routine, he had gone running with the fellas and would probably work out on the basketball court afterward.

Skylar had been thinking a lot about the conversation she'd had two weeks ago with Nettie. Maybe she had been too hard on Storm. But was it so bad to want the best for her family? Hadn't Dutch taught them to be the best women they could be? At any rate, she planned to talk to Storm and maybe try to reach some happy medium. But first, she needed to make some calls to get a few servers and an additional bartender for the evening's affair.

• • •

Storm tossed and turned all night. After checking into the Ritz-Carlton, she refused to leave her bed. She closed all the blackout drapes in the room and had no sense of time. She'd broken her cell-phone beating DuBoy's ass.

Just the thought of him pissed her off even more. "I should have shot his ass when I had his gun in my hand," she said out loud. She would have, too, if she wasn't scared of going back to prison. Yes, she was just that mad!

And Pia, that dirty bitch! How could she even think that Pia and she could have become friendly? Hadn't Lenora warned her? *And the nerve of her to be in the bed where I slept.*

Most women, when they catch their man cheating, attack the other woman. Storm thought that was bullshit! "He is the one you need to be jumping on," she always said. And she wasn't gonna be that woman who, at the end of it all, took his cheating ass back. *Hell to the naw!*

But as her thoughts turned toward how long DuBoy and Pia had been together, Storm felt more hurt than angry. She cared for DuBoy. True, she wasn't in love with him, but there were some feelings. Or maybe it was that she hadn't been with a man in three years. Whatever the case, she was glad that she had found out what she did, when she did.

Storm might have been down, but she wasn't out. She would rise again, stronger than ever. She had to. She was all she had. Yes, Nettie loved her, but now that there was no Dutch, she felt more alone than ever. Her relationship with Skylar barely existed, and considering how things had been going since she got home, she doubted if it would get any better. For now, she needed to think about what she was going to do.

Facing DuBoy was inevitable because most of her belongings were still at his place. She knew that she had to see him again, but she wasn't afraid of him. DuBoy had never laid a hand on her, and after last night she doubted that he would try. But she couldn't promise what she would do or say if she saw Pia. It's not about her being with DuBoy. No, she'd already dealt with that. It was how Pia had disrespected her. *It's bad enough to see her with my boy—'cause a man, he ain't—but to screw him in our bed? There's not a dirtier bitch that walks this earth than one who does that.* Deep in thought, Storm dozed off and spent the rest of the day in bed.

An affluent, sophisticated crowd representing Philadelphia's elite paid two hundred and fifty dollars a plate for the black-tie fundraiser. Guests dined on a special menu prepared and catered by the highly regarded Devon Seafood Grill. Sounds of jazz and easy listening filled the club. Neo-soul duo Kindred was scheduled to perform, and Skylar was told that superstar singer and Philly native Patti LaBelle might make an appearance if she got back to town in time. Sidney was acting as MC tonight, since Flynn left word that he wasn't feeling well enough to come in. The ceremony was scheduled to start immediately after dinner.

Growing ever more concerned about Nettie's absence, Skylar called her house phone several times but got no answer. She tried her cellphone, and not only was there no answer there as well, but her voice mail was full. Skylar tried June, who told her that she and Nettie had broken up last night after the fight at the club. Skylar told her that Nettie had not come in or called.

"I've called her several times myself," June said. "But I figured she wouldn't answer. You know how she likes to be dramatic, ma'. She was pretty ripped last night, so she's probably sleeping off a huge hangover." June told Skylar everything that Nettie had done the night before. Skylar was shocked. Sure, Nettie had a mouth on her, but hitting a girl in the head with a bottle didn't seem like something she'd do.

After speaking to June, Skylar decided not to bother Nettie tonight. She was sure that Nettie would call her later on tonight or tomorrow. The affair was going well, and the temporary staff were doing a good job. Thank God for Sidney, who always knew how to calm her down. He was the voice of reason. Stepping up to the plate as Master of Ceremonies was a major help—even though she had to shake her head at him trying to crack jokes during his opening. He was lucky no one heckled him.

"Just make the introductions, honey," Skylar said loud enough for only her man to hear.

Kindred performed a great set of songs and the crowd loved them. Patti LaBelle did manage to stop by and dedicated her rendition of "Over the Rainbow" to anyone fighting the fight. "No matter what the fight may be, you gotta fight the fight," Patti said. These words couldn't have rung more true. Skylar felt this way now more than ever.

The evening began to wind down and many of the guests filtered out. Skylar noticed a man sitting by himself at one of the back tables. Dressed in a pair of black baggy jeans, a black hoodie, dark glasses, and black Timberlands, he nursed a drink as he took in all the activity around him. He wasn't exactly in black tie, but he was in black nonetheless. She planned to send Sidney over to him to check things out.

Kindred were breaking down their equipment, so she figured he was with them. Less than twenty guests were still in the club, and Skylar thanked God that they had been able to get through the night, which had been a success for Bebashi, raising more than $15,000 in the silent auction alone. Sidney had even convinced Patti LaBelle to auction herself off for a lunch to the highest bidder. Miss Shoes won that honor with her bid of eight thousand five hundred dollars. That should be some lunch, they all thought, because Patti was known for wearing unique pumps. Skylar was sure they would have a lot to talk about.

Torch and Cleet were also in attendance, and as much as Skylar wanted to bar them from the club, they obviously had purchased their tickets for the event and remained quiet throughout the evening. Skylar still placed Head by their table for the entire evening just in case there was any trouble.

"You talk to DuBoy today?" Cleet asked Torch.

"No, but that nigga gon' come through, you can believe that. I didn't see Storm tonight either. They're probably together somewhere making sure that shit was right. I can spot a greedy, dumb muthafucka a mile away. That nigga's been off the streets too long. He don't even know what's up. He ain't seen no paper, no nothing. Nigga will do anything to try and be somebody. This shit is funny to me." Torch and Cleet laughed as they downed bottle after bottle of wine.

With only an hour or so to go before closing, Sidney closed down the kitchen and dismissed all the servers except for one. Only three tables were still occupied. Torch and Cleet were at one, a middle-aged man and a twentysomething young lady who appeared to not want the night to end were at another, and the strange dude in all black sat at the third table in the back. Skylar went over to him and asked if everything was okay. He nodded his head affirmatively.

Cleet stood up and stumbled toward the restroom. Seeing this,

Skylar signalled to the bartender not to serve Torch's table any more alcohol. The brotha all in black got up and followed Cleet into the restroom. Emptying the last of the alcohol in his glass, Torch pulled out his BlackBerry to make a call. Skylar noticed the couple preparing to leave and went over to thank them for coming. When she turned to do the same to the table in the back where the guy was sitting, she noticed that he had gone. For some reason, she felt relieved. She hadn't realized how much he had made her uneasy. She was ready to go home. It'd been a long day. Making her way back into the kitchen, she thanked the staff for all their help.

The bathroom door opened, and the dude in black emerged. He walked over to Torch's table with something concealed in his hand. Torch looked up and saw someone standing directly in front of him. "What the fuck do you want, nigga?" Torch asked, seconds before a jar of clear liquid was thrown into his face.

"Nigga, are you crazy?!" Torch stood up, but before he could reach for his gun, the stranger had tossed the lit candle from the table into his face. Torch fell to the floor, flailing and screaming. He pulled the tablecloth up to cover his face, but the gasoline on his face caused it to catch fire as well. Head and Sidney rushed over to help Torch as Skylar and the kitchen staff ran out to see the commotion. Someone called 911 as others worked to make sure the fire didn't spread. No one noticed the brotha in all black as he calmly walked toward the exit.

Once outside, he adjusted the hood of his jacket, and under the black stocking cap, traces of platinum-blond hair peeked out. The sound of a siren was heard in the distance as he turned down the darkened street and disappeared into the night.

< TWENTY-SIX >

Alone Again, Naturally

Skylar entered the building that, just months ago, had been Legends, the most thriving, successful nightclub Philadelphia had seen in decades. The decision to let it go had not been an easy one. In fact, she'd agonized over it for quite some time. Despite encouragement from Sidney, Flynn, and the community to keep it open, her mind was made up. There were too many painful memories. Walking around the empty building was surreal for her. She had been notified that there was a buyer for the place. The new owner wanted to put a restaurant here.

What had happened? Why was this happening to her of all people? All of her blood, sweat, and tears had been put into this place. And before that, her family's. It was her legacy. But it would soon be only a memory. She thought of Dutch and how sad all of this would have made him feel.

Glancing over where the bar used to be, she thought of Nettie and tears started streaming down her face. Skylar couldn't believe that she would never see her again. Nettie's murder made headlines in the local papers; *The Philadelphia Tribune* tried to sensationalize it with a headline banner on its cover, which read: "Lesbian Barmaid with Sordid Past Found Slain in Lover's Apartment." *What did Nettie's past have to do with anything?* Skylar thought. It was also the lead-in story on local television for several days until the killer was caught.

The entire neighborhood was stunned about what had happened to Nettie, but there was no public funeral. Nettie's wishes, according to June, were that if something ever were to happen she wanted to be cremated. Skylar and Storm oversaw a memorial service at a local church and there were tributes at Legends and Deana's. A candlelight vigil was held in her memory, and more than five hundred people came to pay their respects.

At first most thought that June did it. She was a prime suspect—their legendary fights were no secret—but was ruled out after she produced a solid alibi. Everyone was questioned, including Skylar, Storm, and Sidney. One by one they, along with all of the employees and staff, were summoned downtown to police headquarters for questioning. Skylar remembered being asked if she knew of anyone that might have had a reason to kill Nettie. Was there someone from her past? A jealous lover? A disgruntled customer? Or could it have been just a random act of violence? Skylar gave a sworn statement indicating what June told her about the fight Nettie had had with Candice the night she died, but Candice, too, was ruled out after an investigation. Then she remembered Nettie telling her about the run-in she'd had with Pia. Pia had threatened Nettie. Skylar vaguely knew that there was some type of relationship with Pia's mother, who had previously passed away. She told the detectives that Pia held a deep resentment for Nettie because of that history, and that they should check her out.

Pia didn't lie to the detectives: She told them clearly and plainly that she despised Nettie, but didn't kill her. But after a thorough investigation, Pia was also removed from the list of suspects. "Frankly," Skylar told the detectives, "even though Nettie was widely loved, she had an acid tongue. Her mouth got her into trouble more than once. But anyone who really knew her knew she was harmless."

Skylar called the precinct daily to ask about new leads or developments in the case. But nothing turned up until a tip came in from an unlikely source. Lovely. Although Lovely still hadn't returned to the club, she did keep in touch with Skylar and some of the other staff. One evening while watching the news, she remembered something, and although it was minor, she thought she should at least report it. After phoning the tip line, her story checked out and within three days a suspect was apprehended. Elliott Stevens, also known as Treasure, of Atlantic City, was booked and charged with the murder of Nettie Flowers. It was clear that Treasure made good on threats. She had never gotten over how Nettie had publicly embarrassed her during those auditions held at the club several months before. Her final words to Nettie were that they would meet again, and they did.

Nettie had not noticed that Treasure was one of the female impersonators in the Destiny's Child act that performed for the special evening honoring June. But Treasure recognized Nettie as soon as the fight broke out with Candice. Even though the place was jampacked and it was hard to see who was fighting, the sound of Nettie's voice rang loud and clear. Treasure made her way down from the stage into the mass of spectators. Looking over the crowd she saw an out-of-control, intoxicated Nettie being escorted out of the building. She had never forgotten what Nettie had done and knew that their paths would cross again.

"That bitch needs to learn her lesson once and for all," Treasure said to Cinnamon, the Kelly Rowland look-alike, who was standing right beside her. But Cinnamon didn't hear her. She was too busy watching and listening to the fight. If she had, Cinnamon would have paid attention, because everybody in Atlantic City knew that Treasure was crazy and would *act out*.

June did not notice the 1988 Toyota Camry with New Jersey plates following Nettie's car on their way home. She was far too busy trying to salvage her relationship and calm a drunk and belligerent Nettie. June was pissed at Nettie for ruining the night, and Nettie was cussing her out, telling her that if she didn't like it, she could leave. These threats were familiar and usually meant Nettie was just lit and running off at the mouth. However, this time they struck a different chord with June. She decided that it might be over between the two of them. Sure, she loved Nettie, but she was tired of the jealousy, the fighting, and the arguing. She was also tired of being threatened with being put out of the place she called home. "Nettie, you *know* that Candice means nothing to me. You know she is just a part of my past," she said. But it didn't matter. Her words fell on deaf, intoxicated, angry ears.

Treasure watched as June parked the car, sliding down in her seat just enough to keep both women in view so that she could see which apartment they went into.

June attempted to help Nettie get in the house but Nettie would not allow her to touch her and stumbled up the stairs and into the building. After a few moments, a light went on and the women were visible from the street. June left no more than five minutes later. As Treasure sat in her car fingering the razor she kept tucked under her wig, she relived that embarrassing day at Legends and got angrier by the second, her eyes glued to the third-floor window. She assumed it was the bathroom because the shadowy outline of Nettie's petite figure disrobed and descended into what must have been a tub. This was it. *This is what bitches get,* Treasure thought.

Skylar knew it would take a long time to come to grips with the loss of Nettie. Not just because Nettie was a dear, close friend who had died, but because of how violently she had died.

If that weren't enough, Alexia was now being charged with the attempted murder of Torch, who spent three weeks clinging to life in intensive care and was now at the Lehigh Valley Burn Center, suffering from third-degree burns on his face and neck. He was expected to live, but had suffered severe damage to his face. Skylar was told he was unrecognizable. His lips had melted together, and he'd lost vision in his left eye. He would eventually have to have multiple surgeries to reconstruct his face and left ear. Because he went into shock and his lungs collapsed, he was now breathing with the help of a tube inserted down his throat. He was spending at least twelve hours a day in a hyperbaric chamber in an isolated dark room and would never know life as it was. An ironic twist for a man named Torch.

Skylar definitely felt Alexia was wrong—dead wrong—to have done what she did. She just snapped. But she also believed Alexia had been a victim, too. Even the strongest person can only take so much. Alexia was just tired and fed up. All she wanted to do was live her life and start over. Skylar remembered something Nettie used to always say: "Everybody don't go looking for trouble, sometimes trouble find them." How true that had been.

Yes, too many memories were in the place. Although Legends had been cleared of all liability, the press had not been too kind with its coverage of the unfortunate circumstances. Skylar even heard that Legends was to be in *Philadelphia* magazine again. This time it would be the cover story. "The Rise and Fall of Legends: Was This the End?" How quickly things could change.

Lost in thought, Skylar didn't notice that Flynn had come in.

"Hey, Sky," he said softly.

"Flynn! Hey." She went to him and they gave each other a long hug.

"Well, I'm on my way," Flynn said, looking at her and holding her hands in his.

"I'm going to miss you, brother," Skylar said, tearing up.

"Not as much as I'm going to miss you." He smiled.

"Have you decided where you're going, Flynn?"

"I haven't. I saw that Amtrak commercial about the 'See America Our Way' campaign, where you pay five hundred dollars and you can see the whole country, and I thought I'd give it a try. I'm not sure where I'll end up, but anyplace is better than Philly right now."

"Boy, do I understand what you mean," Skylar said.

All kinds of rumors had surfaced after the Alexia fiasco and Flynn had become the butt of many jokes by fellow comedians and everyday folks. No one was louder about it than Beatrice, who was headlining at the Laff House on Sixth and Bainbridge. Half of her material was about Flynn and Alexia. None of it was true, of course, but it didn't matter now. He had to go. "Sky," he said, "you have Sidney, and he's a really good man. I'm leaving you in good hands, baby girl."

"What about your comedy, Flynn? You think you'll hit a few clubs on your cross-country journey?" she asked him.

"I doubt it. Ain't got too much to laugh at anymore, Skylar. Besides, I ain't that funny. You know it and I know it. Hell, the crowds know it, too."

"That's not true, Flynn! This city loves you! Everyone enjoys your act."

"There's a big difference between people laughing with you versus at you." His voice seemed to mellow with each word. "But I'm cool with that. If nothing more, I enjoyed myself. And I thank you for giving me a home to do my thing for the past two years. I'll never forget that. So many people go through life never having the chance to follow their dream. I had mine. Tell Storm good-bye for me and that I'm sorry I didn't get a chance to say good-bye in person. And listen, baby girl: I know shit ain't right between you and your sister. But try and work that shit out, Skylar. Family is so important, you know?"

"I sure will. Take care, Flynn." They embraced and then Flynn started toward the door. He put his hand firmly on the knob and, without turning around, said, barely audibly, "I've always loved you."

"I know," Skylar said.

As the door closed behind Flynn, Skylar knew that another chapter in her life had come to an end. People had been leaving her life in one way or another for as long as she could remember. At least she still had Sidney. Having a man so gentle yet so strong who loved her unconditionally, who was her support system, was so important. Sidney was the one person she could always count on.

Skylar decided to take one last walk through the building that held so many memories for her. As she walked through the kitchen, her mind went back to the days when she and Storm would run around and watch Dutch prepare the latest soul food dishes for customers. She thought about how excited she had been going over the layout with the contractors for the new kitchen she had planned for Legends. She wondered what kind of kitchen the new owners would have. Wiping away a tear, she clicked off the light and reentered the main area of the building. An unlikely visitor stopped her in her tracks.

"Hey, sis," Storm said.

"Storm? What are you doing here?" Skylar said softly.

"I figured you'd be here." Storm closed the door behind her and walked closer to her sister. For a few moments there was silence. Skylar decided to speak first.

"I . . . I want to say I'm sorry, Storm," Skylar said.

"Sorry? For what? I didn't come here to get an apol—"

"Let me finish," Skylar said. "I've spent all my life trying to be perfect. It started with Dutch. I always wanted to make sure that I was doing the right thing. Dutch could always count on me. When I was fourteen, he taught me how to run this business, while you were out running with your friends having fun. I never questioned it because I felt that he probably thought I was better at handling responsibility. That made me feel good, feel worthy. When errands were to be run, I was the one Daddy sent. You, on the other hand, stayed at home and rode your bike." Skylar chuckled. "At church, I was on the youth usher board, ran the fellowship program, and sang in the choir. Not Storm. You sat uninterested in your seat, waiting for the service to be over so you could go join your friends. When some of the church ladies would ask why you were not involved in the same things, you'd reply without missing a beat, 'Because I don't want to!' "

Both sisters laughed. "But," Storm added, "don't forget that my flip-ass tongue also got me many an ass-beating from Dutch. Many a time."

"True, but you had the balls to speak up," Skylar told her. "It took me a long time to admit it, but I was jealous of you."

"What? Be serious." Storm was shocked.

"You were always so free. I wanted to be that way. I wanted to be that open to life."

Storm looked at her, totally confused.

"Storm, you dance to the beat of your own drum. You always spoke your mind, whenever you felt like it, even to Dutch. If it didn't feel right to Storm, she'd let you know it. When I look back on that, I'm envious," Skylar said.

Storm was speechless. Never in a million years had she expected to hear her sister say such things. She wanted to interrupt but didn't. This was too good to be true.

"No one ever thought to ask me if I wanted to do all those things. Everybody just assumed I was fine with it all. There were times I wanted to tell Dutch, 'No! I want to go the park and just hang out sometimes, too.' Or when the church wanted to add yet another responsibility to my overflowing plate, I could've said, 'Please get someone else.' But I didn't. I made everybody else happy except for myself." She seemed to drift for a moment, thinking about all of this, before looking up at her sister. "And yes, I did grow up thinking I was better than you. That I would be the success of the family while you continued to fail," Skylar whispered.

"Well, I'd say by the way things turned out, you were right," Storm said.

Moving closer to her sister, Skylar said, "No, Storm. I was so wrong. I was the one who failed. I failed you."

Storm searched her sister's face for some sort of explanation. She wanted to speak but didn't know quite what to say.

Skylar continued, "I should have been there more for you. I never took the time to find out what you thought, how you felt, where you wanted to go. I never asked about anything you had going on in your life. I was too busy doing *me,* I guess. Believing my own press releases.

"So now, here we are, almost thirty, and we don't even know each other. I don't think we ever did. Losing Dutch and now Nettie makes me feel that all this fighting and discord between me and you is crazy! I resented you coming back trying to change things, claiming things that I felt you had no right to possess. I was wrong. Whatever Dutch left, whether you were here or not, is just as much yours as it is mine. The selfish side of me didn't want to believe that." Skylar felt a lump forming in her throat. It's hard to swallow guilt.

Storm took a deep breath before starting. "You know, Skylar, regardless of our paths, you are still my sister, my blood. Now, we can spend the rest of our lives trying to apologize for what went wrong, rehashing the past and feeling bad for every little thing we've done to each other, or we can nix the shit and start living for today . . . right now," Storm said with conviction.

"Why you gotta cuss?" Skylar teased.

"What? Shit, you know I talk like that." Storm playfully hit her.

"I . . . I have something I need to tell you. About your arrest," Skylar said nervously.

"So, what's your plan, sis, now that you've sold the place? Because I have a few ideas—"

"No, Storm, you have to hear me on this," Skylar said, grabbing her arm—and her attention. "I don't want to talk about that right now. I just want to make things right. So I need you to allow me to say what I need to say."

Storm took a step back from her sister and said, "Wait one more second. Being locked up for so long, you tend to get easily bored. So you spend a lot of time reading as much as possible. Mostly it was the Bible or the dictionary. One day, after going over my case with my lawyer, I did something that I hadn't done before. I read my file. Seriously, I sat myself down and really read my file. There were so many inaccuracies; and I uncovered information that I never knew. I gotta tell you, I was pissed."

Uneasiness overtook Skylar. Feeling somewhat faint, she braced herself against one of the tables and the wall. This went unnoticed by Storm, who was looking away.

Storm raised her voice, not out of anger, but frustration.

"Then, I looked up the word 'forgiveness'. Now, according to *Webster's,* it said, 'to give up resentment against; or the desire to punish. To pardon.' What tripped me out even more was in the Bible. Jesus said in Luke 6:37: 'Judge not and you shall not be judged. . . . Forgive and you will be forgiven.' I realized then, what's done is done and can't nobody do nothing about it. Like I said, Sky, I'm willing to start living for today . . . right now."

With that, Storm opened her arms to her sister. Skylar, tears welling in her eyes, brought both of her hands to her lips as if to pray. She gently closed her eyes as a tear fell down her cheek. Slowly she began walking toward her sister. After a few steps, Storm did the same. The sisters embraced, collapsing in the moment. Holding on to each other for dear life, they sobbed uncontrollably, letting go of every hurt, every pain, all those feelings of abandonment that had been bottled inside for years. Cleansing their souls and spirits, the two sisters became one. Composing themselves, they wiped away each other's tears.

"Oh, girl, you look bad!" Storm playfully told her sister as she stood back and gazed at her.

"I was just thinking the same thing about you," Skylar replied.

With that they both started giggling, and they ended up on the floor, still holding on to each other, neither wanting to be the first to let go. Skylar jokingly told her they probably hadn't had this much fun since they were in the womb.

"Naw, we was fighting even then. Trying to be the first one to see the light of day," Storm told her.

For the next hour or so the two sisters remained seated on the floor in the empty building, forgetting about the time and revisiting childhood memories good and bad. Realizing that they had been on the floor long enough, they helped each other to their feet.

"So, sis, are you going to answer my question?" Storm straightened her clothes with her hand.

"About the future? Not quite sure as of yet. Everything is up in the air. Sidney and I are going to take a much-needed vacation first before deciding anything further. And you?" Skylar asked her sister.

"I've decided to invest in real estate. Actually, I put a little money down on a building already," Storm said proudly.

"Really?"

"Yes, I'm opening up a restaurant. Especially since I am serious about culinary school," Storm told her.

"Wow, that's great, Storm. If you've really thought about it, I say go for it. But I thought you had given your money to DuBoy with that whole Torch idea thing?"

"Girl, hell no. I ain't that damn stupid. When I had a lawyer look into what they were really talking about, not only was it not feasible, it was a bad business deal from jump! Torch never really planned on making DuBoy or anyone else a partner. He just said that to DuBoy to get the money. It didn't matter anyway. Everything was over once I realized DuBoy was playin' me. I might have been a little sideswiped for a minute, you know, thrown off-track because of my feelings for him. But chile, that was just because it had been a minute, you feel me?" Storm laughed. "To think that I was becoming friendly with that girl Pia again! Her and DuBoy deserve each other, so that's that. It might take a while for me to see shit for what it is, but eventually I do see that it is shit. Everyone knows shit stinks, no matter whose it is."

"Well, let me say I'm proud of you, and be the first to congratulate you on your new venture." Skylar smiled and hugged her sister. It felt weird to hug her but it felt right.

"Sky, would you have a problem if I named it Morrison's Family Restaurant?"

"Of course not. That is your last name, so why would I object?" Skylar folded her arms across her chest and looked at Storm.

"But you know, in order to call it Morrison's Family Restaurant, I need some family on board. Wouldn't want to deceive the public, you know what I mean?" Storm turned away with a sly smile on her face.

"You and me? In business together?" a stunned and shocked Skylar remarked.

"Yeah, why not?" Storm sounded excited about the idea. "I could learn a helluva lot from you. Just look at what you did with Legends, sis. Imagine the kind of success we could have with both of us at the wheel of Morrison's. We'd blow up!" Storm became more and more animated with each word. "I'm seeing a chain, Skylar. Morrison's all over the East Coast."

Skylar couldn't believe what she was hearing. "Storm are you serious? There is no way we can even think about working together," Skylar said, smiling.

"Why not? We could do it, sis!" Storm said, taking hold of both of her sister's hands and jumping up and down like a child. Skylar was not quite sure what to make of Storm's behavior. This was foreign to her. Dazed for a few seconds, she looked deeply into her sister's eyes. Storm was serious.

"But where, Storm? We don't have a place. Legends was put up for sale, and as of yesterday they called to say there was a buyer," Skylar said.

"I knew the place was up for sale," Storm said while pulling an envelope out of her purse. She handed it to Skylar.

"What is that?" Skylar inquired, bewildered.

Storm told her to open it. Skylar slowly opened the envelope and took out a letter. She read it carefully, periodically glancing up at her sister in wonderment.

"You're the buyer?" a wide-eyed Skylar asked.

"Yeah, and I'd love it if you would add your name to that piece of paper, right there with mine," Storm said softly as she took her sister's hand.

Looking up at her sister with her mouth open, Skylar was speechless.

"All that is needed is for you to say yes, and we're good to go."

Skylar asked again, "Are you sure, Storm?" Storm's mind was made up. She knew coming in what her plan was. She just wasn't sure Skylar would entertain the thought.

"I must be a little crazy, but if you think it'll work, I'm willing to give it a shot," Skylar said as she sighed heavily.

"That's what I'm talking about!" a hyped-up Storm replied. Grabbing Skylar's hands, she began twirling their bodies around and around in a circle.

Skylar became dizzy and stopped Storm. "But with one caveat. As much as I appreciate your offer to be a co-owner, I want to wait a while before doing that. Let's take it day by day, Storm. For now, I want you to enjoy being the sole owner of your own business. I'll be there beside you and will help with any- and everything I can. It's your time to shine, sis. You deserve this. I'm so proud of you." She embraced Storm, who teared up and thanked her sister for believing in her.

While she was very happy for Storm and truly sincere about her willingness to work beside her, Skylar's reasons for not signing on as co-owner had less to do with courtesy and more to do with reputation. Storm might be turning over a new leaf, but Sky would just wait and see how everything played out before she got in too deep.

Embracing her sister, Storm was happy she and Skylar would be working together as a team. But she wasn't stupid. She knew the real reason Sky was holding off from signing on, but that was okay. *All things in time,* she thought to herself.

"You know what I'm thinking about right now?" Storm said, giggling.

"What?"

"What Dutch would say if he saw us," Storm said.

"He'd probably just stand here, smiling, thinking to himself, 'Lord, look at my girls.' And Nettie, sweet Nettie, what do you think she would say about all of this?" Skylar and Storm looked over to where the bar used to be.

"It's about time you bitches got yo shit together! Now leave me alone and let my ass rest."

Hand in hand, Skylar and Storm emerged from the building just as they came into this world: together, as sisters.

< EPILOGUE >

While combing her hair in the bathroom, Skylar suddenly stopped, and for a moment stared blankly at her reflection in the mirror. A lot had happened in a year's time. Her eyes welled up as she thought of Sidney. Somewhere along the way, their fairy tale romance had morphed into a movie-screen fantasy. She knew they were growing distant when she was no longer dazzled by that smile of his, and when she silently wished he would change his signature cologne. *Hadn't Sean John moved on to another fragrance anyway?* Skylar thought to herself. But what had happened? She wasn't sure, but she knew that neither one was at fault. It was just the way things were. She did wonder, however, if Sidney felt it all was a mistake. Had the two of them really been in love or were they both caught up in the search for temporary companionship? Pulling her hair back into its signature loose ponytail, she made a mental note to ask Zenora to suggest a new style. Perhaps this form of exhaling would help her deal with her personal life. The breakup had been amicable. Both made a solid promise to remain friends, even though secretly they knew that they couldn't. How could they replace the intense passion they had once shared with friendly pecks on the cheek? They knew each other too well.

• • •

Just as she was topping off her look with a hint of lip gloss, Skylar heard a recognizable voice coming from her answering machine. "When did my phone ring?" she said out loud. "Hey, Sky, it's Storm. Can you stop by the bank on your way in today and pick up the cashbox change for the weekend? It's ready. I thought I was going to have a chance to do it, but I'm running a little late. Shut up! I know what you're saying, 'Girl, you're always late' . . . Okay, sis, thanks, see you in a little bit. Love ya!"

"That girl will never change," Skylar blurted out with a wide grin on her face. Who would have thought these two would be this friendly toward each other? She and Storm still shared management duties, working side by side at Morrison's. Surprisingly enough they got along quite well. Sure there were still differences—several—but they always managed to work things out. Skylar still had not signed on as an official partner in the business; she wanted to give their relationship a little more time to heal before committing to it. She had to admit that Storm's dedication, hard work, and perseverance had not only surprised her but left her intrigued. Guilt from what she had done to Storm still poked its ugly head into her thoughts periodically, but for the most part, the inner pain that she'd endured over the years was subsiding. Thankfully, Storm never, ever once brought it up. She felt that her sister had indeed forgiven her and moved on. That was something she was attempting to do, too: forgive herself.

Although the economic climate was still just above Depression-mode in America, with most small businesses suffering to the point of going under, Morrison's remained sovereign. Business couldn't be better for the two-story, newly painted red brick building that sat on the corner, flanked by a gigantic neon signed that flashed MORRISON'S: A FAMILY TRADITION CONTINUES. The sisters had even been able to bring back Head as security and Ruta Lee as house manager.

The friendly neighborhood seemed alive again. So much tragedy had plagued the community recently that the sight of this South Philadelphia landmark restaurant returning only brought joy and harmony. Many still found it hard to come to grips with Nettie's slaying, especially Storm and Skylar. Treasure had been apprehended, charged, and convicted of first-degree murder and likely would spend the rest of her life in prison. On the day of sentencing, she showed no signs of remorse. The judge asked if she wished to address the court before her final sentencing. Free of her hair weave, fake nails, and makeup, she tilted her head back in full *America's Top Model* affect, and softly replied, "Yes." A hush immediately came over the packed courtroom, filled with Nettie's friends and loved ones, as well as strangers. Each ear pricked up, and every breath was held. Skylar closed her eyes as she held on tightly to Storm's hand. Storm fixed a deadly ice-cold glare at Treasure, expecting to hear some "I'm sorry, woe-is-me" sentiment, complete with crocodile tears and a plea to be forgiven in the name of Jesus. However, no one was prepared for Treasure's statement. "I'm glad that bitch is dead! And the only thing I'm sorry for is that I didn't do it sooner and not get caught." Gasps and uncontrollable outbursts filled the courtroom as the judge banged down the gavel and ordered guards to have Treasure taken away. June bolted toward her as she passed by the family seating area, only to be restrained by several friends and another guard. June had moved on with her life, but she would always love Nettie. And she knew that Nettie had loved her, regardless of the problems they had. Secretly, she agonized over the fact that had she not left Nettie that night, she might still be alive. Skylar raised her hands to her face in prayer and sighed heavily. Tears rolled from her eyes. Storm quickly retrieved a tissue from her purse and dabbed her sister's cheeks. Neither could say justice had been served, because their good friend was no longer here, but at least it was over.

Assuring Storm that she would be okay, Skylar excused herself to the restroom and told her sister that she'd join her in the hallway outside the courtroom. As the spectators cleared out, Storm sat still. At that very moment she longed for her mother—no, not Nettie, whom she loved like a mother, but the birth mother she never knew. Her touch, her smell. She wished she could remember how it was to be cocooned in her mother's womb, sucking on her thumb and her mother's nourishment. Perhaps that was why she had worked so hard this past year on reconciling with her sister. It was the only connection to the beginning of her life. Loving her sister was a new feeling for Storm. But it was a feeling that she welcomed. Watching how Skylar conducted herself as a businesswoman day to day only encouraged her to learn and do better. Owning and operating a business was new to Storm; in fact, at times it downright scared her. But she knew she could count on Sky to help her through it all. Skylar was a totally different person ever since the two had gone into business together. She treated Storm as her equal, not just in their professional lives, but also in their personal lives. Storm had never revealed to Skylar that she knew her sister's role in her incarceration, and frankly, at this point she didn't feel it would do any good to let her know. Besides, Storm knew that the guilt her sister felt was far more painful than any tongue-lashing she could give her. This was about forgiveness, for both sisters. Hell, she had even forgiven DuBoy for all he had done. But forgiving did not mean she would forget. In fact, she had no desire to ever see him again. Strangely enough, even after all that went down, he attempted to reconcile with her on several occasions, leaving pitiful messages of desperation and stopping by the restaurant. But it fell on deaf ears. Storm was moving forward in her life and any association with DuBoy would deter that. He eventually got the message because she heard less and less from him. Then one day she received a collect call from Graterford prison for men. Curiosity caused her to accept the call. Seems after several complaints from his upstairs neighbors about a marijuana stench, police barged in and found not only several blocks of weed in plastic bags, but plants growing under special lights in a hydroponic system in his bathroom. He was given five years for possession and intent to distribute a controlled substance. He asked Storm to come and see him, or at least put a little something on his books 'cause he hadn't "heard shit from that bitch Pia" since he was down. Storm wouldn't go to see him, but she did put a hundred on his books. It was the least she could do; after all, he had held her down when she was in Muncy. She had to admit that hearing how Pia had given him her ass to kiss made her feel kind of good. "They deserved each other," she thought out loud. And anyway, Storm was dating again. Matt Chin. A nice guy and the brother of Michael Chin, Sidney's partner. If anyone had ever told her she would be dating an Asian guy, or any other race than black, she would have laughed it off. Wasn't nothing like the brothas—still wasn't, but Matt was different. He was self-assured and bright, and he accepted her for who she was.

Torch was released from the hospital after about three months and was housed at Magee Rehabilitation Center, on his way to a slow, ever-painful recovery. Eventually, it all became too much. He took his own life with the gun he'd once showcased to DuBoy. The only person at his funeral was the undertaker. Gidget didn't even make an appearance. She was now turning tricks on Thirteenth and Locust at night and strung out on crack.

While waiting for Storm to join her in the courtroom lobby, Skylar turned on her cellphone and saw that she'd received a text from Princess. "Hey, how did everything turn out today?" Skylar planned to give her the update when she got home. She hadn't heard much from Princess in the last few months. She had left Philadelphia and secured an on-air job as a celebrity dance judge on MTV's reality show *Dance Like U Wanna*. Princess was now a national star.

She would also hit up Lovely and let her know how things had gone. Lovely had hung up her dancing shoes, returning to the hospital full-time as a nurse and dedicating all her free time to her son. The last they talked, she informed Sky that she was up for the head nurse's position.

Out of nowhere, Skylar longed to hear Flynn's voice, if only to make her laugh again. *My brotha, where are you?* But she had not heard from him since the day he left Philly. Somehow, she knew this would be the case. Wherever he was, she hoped that he was laughing and enjoying life. Alexia was never caught; she was on the most-wanted list for Cleet's murder and the attempted murder of Torch.

As Skylar looked up, she saw a smiling Storm approaching her. She returned the gesture. It was the first time she'd witnessed her own image looking back into her soul. . . . Without uttering one word, the sisters wrapped their arms around each other in a tender embrace that would last forever.

< ACKNOWLEDGMENTS >

Let me begin by thanking God for continuing to grant me grace! I have no idea how anyone can go through this life and not acknowledge Your existence. To my family (and that includes *all* of you that I listed in the first book, so don't call me up and ask me how come you didn't see your name): You know I know y'all love and support me. To Melody Guy, my editor: Thank you for allowing me to be me, and for letting my wild imagination come to life on paper. I know sometimes you just shake your head. . . . LOL. To Porscha Burke: Thanks for always laughing at my jokes . . . all the time . . . and for being on top of things!

To One World/Random House: Let's climb to the top with this one! To Jonathan Welch: Hey, cuz, I didn't forget you this time. Special thanks to Harry Smith, Alex Fisher, Alexander Hamilton, Danny Arroyo, Valeria Moore, Carol Roberts, Brandon Fobbs, Carla Stit, Jermaine Jacox, Christian Keyes, Sandra Hodge, Terryl Daluz (spelled it right this time), Jennifer White, Antina Campbell, Todd Thomas, The Living Waters Family, Keely Watson, Reggie White, Jr. To all the actors (too many to list) that have graced the stage in a Don B. Welch play, thank you for sharing your talents.

Stephen Slates: U already know that this friendship is for life.

Danny Berrios, the girls at City National Bank, Chico Benymon, Hattie Winston, Harold Wheeler, Diana Charles, Robsol Pinkett, all my Facebook friends, MySpace friends, fans, and the people of LA and Philly, my two homes. Patty Jackson of WDAS (Philly), Tammi Mac, and the KJLH family (LA). All my friends in NY, ATL, and Miami. To Jana Babatunde-Bey: Yeah, I know I acknowledged you in the first book, but you mean so much to me and my life, I had to do it again. Will and Jada: You've been a lifeline for me and so many others, but since I'm talking about me right now, know that I love and admire you both for so many reasons. Is thank you really enough? Debbie of Diamond Dust, Guy Black, Kieren Boyce, Ken and Brenda Gober, Leslie Magnum, Mike Davis, Vivian Vanderwerd (you went all the way in making those typing deadlines for me. I appreciate u so much). Farley Jackson, Vincent Ward, Kwame Patterson, Nile Taylor (Aaliyah in da house!). To Eric Benet: Is the script finished yet? (smile). A new friendship I graciously accept. Many thanks to: Adrianna Porcaro, Sandy Johnson, and "Q" the Barber. Thanks to Rodrick Paulk for coming up with the title. To my trainer, Verlondon: Stop counting! And I'm tired of working out! LMAO. To Eleanor Garcia, Dawnn Lewis, Vanessa Bell Calloway, Ananda Lewis, Callie Rogers, Ruth Blake, Sharon O. Walker, Freda Payne, Hill Harper, Loretta Devine, Glenn Marshall, Kenny Lattimore, Dorien Wilson and Obba Babatunde, Tasia Sherel (Thanks for spreading the word about my book in Chitown), Thomas Duckett, Scherrie Payne, Anna Maria Horsford (Where are u?). Tatyana Ali, Julian Johnson, Anthony ("Wayne") Burley, DeVon Franklin, Jett Lake, Shannon Wiggins, Henry Johnson, Debbie Feagins, Luis Rodriquez, Catareh Hampshire, Naeem Congo (I forgot u in the first one), John O., Tony Adams, Tri-Destined. To my Brenda (Vivian), who I know just loves me to death! To Fred and Shoneji: Hmm, my next birthday, I want to go to Boa for dinner; get yo' pennies together. . . . LOL. I dedicate the audio version of this book to my brother Vernon, who cannot sit still long enough to read a book!

Okay, for those I forgot this time, I'm sure I'll hear from you, so I'll catch u on the next one!

Living my life like it's golden,

Donald Welch

< ABOUT THE AUTHOR >

DONALD WELCH is an accomplished singer, actor, director, and producer, and the writer of eighteen stage plays, two television pilots, and several screenplays. He has also written for his friend the actor Will Smith, and recently sold him the film rights to *The Bachelorette Party* for a feature film. As an actor, he has costarred in *The Fresh Prince of Bel-Air* and *Cosby.* Don served as a celebrity judge for the Miss America Pageant (2000 and 2004). *In My Sister's House* is his second novel, following his 2007 One World release, *The Bachelorette Party.* He divides his time between Los Angeles and Philadelphia. Visit the author at myspace.com/donbwelch or email him at info@donbwelchproductions.com.

My mother made my dreams possible,
Will & Jada made them probable,
but my faith made them a reality.

—DONALD WELCH